The woman moved her rifle so that it pointed at Brian's chest.

"No go Lampang," she said. "Go Nan."

This was good news. The city of Nan was in the far north near Laos, much nearer to the Golden Triangle.

"Will you take me there?"

A fleeting smile wrinkled the woman's broad face. She turned to interpret to her guerrilla companions, mimicking Brian's tone. What she said struck them as hilarious. They laughed and slapped their thighs.

Smiling, the woman leaned toward Brian. "You go Nan to die," she said. . . .

Also by William Woolfolk
Published by Fawcett Books:

THE ADAM PROJECT

THAI GAME

William Woolfolk

FAWCETT GOLD MEDAL • NEW YORK

A Fawcett Gold Medal Book
Published by Ballantine Books
Copyright © 1989 by William Woolfolk

All rights reserved under International and Pan-American Copyright
Conventions. Published in the United States by Ballantine Books, a
division of Random House, Inc., New York, and simultaneously in
Canada by Random House of Canada Limited, Toronto.

Library of Congress Catalog Card Number: 88-92200

ISBN 0-449-14569-7

Manufactured in the United States of America

First Edition: April 1989

ONE

THE ELEPHANT'S HEAD WAS COVERED WITH A WOVEN YELLOW cloth fringed with bells. Holes were cut in the cloth for the elephant's eyes, its huge sides were covered with a metallic-looking green material bordered in vivid red, and its long tail was braided with purple ribbons.

The pachyderm's shambling rubbery feet made soft plopping sounds, and teakwood bells hanging from its neck sedately jingled to warn pedestrians out of its way.

Riding on top in a gold-painted *howdah* beneath a blue canopy were two young girls who giggled and waved at passersby. A young man rode bare-legged astride the elephant just behind its fan-like ears. He carried a birdcage with a bright-colored parakeet inside.

Joyously prancing alongside, three other young men were carrying poles festooned with gaily colored banners and sheaves of wheat.

They were celebrating the end of the harvest season, a time when farm folk come to Bangkok to spend the money they earned, to buy clothing, shoes, sandals, wristwatches and fountain pens, cooking utensils, lanterns for homes rarely wired for electric lights, and all the other sundry marvels offered by a big modern city of six million inhabitants.

A white Mercedes was held up in the traffic maneuvering out of the elephant's way. The young woman in the driver's seat gripped the steering wheel and stared straight ahead, ignoring the feints with festooned poles being made at the car, not reacting even when one pole came so close it seemed likely to break through the windshield.

When the traffic jam cleared she swung out around the gaily caparisoned elephant and drove across the wide square to the entry to the Royal Palace. At the first gate a uniformed guard, rifle grounded and held by one stiffly extended arm, stood by the sentry box. She showed her permit, and he nodded permission for her to go through the gate.

Directly ahead was the Chakri Maha Prasad, the three-storied Reception Hall. On its second floor, in the central throne hall, the new French Ambassador was presenting his credentials to King Bhumibol Adulyadej and his lovely Queen Sirikit.

The Mercedes parked in front of two stone lions guarding a small entrance at the right.

The explosion was a shattering, bursting, overwhelming, thunderclap.

Where the white Mercedes had been a mighty gout of flame geysered. Brown-red earth shot up in a torrent.

A great hole yawned in the palace courtyard.

Nothing was left of the white Mercedes. It had totally disintegrated. Fragments of bone and blood and metal were drizzling through the air.

Inside the Royal Palace many voices began to scream.

IN THE MIDDLE OF THE NIGHT BRIAN BUCKLEY WAS CARRYING the football close to his chest and buffeting his way over right tackle. Red jerseys rose like a wave, then the wave shattered and he was going through.

The referee's whistle shrilled again and again.

Brian did not know how long the telephone had been ringing. He reached toward the night table and his fingers stumbled to the receiver.

"Mr. Buckley?" The voice was masculine.

Brian could almost feel the impact bruises from his dream; his ribs ached. "You know what time it is?"

"I'm calling about Diane Hollings."

There was a perfume scent in the air, faint but unmistakable. Not secret or mysterious or memorable—it was the kind of scent available at any drugstore counter. A small puddle remained in the bottom of a champagne glass on the night table, and a cigarette butt stained with lipstick was drowning in it.

"What about her?"

"According to our information, she's your wife."

"What business is it of yours?"

"This is Reuter's News Agency. An hour ago, three o'clock in the afternoon Bangkok time, she drove a car into the courtyard of the Royal Palace. The car was loaded with five hundred pounds of dynamite. She was killed in the explosion along with . . ."

"Are you crazy?"

"Is this B.T.B. Buckley? The former All-American?"

Brian pushed down the button to break the connection. He left the receiver off the cradle. This was someone's idea of a practical joke.

His heart was pounding, his head ached, and he felt sick. His body was listening to what his brain would not.

TIM AND NANCY HARTEN LIVED IN AN OLDER, WELL-KEPT apartment house on Eighty-seventh Street between Second and Third avenues. Nancy, a small, trim-looking blonde who wore a blue terrycloth robe, opened the door.

"Tim's on the phone in the living room. He began checking as soon as you called him."

Brian went in as Tim was hanging up the phone. He and Brian had been friends since Tim covered Yale's football games for the *New Haven Register*.

Tim looked at him through thick eyeglasses. "It's true. Six people dead, twenty hurt. She was driving the car."

Brian sat down in the nearest chair.

Nancy brought a cup of coffee on a small tray. His hand was trembling, and some liquid spilled into the saucer.

"It doesn't make sense," he said.

How could he accept or believe in a tragedy that had happened in a city halfway around the world?

Tim asked gently, "When was the last time you saw her?"

Brian put down his cup of coffee. "Almost two years ago."

October 10th, a Saturday, half past four in the afternoon. They were in the hallway of the apartment. His bags were packed and standing near the door.

Nancy said, "We never really got to know her. She was always something of a stranger to us."

He thought, I never really got to know her either. Only to love her.

* * *

I HAVE TO GO THERE.

A tiny madness crept in like a red tinge on the margin of his brain. Out of a disorderly rush of emotions he chose one in particular. I have to find out what happened. This is something I must do, he told himself.

He knew that he was not thinking rationally. It would be a waste of time to travel halfway around the world. He would accomplish nothing.

Ritual logic led to the wrong conclusions.

A few minutes later he left the apartment. He took the Lexington Avenue subway downtown and walked across to the Chase Manhattan Bank at Fifth Avenue and Fourteenth Street.

He closed out his account, taking most of the money in traveler's checks. The sum was not impressive. From his safe deposit box he took his passport and life insurance policy.

At the airline office he was informed that there were three flights a week into Bangkok. The earliest left at midnight, with a stopover in Tokyo, arriving at eleven o'clock the next morning. He booked the flight and paid for it with his Visa card.

At the post office he left instructions for his mail to be forwarded to the Harten residence. He wrote a short note to Tim and Nancy, thanking them for their sympathy and help, and enclosed the insurance policy that named his brother Martin as beneficiary.

Then he called Cochrane, Stevens, Elliot & Alkorn to tell them he was taking an indefinite leave because of a family problem. Word had not reached them of Diane's death, so there was no need to explain further. There was no objection to his leaving so abruptly; after nine years he was still a spare cog in the machinery.

Brian returned to his apartment, taking the elevator to the floor above and watching the hallway below for a minute to be sure no reporters were lying in wait.

Inside the apartment he bolted the door and began to pack.

HE TOOK THE SUBWAY TO GRAND CENTRAL, CHANGING AT Forty-second Street to the shuttle to the West Side. In Penn Station he checked his luggage in a locker. He was in time to catch the train to Islip on Long Island.

A short taxi ride brought him to a familiar gray building set back over a wide lawn. The taxi went between stone pillars that read: "Veterans Hospital, Extended Care Division."

Martin's bed was beside a window. He was strapped in and trying vaguely to loosen the straps.

"How is he today?" he asked the nurse.

"Not well, I'm afraid."

He moved to the side of the bed. "Hello, Martin."

Martin made a little gesture with his head—more questioning than recognition. His breath moved a black handkerchief that concealed the lower part of his face. The ligaments of his neck were like visible strings beneath a thin covering of skin.

Martin was four years older than Brian. He was so talented he could have been anything he wanted, a doctor or a lawyer or an engineer; he chose to be a minister. When he was ordained the war was on in Vietnam and he volunteered as a chaplain. One morning he was watching a few men remove a land mine from a road. The lucky ones were killed.

Martin was staring at a spot a little beyond Brian's shoulder. He was looking at the pitcher of water on the nightstand. Brian poured a glassful and lifted him to a sitting position. Martin fumbled for the glass with his stumps, but Brian kept the glass until he could lift the handkerchief that covered part of Martin's face. He poured it into a black gaping hole. Suddenly Martin started to cough and splutter. His head bobbed as though it were on a stick that somehow had worked loose.

Brian was as shocked as if he had committed an inexcusable act.

"Nurse!"

Gasping breaths fluttered the handkerchief over the lower part of Martin's face. When the nurse came and saw what was happening, she went quickly to summon the doctor.

Brian muttered, "Oh, Martin, I'm sorry." Holding his brother upright in bed, he willed to him some of his own strength.

When the doctor arrived Martin was gargling and snuffling. Frightening sounds came from his throat.

"You'd better wait outside," the doctor told Brian.

In the corridor outside, Brian was so unnerved he could not stand still, but walked rapidly up and down.

After twenty minutes the doctor and nurse emerged. Brian offered a deal to God. I will do any penance.

"Is he all right?"

The doctor nodded.

"Can I see him?"

"Only for a minute."

Martin was lying quietly in bed, his face turned toward the

window. Brian touched his shoulder gently, careful not to startle him.

"I came today because I have something important to tell you." He spoke as if his brother understood. It was important to him to speak to his brother as if he understood. "I have to go away for a while. You remember Diane—the woman I married?"

Martin had never met her.

"Well, a terrible thing happened. She was killed in an accident."

Martin fretted with the straps that held him in the bed.

Brian said, "She was someone I cared about very much, and this is something I have to do. I have to find out what happened to her."

In an odd way he felt as if the situation were reversed and he was sending his brother away.

He stood up. "I'll be back soon. And I'll come to see you."

He spoke to the nurse on the way out and explained that he was leaving on a trip. "If there's anything he needs, please get it for him." He slipped her a fifty dollar bill. She put it into the pocket of her white starched uniform.

"We'll look after him."

"My mail is being forwarded. I'll leave a telephone number in case of emergency." He wrote down Tim and Nancy's number and gave it to her. "They're good friends of mine."

She nodded. "Have a pleasant trip, Mr. Buckley."

From the driveway outside, while waiting for the taxi, Brian stamped his feet and rubbed his hands. The air glimmered with cold. He looked back once at the monolithic gray building. Strong as it was, it did not seem strong enough to contain its burden of pain.

The taxi came.

TWO

A STEWARDESS WEARING A COLORFUL SILK SARONG WHEELED a cart to Brian's seat in the 747 racing across the Pacific. She had a thin body, a flat sallow face, and bony hands.

"Tea or coffee, sir?"

"I'd like a drink."

"The other stewardess will come by in a minute."

Brian chose two cookies from the bowl the stewardess was holding. "Are you Thai?" he asked.

"Some mix."

"Mix?"

"Chinese and Shan."

"A nice mix," he told her.

She smiled, excused herself, and pattered down the aisle.

"Interested?" asked the man seated on Brian's right. He wore metal-rimmed eyeglasses and had been reading *Money* magazine and the *Financial Times*. "You can do a lot better in Bangkok. Some Thai women are knockouts."

Brian smiled noncommittally. He opened the *New York Times*. The report on the bombing in Bangkok took less than a column. There was a photograph of the shattered courtyard of the Royal Palace and an interview with an English-speaking Thai woman who was across the street when the dynamite went off.

"So much noise. I was knocked to the ground. I thought it was an atom bomb."

The news account reported that a police investigation was underway, and an "American woman" was mentioned as having been the driver of the automobile.

7

"Not too many tourists come here in the monsoon season," said metal rim spectacles. "It gets pretty wet. You been in this part of the world before?"

"Only once."

"Where was that?"

"Vietnam."

"You were in that? Don't pass it around. Believe it or not, a lot of Thai people don't understand. In Bangkok they're mostly pro-American, but you go upcountry to Korat or Singkhla and it's a different story. By the way, my name is John Nixon."

"Buckley." Brian took the hand that was offered and gave it an awkward shake.

"No first name?"

"Brian."

"B.T.B. Buckley?"

Brian nodded.

"I'm sitting next to a celebrity. Wait'll I tell my wife and kids."

Nixon showed a color snapshot of his wife and four daughters standing on a lawn in front of a yellow frame house. Everyone in the photograph was carrying little American flags. The girls ranged from six to twelve years old. His wife's hairdo looked like a wasp's nest.

A stewardess came around with drinks. Brian ordered two of the sample-size Martinis, finished them, and gave the serving tray back to the stewardess. He closed his eyes and pretended he was going to sleep.

WHEN BRIAN EMERGED FROM THE PLANE AT DON MUANG AIRport, a hot humid wind was blowing, and the sky had the look of imminent rain.

Nixon fell into step with him as they crossed the tarmac. Inside the airport three Thai customs officials were checking baggage at a long counter.

Nixon was at Brian's shoulder while his luggage was being examined.

"You have to declare all the money you bring in. You can spend as much as you like, but you can't take out more than you brought in."

"Thanks."

Nixon followed him to the currency exchange booth where

Brian turned in five hundred American dollars for a pile of green, red, and purple bahts. Thai money.

"Better count it," Nixon said. "Don't take anybody on trust."

Nixon apparently shared the feeling of some Americans that the danger of being in a foreign country increased in direct proportion to its distance from their own, their native land.

"What's the cheapest way downtown?" Brian asked.

"The bus. It'll take you to the downtown terminal. If you're looking for a nice quiet hotel, not too expensive and near the American Embassy, try the New Thonburi."

"Thanks. I'll look into it."

Brian waited twenty minutes for the bus, and then signaled a taxi, a high-bodied car of undetermined ancestry. The driver wore a brown bandana around his head.

"American Embassy?" Brian asked. "How much?"

After a moment's consideration the driver held up ten fingers. "American dollar."

Brian consulted the vocabulary in his little guide book and found the words for too expensive. "Paeng mark."

The driver folded one finger. Brian shook his head. The driver folded another finger. Eight dollars seemed fair, so Brian got in. The interior of the taxi was stifling.

"Air conditioner?"

"Oh, yes, sir."

Five minutes later the interior of the taxi was muggier than before. Brian felt as if he were sitting inside a dryer with a fresh load of wet sheets.

"Air conditioner," he said firmly.

The brown bandana shook negatively. "Very sorry. Not work today."

Brian took off his jacket. "Swindler."

The ride from the airport was dispiriting. Open fields were divided by long narrow ridges of earth and separated again by still narrower ditches that resembled mud quagmires. An occasional billboard seemed to have been transplanted from an American highway—advertising Coca-Cola, Pepsi, Seven-Up, and Fanta.

The sky was gray with dark, threatening clouds. In moments a few raindrops spattered down, then the rain came. Cascading water swamped the windshield wipers, and the roof of the taxi resounded with volleys of what sounded like musket fire.

The taxi passed a rain-shrouded shape that Brian identified

from his map as the Victory Monument. They turned down Raj Damri Road past the Suan Pakkard Palace, turned left on Ploenchi Road and right on Wireless Road. As they pulled up in front of the American Embassy, the torrential rain stopped as suddenly as it had begun.

Brian gave the driver some red bills and some green.

"Khob khun krap," the driver said. "My name is Phibul. You want me to wait on you?"

"I don't know how long I'll be."

Phibul smiled broadly. "I wait."

Brian wondered if he'd overtipped him.

The gutter was overflowing and streaming water onto the sidewalk. Hefting his bags, Brian entered the Embassy building. He asked the woman at the reception desk if he could see someone in authority.

"Are you an American citizen?"

He showed his passport and the fifteen-day transit visa he'd picked up at customs.

She dialed a number on a desk telephone and spoke for a moment. She looked up, and her dark brow knitted.

"Are these the correct initials? B.T.B. Buckley?"

"That's right."

She returned to the telephone. "Oh, yes. Very big." She hung up, smiling. "Mr. Calisher will be right out. He thinks he knows you."

Calisher was a middle-sized, middle-aged man who walked with the thrusting aggressive stride many bowlegged men seem to have.

"Well, I'll be damned. Brian Buckley!" He shook hands with enthusiasm. "You've made my day!"

"I'm not sure I remember . . ."

"We never met. I graduated two years before you got to Yale. I was just an alumni rooter. Come into my office. We have a lot to talk about." He turned to the receptionist. "Cancel my next appointment and hold any phone calls."

Calisher's office contained a solid teakwood desk, several dark cane-bottom chairs, and a wall lined with bookshelves. Fat, official-looking volumes cheek-and-jowled on the bookshelves. Rolled-up bamboo shades partly covered the two windows.

Brian settled into a cane chair that was too small for him. Calisher opened a humidor and offered a cigar.

"No, thanks."

"Mind if I do?"

Calisher sat down behind the desk and made a small ceremony of clipping the cigar with gold scissors.

"I'm the senior consul here," he said, as though replying to an unspoken question. "That rates a private office, a fancy title, and a salary level ridiculous for anyone who hasn't got money of his own. Only rich people can afford to work for the government."

He lighted his cigar, sucked until the other end was glowing, and breathed out smoke with deep satisfaction. "May I call you Brian?"

"Of course."

"You earned All-American. The way you'd break through the line. They knew you were coming, but there wasn't a thing they could do to stop you. You went through like a locomotive."

"I got derailed pretty often."

Calisher sat back, puffing at his cigar. "If it hadn't been for that leg injury, you'd have been up there with the great ones. With Bronco and O. J. and Jim Brown. But you did the right thing, signing up for duty in Vietnam."

A spiral of smoke rose and settled around Brian's head like a laurel wreath.

"That was a long time ago."

Calisher leaned back in his chair. "What brings you to this part of the world? Vacation?"

"I want to find out more about the bombing at the Royal Palace."

Calisher was surprised. "What's your interest?"

"Diane Hollings was my wife."

Calisher was startled. "I had no idea. I didn't realize . . ." He suddenly seemed to have trouble drawing on his cigar. "It was a terrible, terrible tragedy. I met her casually. At one or two Embassy functions." Calisher was still trying to regain his composure. "An extremely clever, attractive woman."

"I don't believe it happened the way the newspapers say. Diane wasn't a terrorist."

Calisher said sympathetically, "People close to someone who commits a violent act rarely can believe it."

"What motive would she have?"

"I have no idea. This is outside my domain. It's in the hands of the police. I realize it's a personal tragedy, but you can see that it puts us in a very sticky situation. An American woman. Frankly, we're anxious to play the whole thing down."

"I don't see this as just a diplomatic embarrassment," Brian said.

Calisher's tone reflected a cautious new appraisal: "In our view, this kind of dreadful event shouldn't get further publicity. If it had been leftist guerrillas trying to harm the royal couple, that would be a different matter."

"Who says she was trying to harm the royal couple?"

"Queen Sirikit was injured in the explosion. A sliver of glass from a shattered window." He touched his elbow. "Entered her arm just about here. She had to have an operation, but she's all right, thank God."

"Are the police investigating?"

"Yes, of course, and they're quite efficient. You can leave it in their hands. I'm speaking to you as a friend." Calisher surveyed him from behind a drifting veil of blue smoke. "I'll keep you informed if there are any new developments. Meanwhile, enjoy your visit to Bangkok. Marvelous restaurants, interesting places to see."

"I didn't come here as a tourist."

Calisher was looking at a spot on the ceiling. "This has been a hard time for the Embassy. You won't make things any better if you go fishing in troubled waters."

Brian stood up. "I'll try not to make things worse."

BRIAN'S ROOM AT THE NEW THONBURI WAS MODEST, WITH A bathroom featuring a gilt spittoon discreetly tucked under the washbasin. There was a shower, but no bath. The room was colored a pale orchid, and paint was peeling in a corner near the window.

He had just unpacked when the telephone jangled.

"Someone in lobby, sir. Wish to see you."

"Who is it?"

"Shall I ask name, sir?"

"Never mind. I'll come down."

In the lobby, beneath wooden carvings on the wall depicting the abolition of slavery in Thailand, John Nixon was seated in a teakwood chair with soft cushions.

Nixon stood up to shake hands. "I'm pleased you took my recommendation. You like the hotel?"

"It's fine."

"Can I buy you a drink?"

They went into the bar lounge. A party of Thais, just leaving, smiled and bowed graciously. Polite little people, Brian thought.

Nixon chose a small table in a quiet corner. A waiter brought a small tray of refreshments. Nixon ordered a vodka and tonic, Brian ordered a Thai beer.

Nixon's smile went well with his steel-rimmed eyeglasses. "I'll dispense with the buildup. I'm a United States Treasury agent, and our meeting on the plane wasn't accidental. I went to some trouble to arrange it."

Brian took a swallow from his beer glass. Thai beer tasted like Canadian ale.

"What do you want?" he asked.

"Actually, I was introduced to you by a computer. Your name came up when we were inquiring into Diane Hollings. You filed a couple of joint tax returns."

"Married people often do."

"Let me put it this way. We don't care what kind of crooked deals Americans get mixed up in over here. But Uncle Sam doesn't like being cut out of his share of the profits."

"I don't like what you just said about crooked deals."

Nixon's smile became even more tightly controlled. "Your wife was a partner in the H & D Trading Company. They were engaged in a very profitable smuggling operation and paying plenty in bribes to Thai officials to forget about taxes and duties owed their government."

"I suppose you can prove that."

"We've done our homework. We were ready to close in, but everything took an unexpected turn when your wife was killed. I hope we can count on your cooperation."

"Name, rank, and serial number."

"I'm not your enemy."

"If you're trying to incriminate my wife, you're not my friend."

"Her case is moot. A lot of money is involved. Would you be willing to talk to her partner? A man named George Denison. He wouldn't talk to me without a lawyer."

Brian finished his beer and put the empty glass down precisely within the circle it had made on the table. "If I talk to him, it'll be for my reasons. What makes you think he'd tell me anything?"

"The human factor. You were her husband." Nixon took out a small notepad and scribbled on it. "I'll give you his address and the address of the company, too."

"Funny. The man I spoke to at the Embassy didn't want me to do anything."

"We work different sides of the street. They care about diplomacy, we care about money. Anything you find out may be useful. A reference to a business transaction. A casual comment. Anything. If you help us, there could be a finder's fee."

"I came to Bangkok for only one reason. To find out what really happened to my wife."

"Maybe we can help each other. She didn't live far from here. I'll give you her address, too." He finished writing, tore off a page from the pad and gave it to Brian. "Keep in touch."

Nixon left, steering carefully around a man in the lobby who was chewing betel and expectorating its red juice into an ornate gold spittoon.

Brian stopped at the lobby newsstand. He picked up a copy of the *Bangkok Post*, an English-language newspaper. In his room he settled down to read about the bombing of the Royal Palace. The story was on the front page, and featured an interview with George Denison.

Denison said Diane had left the office of the H & D Trading Company an hour before he did. At a bar he had a few drinks, then went to a friend's house for dinner. He didn't get home until after nine o'clock. The television set was on when he got there, showing pictures of the bombing at the Royal Palace, and a reporter said that an American woman, Diane Hollings, had driven her car loaded with dynamite into the palace courtyard. Denison didn't believe it; he tried calling her home, but the line was busy. He drove there, and when he saw the crowd of reporters and police, he knew it was true.

The telephone jangled.

Calisher asked, "How do you like your accommodations?"

"They're okay."

"The New Thonburi is an excellent choice in its price range. I hope you enjoy your stay."

"How did you know where I was?"

"We try to keep track of important American visitors." After a slight pause Calisher said, "Think about what I told you earlier. It's really in your best interest."

That night Brian slept poorly. The twelve-hour time difference between New York and Bangkok was hard to overcome. He awoke before daylight. A single streak of silver moonlight cut into the dimness of a pillow, and for a moment he thought

Diane lay awake beside him, breathing softly, unhappy for reasons he did not understand.

The other side of his bed was empty. He got up and stared out the window at the strange night shapes of flat roofs and a single distant conical temple.

Memory contracted into a hard knot of pain.

AT THE BROKERAGE FIRM OF COCHRANE, STEVENS, ELLIOT & Alkorn where Brian plugged away at selling mutual funds, Diane was hired to handle the accounts of foreign investors, mostly from Far Eastern countries. She could speak several languages and often had to do so during a busy morning.

Brian thought her very attractive and full of vitality. During her first few months with the firm, several men tried to date her, including Frank Cochrane, a married partner of the firm. None succeeded.

Brian discovered that Diane went for daily morning jogs around the Central Park reservoir. At dawn one morning he put on a gray sweatshirt, long cotton trousers that bagged at the ankle and sneakers, and took the subway uptown from Greenwich Village.

He waited until he saw her. She was a lithe, strong runner and had a trim shape in her jogging suit. He fell in about twenty yards behind her on the running track, intending to wait for the right moment to pull up beside her. Within a short distance, he discovered his mistake. He was out of condition, breathing heavily, and his bad leg was sending signals of pain.

He ran off the track, limping slightly, and sat on a bench for awhile trying to coax his knee to stop throbbing.

"You're Buckley, aren't you?"

She was standing near the bench, looking at him curiously.

"Yes."

"I haven't seen you here before."

"I haven't been here. I decided to give it a try."

She sat down on the other end of the bench. "All the way from Greenwich Village?"

"How do you know where I live?"

"I made it my business to find out."

She made it her business to find out.

"How were you going to get into the office?"

He responded tardily, "I was going home to shower and change."

"All this just to meet me?"

He decided against foolish denial. "Yes."

"Your leg is hurting you. Is that the one you injured playing football?"

"It wasn't football. It got shot up in Vietnam." Suddenly everything seemed possible. "Will you have dinner with me tonight?"

She smiled. "How about eight o'clock?"

She lived in a new condominium building just outside the boundary of real affluence. Only a few blocks farther downtown began the coveted land of art galleries, brownstones renovated into expensive studios and apartments, antique shops, museums, boutiques, where two-bedroom apartments sold for half a million dollars and more.

In her living room that evening he felt like Caliban summoned from the lower depths to sit uneasily among gracefully arched chairs, a low-backed French sofa placed against an array of green and flowering window plants, gold-flecked wallpaper, an oval glass coffee table, diffuse lighting. They had a drink, and went out to dinner at a nearby, moderately expensive restaurant.

"You were Princeton, weren't you?" she asked.

"Yale. My family always went to Yale."

"You see? I'm not infallible. Your father was a good friend of Sy Alkorn."

He had been hired because of his late father's friendship with Sy Alkorn, and because his fame as a football player would give him entree to sports-minded clients. After his career as an athlete ended, he had worked as an assistant football coach and a sporting goods salesman. Neither job paid much, or offered much of a future. He had no talent for making money; it was like drilling for oil in the Rock of Gibralter. He was glad to discover he could make a better living by sitting in corporate offices and talking football, trading stories of past exploits for a chance to sell mutual funds.

"That's how I got my job."

"Sy is only friends with rich people. Was your father rich?"

"At one time." Suddenly he decided to tell her. "My father was involved in a big Wall Street scandal. He lost everything."

"Oh."

"I was a junior in college at the time. I couldn't believe my father did anything wrong. One day he went out in his motor cruiser and disappeared. His body washed up a week later on the other side of the lake."

A freak accident, the coroner decided. At the funeral Martin sprang his own verdict like a concealed handgun: *If Dad had been around when Jesus was alive, he'd have been one of the moneychangers chased out of the temple.*

"You don't think it was an accident?"

He answered bitterly, "It wasn't. He had a heritage to live up to. He paid his dues." He thought about it, and added, "I loved him very much."

"Did your father give you those impressive initials?"

"B.T.B. ?"

"What do they stand for?"

"Brian Thomas Boru. I've always thought somebody should jack up that name and slide someone important under it."

"How did you get it?"

"That's a long story. It starts with my not being a member of the family. Only halfway, anyway. I was born on the wrong side of the bed."

"Adopted?"

"Yes and no. My father was my real father. He had an affair with my mother, but they couldn't marry because he was married at the time. My real mother died when I was four, and my father insisted on adopting me and making me part of his family. I was always the outsider. My father's wife never really accepted me. She was an Irish beauty, proud of her ancestry, and it was partly to win her over that my father tried to rename me Brian Boru. She wouldn't hear of it. She insisted on keeping my original name Thomas. But my father could be stubborn, too, so in the end I got all three."

She looked at him with an odd expression. "You know I'm Jewish, don't you?"

"Hollings?"

"Hochberg."

"Why did you change it?"

Diane said, "There was this nice Jewish boy, Saul of Tarsus. Why did he change to Paul?"

"You didn't change your religion, too?"

"That wasn't a problem. I belong to that branch of Judaism known as Jewish Agnostic. I can't accept God in the Old Testament. He's too fierce and unforgiving. That business about Sodom and Gomorrah. There had to be good people there, even if they were just passing through. There must even have been some doing His work, trying to save the heathen, but they got wiped out, too. It wasn't fair."

He was amused and fascinated by her, and his imagination swirled with desire.

In the lobby of her building they were under the watchful eye of a doorman whose stubble of white beard and deep searching gaze gave him the whiskery look of a walrus. A security guard seated at a semicircular booth was facing a bank of TV monitors that showed different floors of the building. The screen images changed every few seconds. Lack of privacy is the price of security in Manhattan.

She said goodbye and shook hands and told him she had enjoyed the evening (she's being polite, he thought), and then she disappeared into an elevator.

The next day at the office he saw her with a coat thrown over her arm and carrying a small overnight bag. Top executives at the firm kept a traveling bag fully equipped so they could take off for anywhere at short notice.

"Leaving?" he asked with a tentative smile.

She nodded. "Chicago."

"When are you coming back?"

"I have an early flight Thursday. Are you free for dinner that night?"

No one has this kind of luck, he thought.

"Where would you like to go?"

"Believe it or not, I'm a good cook. My place at seven."

The firm frowned on dating between employees, fearing some kind of corporate incest. But she asked within hearing range of several people, including Frank Cochrane.

Thursday finally came. He brought champagne—the Pied Piper of Heidseck. She made a delicious dinner of cornish hens and mushrooms. He felt more at ease. He told funny anecdotes, and she laughed in a hearty open way.

Tall candles were on the small dinner table pulled out from the wall, and their light played teasingly with the silver forelock of her hair. A candle's reflection burned in her right eye, making it appear illumined from within. Little details merged and grew into an obsession that was like a live wire incandescing in his brain.

At one point she leaned toward him to make a point while they were talking. A warm perfume scent rose from her. Her forearm had nearly invisible floating light hairs. When her fingertips touched the back of his hand his nerves tingled where her touch had been.

He put his arm around her. She offered no maidenly demurral. They kissed, tentatively at first, then with passion.

Very gently he began to make love to her. When she lay sleek and arrowstraight on the bed with one arm draped across her bare breasts, he lay down beside her and drew her to him.

Her eyes closed and her mouth opened slightly. She seemed to fall into a rapt state. He heard her hissing breath. Then she began to writhe. He twisted deeper, drove hard. She turned her face deep into the pillow to stifle a cry rising far back in her throat.

Everything went out of control. It was frighteningly intense. It was far, far beyond anything he had ever known.

It was the single most important event of his life.

THREE

IN THE MORNING A TORRENTIAL MONSOON DOWNPOUR BE-
gan. Brian went to breakfast in the hotel dining room. The
coffee was very black and too sweet, the waffle and bacon
strips he ordered were cold. The waitress stood nearby with
wide brown eyes, watching him. He was conscious of being
exotic and interesting.

After breakfast he spent an hour in his room reading the new
edition of the *Bangkok Post*.

The newspaper had gathered more information about the
identities of those dead and injured in the bombing, and there
was a sidebar story about Diane with some speculation about
the reason for her action. The speculation centered mostly about
the rumored illegal trade of the H & D Trading Company.

When the rain stopped he ventured out into the street. Within
a block he had to take refuge beneath the awning of a spice shop
while Niagara flowed down an inundated sidewalk. A small
concrete dam in front of the shop kept out the flood.

A woman came to the screen door of the shop, and with a
polite gesture invited him in. The mingled sweet pungent
aromas from inside were tempting, but Brian resisted. He
showed her the slip of paper on which Nixon had jotted addresses.

"Do you know where?" he asked, pointing to the first.

The woman nodded and with several winglike motions of her
hand indicated the route he should follow. He followed her directions, picking his way through large puddles on the sidewalk.
Other pedestrians were carrying their shoes in their hands.

He turned off the main avenue onto a gently ascending road

lined with coconut palms, where pastel houses were hidden behind high hibiscus hedges.

The American sector lay beyond a wide traffic circle. Spacious houses were set deep in gardens that rambled among orchids, red, orange and purple bougainvillea vines, and rain trees. Behind barred gates fierce-looking dogs barked as he passed. On a verandah a surly man in white shorts and a colorful T-shirt sat in a chair, drinking from a tall amber glass. He stared at Brian challengingly, as if to say, "I belong here and who the hell are you?"

The house Brian arrived at had a broad patio of red tiles, a low brick wall, and palm trees, hibiscus and bougainvillea growing on the expansive lawn. The name set on a metal plate in the wall was *Hollings*.

The house had an empty look. Windows were shuttered, the front door closed, and there was no sign of habitation.

As he was going across the patio the front door opened. A small dark Thai, with heavy pouches under his eyes, looked out narrowly. He wore a holster and belt over a pajama-like outfit.

Brian gave him his business card. The man looked at it so studiously that Brian realized he couldn't read the English script. From inside the house voices were speaking in Thai, a male voice questioning, a woman's responding.

The man at the door stepped back, moving aside, and waved Brian through.

In the small living room, seated in a curve backed cane chair before a small teakwood table, was a slightly built man about sixty years old. He was dressed in a white shirt, and a striped length of cloth was wrapped about the waist of his trousers. He had a long thin brown face with small lidless eyes and a shaved head.

He was interrogating an old woman. She rose quickly as Brian entered. The man in the cane chair indicated that she could leave. She bowed to him, then to Brian, and slippered away.

The man in the chair stared at Brian. "Good morning, sir. Your name, please?"

"Buckley. Who are you?"

"I am Bangkok Police. My name is Colonel Suvit. You will please to say why you are here."

Colonel Suvit's command of English was excellent, but his musical Thai intonation made the words sound as if they were being played on a flute.

Brian chose his reply carefully. "I knew the woman who lived here."

Although furnished in the open Thai manner, the living room had a stylistic similarity to Diane's Manhattan apartment. Lamplight glowed on walls of polished teakwood, and there were lush plantings. Diane had always liked flowering plants.

"How do you know the woman?" Suvit's tone was cool but insistent.

"We were married."

Suvit looked puzzled. "Her name is different from yours."

"That's how she wanted it." Brian did not think it necessary to explain.

Suvit digested this answer before he fashioned a new question. "Do you live in Bangkok, Meestrah Buckley?"

"I live in New York."

"Your passport and visa, please?"

Suvit held the documents in strong-looking brown hands with long, ridged, pale fingernails. He put on thick glasses that sat crookedly on his shaved head, looked from the passport photo to Brian, then gave both passport and visa to the small dark man who immediately left the room.

Suvit continued to regard Brian solemnly. The steadiness of his stare was unsettling.

"I see that you arrived in Bangkok yesterday. Why did you come?"

"I heard what happened to my wife."

"Are you aware of problems which might have led her to do such action?"

"That's what I came to find out."

Suvit received this with interest. "Where do you stay in Bangkok?"

"The New Thonburi."

The small dark man reentered the room and spoke swiftly to Colonel Suvit for half a minute. Suvit waved the man out of the room.

"My assistant has called the American Embassy. A man named Calisher gives you excellent references. He says you are famous and deserve to be treated with respect. Of what are you famous?"

"I used to play football."

Suvit nodded in a way that indicated the answer was irrelevant to his concerns. "Will you care to look at the house? Perhaps you will notice something we have overlooked."

As they made the rounds Suvit was observing him as much as what they looked at. Brian was busily imprinting every detail on his mind. In an enclosed windowless study filigree patterns of light illumined an alcove with a teakwood desk. There was a wooden pen and pencil set on a stand. She must have sat there writing notes in longhand as she did in the New York apartment.

"Did she own this house?" Brian asked.

"She had a lease for three years. There was one year remaining."

Her own lease on life ran out sooner.

"Was there a note? Anything to indicate what she was planning. Or why?"

"No writings."

The master bedroom forced a verandah that overlooked the lawn. One wall was segmented by slanted windows, and a bamboo shade covered another section of the wall.

On the neatly made double bed there was a light blue coverlet and a long white bolster pillow that stretched across the head. A matching bolster was at the foot.

"The closets are empty," Brian said.

"We have taken what may be evidence. We are going through them carefully."

"Her clothing?"

"I myself arrested a man who claimed to be so poor he could not be guilty of dealing in drugs. We found seven million baht sewed into the lining of one of his jackets."

"Are you keeping an inventory of what you've taken?"

Suvit replied coldly, "When we finish we shall return all."

The only object Brian recognized was a silver-backed hairbrush that he had given to Diane as a birthday present. It was on a dressing table, and a strand of hair was still caught in its bristles.

He thought, she has walked these floors, looked at these walls, seen that view of the garden, sat in that chair before the dressing table. This house must carry something of her within it like a portrait within a locket.

They returned to the living room.

With an expression of pained delicacy, Suvit said, "It appears that you and your wife were not together. Are you in divorce?"

"We were separated."

"Will you say that you still had a relation of significance?"

Diane had said, "You're a marvelously uncomplicated man.

We're like two pieces of a jigsaw puzzle that don't match. We have defined shapes that belong in different places."

"Perhaps you were in business together," Colonel Suvit suggested.

"No."

"Have you been in recent correspondence?"

"No."

Suvit nodded resignedly. "It is necessary to ask useless questions. One must accumulate certain amounts of information before arriving at a theory. Are you planning to stay in Bangkok for a time?"

"A few more days."

Suvit dismissed him firmly but politely: "Then we shall talk again."

AFTER THE RAIN THE AIR WAS DANK WITH HUMIDITY. EVEN the short walk back to the hotel left Brian perspiring profusely. He undressed in the bathroom and got into the shower. He held a bar of soap under the spray and began working up a lather. He did not identify with his powerful naked body. That was something that belonged to him rather than something that *was* him.

He remembered one cold Sunday morning when they were lying abed in Diane's apartment. Snowflakes were falling outside the window and whitening other rooftops. They had just made love and her cheeks were glowing against the bedsheet she had pulled up to her chin.

"My fine, lovely animal," she said approvingly.

"Would you like to get married?" he asked.

"That's very sweet of you, darling."

"I'm serious."

"*Semper fidelis?* I'm not sure I can deal with it. In fact, I'm sure I can't."

"The old ways are coming back. People are falling in love and getting married and living happily ever after."

"Bless them." She took a cigarette from the box on the night table. "Isn't it possible for two people to have fun anymore? Is there something evil about that?"

"I love you. I'd like to know what I mean to you."

She lighted a cigarette from a gold lighter with her initials on it: D. H. "You're important to me," she said. "You're a damn satisfactory lover."

"But you don't really love me."

"Everybody uses that word, but nobody really understands it." She puffed at her cigarette. "L-o-v-e. Everybody agrees it's real. But it may not be real at all." Exhaling smoke, she ground out her cigarette. "I don't want to talk about this anymore."

"I do."

She gave an exasperated laugh. "If it makes you feel better, I think I do love you. Just try it my way a little longer, and, damn it, darling, in the end I'll do anything you want."

They were married three weeks later.

Even now he did not understand why they never achieved the unspoken hum of communication that other married couples seemed to. He never stopped being in love with her. He did not know why she stopped. Everyone talks about the end of love, puzzles about it, cries over it, but when love goes there is nothing to do. A relationship often ends not because something important happens, but because nothing important happens.

As HE EMERGED FROM THE HOTEL A FAMILIAR HIGH-BODIED taxi came forward to greet him. Phibul looked cool in white ducks and a red jacket that was too small for him. He wore a white bandana on his head.

"Good morning, sir. I am thinking you will enjoy personal escorting of city today. See many interesting things, sir. Many interesting *wats*."

"Some other time."

"The Wat Arun is special beauty. Wat Arun means temple of dawn. Very much to examine inside. Has school and rooms where monks live and cremation place. Also many small chapels."

Brian had seen the soaring monument from a middle distance. The rounded spire, covered with pieces of porcelain stuck in cement, looked as though it were covered with broken pottery.

He opened his wallet and found the other street address John Nixon had given him.

"Do you know Tamarad Road?"

"Oh, much so, sir. It is of Chinatown."

"We'll go there."

It was past noon. The traffic inched past banks and business buildings and reached an area of stores and movie theaters with large colorful posters in front. These gave way to discotheques, open air cafes, girlie bars, and massage parlors. The city seemed to grow seedier with each passing mile.

The taxi turned onto Tamarad Road. At an intersection with a public fountain the taxi paused for a red light. Children were bathing in the fountain, their wet clothing molded to their bodies.

"Stop here," Brian said.

"Must find place for park, sir."

"I don't want you to wait."

Phibul produced a card with his telephone number and address. "Tomorrow we go on tour, sir, yes? See many sights. Bangkok is topmost civilized. Home of King and Queen."

Brian thanked him for the card but did not commit himself.

Number twenty-six Tamarad Road was a narrow two-story building squeezed in between two equally narrow buildings. The stucco facade might once have been bright yellow but was now streaked by rain and grime.

In a cool dark vestibule, a slowly turning ceiling fan revolved about a floor of polished teak. Brian moved toward the sound of a typewriter rattling. The vestibule widened abruptly into a large room where a pretty young blonde woman was typing. A light-gray radiance from a skylight fell on her desk.

She removed crimson-nailed fingers from the keyboard.

"May I help you?"

"I'd like to see Mr. Denison."

"What is this in reference to?"

"It's personal."

Her tone was just short of a rebuke: "Mr. Denison isn't in. I'll take a message."

"Do you know when he'll be back?"

"I'm afraid I don't."

"I have nothing better to do. I'll wait."

She looked him over with disapproval. "I don't expect him for some time." She took a pen from beside a pad with the heading *Today*. "Who shall I say called to see him?"

"I'll wait," he repeated, and heard a sound from upstairs that was like furniture being moved.

The young blonde woman gave him a quick nervous glance.

"Never mind," he said, starting for the staircase.

"You can't go up there!"

She stood up. She was wearing a silk blouse and wide-legged dark trousers. As Brian was going up the stairs he noticed that she had a quite spectacular figure.

She flicked up the intercom and spoke into it.

On the second floor landing there were two closed doors. A third door at the far end of the landing was just starting to close. Brian arrived in time to hold the door open with one hand.

Someone threw the weight of his body against the other side. Brian gave a strong push back. The door flew open.

A silver-haired, good looking man of about forty was sitting on the floor with his legs stick straight before him. He took his time getting up, and standing he brushed off cream-colored linen trousers.

"Who the hell do you think you are?" His voice was hoarse with anger.

In the office, filing cabinets had been moved away from the wall toward the center, leaving blank wall shapes. The drawers of the cabinets were pulled out, and most had been emptied. Folders were stacked on the floor, and several were jammed into wastepaper baskets.

In one of the blank spaces outlining where a filing cabinet had been there was an open wall safe. An attaché case filled with other folders was open on the floor.

"Moving?" Brian asked.

"Exactly what do you want?"

"My name is Buckley. Brian Buckley."

The man went around a desk and sat in a chair. He folded his hands on the desk in front of him.

Brian said, "That puts you one up on me."

"I'm George Denison. Diane's business partner."

"Just the man I want to see."

"It does not necessarily follow that I want to see you."

Brian squeezed into a chair on the opposite side of the desk. "If you'd like to get rid of me, you can do it by answering a few questions."

Denison's tone became controlled, ironical. "You're probably interested in a share of her estate. Forget it. Our partnership agreement calls for the surviving partner to get everything."

"My questions are about Diane. She wasn't the kind to commit a terrorist act. What made her do it?"

"Damned if I know."

"If you had a guess, what would it be?"

"She might have been feeling pressure. We were being harassed from all sides. The newspapers. The Thai government. The U.S. Treasury Department. We heard a treasury agent was coming to Bangkok just to investigate our business. It wasn't a happy situation.''

''Killing herself wouldn't solve the problem.''

''People don't always act rationally when they're badly upset.''

True enough, Brian thought, or I wouldn't be here now.

''Were you being harassed because of the smuggling business?''

Denison's look said plainly that Brian was asking for more than he had a right to know. ''We're a legitimate business. The *Bangkok Post* ran a series of articles about illegal smuggling and named us. They were wrong, but that's what started the trouble.''

Brian sat quietly, wondering how much he could believe of what this man was telling him.

''The last time I saw her she was crossing the parking lot to her car. I saw her from my window. Before that she was sitting in the chair I'm in now. Making telephone calls.''

''Who to?''

''The U.S. Embassy, trying to get their help. The *Bangkok Post*, trying to get them off our backs. Some friends in the Thai government, asking them to pull wires. Every time I looked in, she was on the telephone. You know what she was like,'' Denison went on. ''She had to be in charge. Brilliant at making plans, but if anything went wrong she blamed herself. Took all the responsibility. Finally I went back to my office and stayed there.''

''You went back to your office?''

''Yes.''

''Then this must be Diane's office. She was making phone calls from here. And those are her papers you've been going through.''

''We were partners. We didn't have secrets from each other.''

''I'd like to look at those folders.''

''Well, you can't.''

''Why not?''

''I don't have to explain anything to you. Nobody invited you here. You're trespassing.'' Denison put his hand warningly on the telephone. ''If you don't leave, I'm going to call the police.''

''When the police come they might want a look at some of the stuff you've been going through.''

''That's ridiculous. Those are business records. I have a perfect right to go through them.'' Denison's hand stayed on the telephone. ''What the hell do you think you're doing?''

Brian was stooped in the midst of the chaotic disorder on the floor, examining some of the folders. One was marked *Office Matters* and contained reports, letters, memos. Another marked *Partnership Matters* had stock certificates, various letters of agreement, and a scribbled note: *George upset about latest Bangkok Post article. Reassure him.*

The handwriting was bold, feminine, familiar. Diane's.

Denison said, ''I warn you. I'm calling the police.''

Suddenly Brian realized that whatever was lying about had been discarded. The bulging attaché case held what Denison chose as important.

He picked up the attaché case.

Speaking with deliberate emphasis, as if each word were a pebble he was throwing, Denison said, ''I wouldn't do that if I were you.''

Something menacing in his tone made Brian turn. The gun in Denison's hand was pointing directly at him, and his attitude had undergone a chameleon change. Brian had no doubt this man could be dangerous.

''Hand it over.''

There was authority in his voice but uncertainty in his eyes. Brian decided that Denison had not made up his mind what to do if his order was not obeyed.

Brian put the attaché case down.

''That's better,'' Denison said. ''Now . . .''

Brian moved with startling speed. Faced with an instant decision, Denison tried to use the gun butt as a weapon. Brian grabbed his wrist and twisted it until the gun fell from his hand.

Denison struck at him with his free hand. Brian moved his head and let the punch whistle by his ear. Denison kept trying to get his knee up into Brian's groin.

Regretfully, Brian hit him.

Denison went down flat on his back and slid. He did not stir. His chin was resting on his right shoulder, and one knee was slightly raised.

He was lying in the same position when Brian left with the attaché case.

Downstairs the pretty blonde was on the telephone. She looked up at him.

Brian smiled. ''Mr. Denison said you can go to lunch.''

FOUR

BRIAN LEFT THE BUILDING AND CUT ACROSS THE STREET TO-
ward a parking lot on the opposite corner. Most cars parked in
the lot were expensive and new: Toyotas and Hondas and Nis-
sans with a sprinkling of Bentleys, Mercedes, Peugeots, and
Cadillacs. There was even a bat-winged DeLorean with several
dents and scratches attesting to its age.

George Denison had seen Diane getting into her car at a parking lot, and this was the only parking lot visible from his window.

A young Chinese man wearing a neat blue jumper and a white
cap approached him. "License numbah?"

"I'm interested in finding out about a car that was parked
here a few days ago," Brian said. "It belonged to a woman.
Probably a regular customer."

The attendant regarded him with a flat, uncomprehending
gaze.

"Her name was Diane Hollings," Brian said. "A very pretty
woman. You may remember her. I don't know what kind of car
she had."

"No English."

"You just spoke to me in English."

Another voice said, "He knows some words, yes, sir. But he
don't have the language." Phibul had joined them. "You wish
me to ask him?"

"Go ahead."

Phibul spoke rapidly to the young attendant, who answered
just as rapidly. Brian knew the answer before Phibul interpreted:

"He says he has many cars. He can't remember all."

30

"I wish I knew what kind it was."

"A white Mercedes, sir. This man and others working here have already been questioned."

Brian stared. "How do you know that?"

"I am police, sir." Phibul reached into the pocket of his tight red jacket to produce a card that he showed as identification. "Phang Eg Phiset will see you now."

"Who is he?"

"You have met him in house of woman who did bombing. Phang Eg Phiset is name of rank in police. Same like colonel your country."

"Colonel is a military rank in my country."

"Here rankings for police and military are same. Colonel Suvit will wish to know what is in the attaché case you carry."

"It's mine."

"You did not have same when you enter building." He put one hand on Brian's arm.

Brian foresaw what would happen. He would accompany Phibul to police headquarters where Colonel Suvit would examine the attaché case. Brian had no intention of letting that happen until he had a chance to examine the contents of the attaché case himself.

"Please do not make trouble," Phibul said.

Sometimes all that is needed is the courage to make trouble when trouble is called for.

He hooked the back of Phibul's leg with his foot and gave him a shove that sent him sprawling.

Traffic had stopped for a red light but surged forward as Brian reached the middle of the street. He made a broken field run, caught up with a small three-wheeled cab, and jumped in. The driver looked back, surprised to find he had a passenger.

"*Bangkok Post,*" Brian told him. "Hurry!"

The sign on the *Bangkok Post* building was a block ahead when Brian paid the driver, got out, and walked quickly to the building. In the lobby, a woman was stationed behind a circular desk.

He said, "Is there anyone who speaks English?"

"What is your wish, sir?"

"I'd like to see the editor. I have some important information to give him."

Ten minutes later he entered a conference room. The room was empty except for a man seated in a high-backed chair at a long table. He had a yellow moist face and lank black hair.

"I'm Harry Lokma," the man said. "I'm the managing editor. What can I do for you?"

Lokma spoke English with a nasal twang.

"You published some articles about the H & D Trading Company."

Lokma looked wary. "Yes, we did."

Brian put the attaché case on Lokma's desk. "I think you'll be interested in this."

Lokma indicated an empty chair with a hand movement as abrupt as a punctuation mark. He opened the attaché case and took out the two top folders. He began leafing through the papers in the folders, then paused to scrutinize a page carefully.

"Where did you get this?"

"From a man named George Denison."

"Surely he did not give it to you."

"Not exactly."

Lokma touched a handkerchief to an oily looking heat rash on his forehead. "Do you know what you've got? A very careful record of transactions that apparently took place outside H & D Company's regular business."

"I figured it was important."

"Why did you bring it here?"

"I couldn't think of any place else. If you're like American newspapermen, you protect your sources of information."

"We try to. I'm going to have to know more about how you are involved in all this."

Brian told him. Lokma listened attentively, occasionally tapping a fingernail on a folder he had on his desk. At one point he offered Brian a drink of "good American bourbon, not Mekong. One fourteen proof." He poured from the silver decanter. The bourbon was fine.

When Brian finished talking, Lokma nodded. "I'll be very interested in seeing the rest of what is in this attaché case. Can you leave it with me?"

"I'm willing to make a deal. I'll trade for information about everything that was going on at the H & D Trading Company. Not just the stuff that's been published. The real inside story."

"What do you want to find out?"

"Why my wife got herself killed in a terrorist bombing. Or why someone tried to make it look that way."

Lokma tapped the folder again with his index finger. "These

records were obviously kept by an experienced accountant. Your wife?''

"Never. She hated detail."

"Then it's a woman named Ellen Peterson. She's the accountant for the H & D Trading Company."

"She'd be worth talking to."

"She's dropped out of sight. It's possible she's left the country. Would you care for another drink?"

"Sure." Lokma poured, and Brian forgot to say when. "Do we have a deal?"

"I'll introduce you to someone who can answer all your questions." Lokma picked up the telephone. "Ask Arunee to come in, please."

A few moments later the door opened to admit a slender, graceful Thai woman who moved with the languid grace of a ballet dancer. Her skirt was wrapped tightly about her hips and fell almost to her ankles.

Lokma said, "Arunee has been gathering material for our articles about the smuggling trade. Arunee, this is Mr. Buckley. He was married to Diane Hollings."

Brian stood up. The woman barely came up above his elbow. Soft brown eyes raised to his.

"I am pleased to meet you, Mr. Buckley." Her voice was low-pitched and musical.

Lokma said, "He's got some valuable information about secret business dealings of the H & D Company. I have a hunch that what he's after and what we're after may fit together."

Arunee looked at Lokma inquiringly. "What would you like me to do?"

"Tell him everything you know. Make sure he gets to see people who can help him, and keep him away from people who can hurt him." Lokma's face squeezed together in a monkeylike grimace. "Above all, don't let him jump in the water with both feet until he knows how deep the water is."

"When would you like me to start?"

"You've started."

"Not until I finish my drink," Brian said.

BRIAN AND ARUNEE LEFT THE *Bangkok Post* BUILDING AS ANother rain-bearing cloud was heading in from the southwest. A gusty wind was blowing.

"Where would you like to go?" she asked.

"I'd like to see the Royal Palace. The place where it happened."

"I don't think visitors are permitted now. But I will see what can be done."

The area around the Royal Palace and the old city, along Rajadamnoen Road, was crowded with government offices. Their taxi let them off near a large oval-shaped field that resembled a racetrack with a wide walk around the periphery. Trees bordered the sidewalk at its edge.

"This place is called the Phra Mane ground," Arunee said. "On Saturday and Sunday it is a market place. Because of what happened here the market will not open this weekend."

Beyond the Phra Mane ground was the Royal Palace, a glittering Thai version of Versailles with golden pagodas and turquoise temples. Barriers were set up along the approaches with warning signs in Thai, English, and French.

A hundred yards from the palace they were stopped by a police guard. Arunee took a card from her purse to show him. He shook his head.

She continued to speak urgently, and after a while the policeman seemed less sure. He left her to consult with another policeman on guard at the barrier. Both policemen looked at Brian curiously.

"What did you tell him?" Brian asked.

"That you are a very important American person connected with television. I hope they're impressed."

"What was the card you showed him?"

"My press credentials. That helped to convince him of your importance. Would I be acting as your escort if you were not important?"

The policeman returned, and gave Arunee her press pass.

She turned to Brian. "He says no one can approach nearer to the palace than this. It is forbidden."

The towers and spires of the Royal Palace showed above gleaming white walls. So near and yet so far.

"There is another way, I think," Arunee said. "I know a restaurant that has a close view of the palace entrance. Will that satisfy?"

"It will satisfy." Brian was suddenly aware of being hungry. "I haven't had lunch yet."

"Do you like Thai food?"

"I don't know. I'm willing to try."

Several persons were at the bar of the restaurant. There were booths on the right side and the place had a pleasantly dim ambiance.

Arunee chose a booth at the rear of the restaurant. In the next booth a turbaned Indian Sikh was in earnest conversation with a woman in a gauzy dress who wielded a heavily ornamented fan. At a nearby table several men in resplendent uniforms were having an animated debate.

Arunee noticed Brian looking at the men. "Don't worry. They're just private guards at business establishments."

Their waiter was an elderly man who wore a bright red cotton skirt under his white shirt. Arunee ordered. As soon as the waiter left, she indicated that Brian should follow her.

A large window at the rear looked out on a garden enclosed by a fence about three feet high. Looking over the fence they had a clear view of the Royal Palace.

A few trucks were pulled up near the entrance, and workers were unloading construction materials. Surrounding the large courtyard were buildings, temples, and pavilions. A painter's ladder was tilted against a pillar supporting an open pavilion. He was touching up burned and blasted spots on the eaves.

In the center of the courtyard, a large fenced area surrounded a deep black hole with jagged edges.

That is where it happened, Brian thought. Right there.

Nearly fifty yards from the palace building.

They returned to the booth. The waiter brought a tray with fried oysters, bamboo shoots, pickled fish, cucumber, and lotus. Brian barely touched the food.

"Am I wrong or did you notice something?" Arunee asked.

He nodded. "That bomb crater is pretty far from the palace. What kind of trigger was used?"

"A timing device. Fragments were found."

"That doesn't make sense. She wouldn't have used a timing device. Too many chances of something going wrong. Suppose there was a delay in traffic. The bomb might have gone off before the car got anywhere near the palace."

"What would be used?"

"Anything that set off the explosion on command. With a hand trigger it could be set off at the last possible minute. Or with explosives rigged to go off on contact the car could be driven right into the palace wall."

"Perhaps she did not think of that."

"There's a more likely explanation."

''What?''

''She didn't put the explosive in the car. She was the victim. It's only *where* the bomb went off that made her look like a terrorist.''

''You mean someone killed her. Why?''

''George Denison told me there's a partnership agreement. The survivor gets everything.''

''It would be most foolish of him. He would be, how you say, killing the golden goose. Only after your wife joined the firm did it really start to make a lot of money. Until then it was just another trading firm, exporting rubber, tin and jute and importing machinery and equipment. She made the deal with Wanchai.''

''Who's he?''

''A warlord who rules over the Golden Triangle. That's in the northeast where Burma, Laos, and Thailand meet. It would be the poorest part of my country—except that the farmers in the Golden Triangle grow opium. That crop brings several thousand dollars an acre and helps Wanchai pay for the goods he has to import.''

''You say Diane made a deal with him? What kind of deal?''

''I don't know the details, but it was immensely profitable. With her gone, I don't think Denison can maintain the relationship. He had more to lose than gain with her death.''

''That doesn't rule him out.''

''There must be more likely suspects. Mr. Lokma may have found a clue in the documents you left with him. I'd better call him.''

She went to a wall telephone near the restaurant entrance. The elderly waiter brought the check and Brian paid. After a few minutes he noticed that Arunee was still on the telephone. She was listening, saying little, and rigidity seemed to have entered her body.

When she returned to the table, she sat down close to him and said in a soft whisper, ''Police have come to the newspaper looking for you.'' She watched him with a curiously intent scrutiny. ''What happened when you took the attaché case away from Mr. Denison?''

''He tried to pull a gun on me.''

''You fought?''

''If he claims assault I'll claim self defense. I don't know the law here, but in the United States it isn't an offense to take a gun away from someone who's threatening you with it.''

She answered, "It isn't as simple as that. George Denison is dead. And the police want you for his murder."

ARUNEE DID NOT THINK IT SAFE FOR HIM TO LEAVE THE RES-
taurant. She left alone and returned in twenty minutes. Harry Lokma was with her.

"We're going to my house," she said. "No one will look for you there."

Lokma had a battered yellow Toyota borrowed from the newspaper car pool. On the way he outlined Brian's predicament. The facts were condemning. Brian was the last person known to have seen George Denison alive. He admitted there had been a struggle, and he had taken a gun away from Denison.

"I didn't kill him. When I left the office he was unconscious, but he'd have come to in a few minutes. How was he killed?"

"Shot through the head. At close range. With his own gun."

"I guess that doesn't look too good."

"No, it doesn't."

"I haven't been in Bangkok twenty-four hours, and already I'm the chief suspect in a murder case. What I'd like to know is why the police came to you. How did they know I was there?"

"That isn't hard to explain," Lokma said. "The police have informers everywhere. There's almost certainly one or two working in our office."

Arunee's home was a small frame structure built on stilts on the bank of the Chao Prya River. It was amid a jumble of similar houses jostling each other for space.

Seated in the living room with Arunee and Harry Lokma, Brian watched through a very wide open window the dutiful ferries plying between opposite banks, and dowager-like barges moving at a stately pace.

Arunee said to Lokma, "We ought to discuss his options now that the police are on his trail. Clearly he can't go back to his hotel."

"I don't see that he has any options," Lokma said, "Other than voluntarily going to the police."

"What kind of story can he tell them?"

"Why not the truth?" Brian suggested.

Lokma said, "I believe your story, but it might be too much to ask the police to. If you tell them what you told us, you'll be a cooked rice bird. Head, beak, and tail. Even if they don't charge you with the murder, they'll hold you for stealing an attaché case with presumably valuable documents and then assaulting a policeman.''

"What do you suggest?" Brian asked.

"There was no fight with Denison. It never happened. He gave you the attaché case because it had your wife's personal papers.''

"Will the police believe that?" Arunee asked.

"Probably not. But they can't prove it isn't so.''

"They'll want to know where the attaché case is now.''

"He lost it in the confusion after he broke away from what he thought was an attempted robbery. He dropped it in traffic, and doesn't know what happened to it.''

"Then why did he come to us?" Arunee asked skeptically. "To place an ad in the Lost and Found section?''

"Good idea. I should have thought of that. The ad will appear in tomorrow's paper. He'll offer a reward.''

"That policeman showed me his ID,'' Brian said. "Why would I think it was an attempted robbery?''

"Anyone can show an ID. Try to remember this. The story doesn't have to be convincing. It just has to sound better than what actually happened.''

"When should I turn myself in?''

"You have nothing to gain by delay.''

"I'd like to talk to someone at the American Embassy before making up my mind.''

"When you're ready you can reach me at the office.''

After Lokma left in the yellow Toyota, Brian placed a call to the American Embassy. In a few moments he was telling his predicament to Horace Calisher.

"It sounds very serious,'' Calisher said.

"Before I go to the police, I want to know what my legal rights are. What kind of system have they got here?''

"Not much different from ours. Same rights and privileges. Same cautions. At a preliminary questioning you won't have a lawyer with you. Bear in mind that anything you say may be used against you in a court later.''

"In court?''

"I hope you're not going to trial, but it's possible. We'll do all we can to help you.''

The wheezing rattling of an old heavy engine came from

outside the house, followed by a faint squeal of brakes. Footsteps approached, walking at first, then starting to run.

"My children," Arunee said. "Home from school."

A boy about eight years of age and a girl a couple of years younger erupted into the room. They were spilling over with energy, chattering and laughing. They fell silent as they saw Brian.

Arunee said slowly in English, "Children, I would like you to meet a friend of mine. Mr. Buckley."

The tall, thin boy stared at him. His short, pretty sister made a *wai* of greeting with her palms together near her forehead.

Brian rose to his full height. The girl's eyes widened in disbelief. The boy faced him sturdily, his stare turning a little defiant.

The girl hid her face against Arunee to whisper something.

Arunee said, smiling, "My daughter Ajana says you are very big. She wants to know if you are a monster."

"I was," Brian said, "but I reformed."

The boy grinned, and, taking her cue from him, Ajana giggled.

Arunee said, "We will speak English so that my friend here will understand."

The boy put his palms together in a *wai*. "I am most pleased to meet you."

"I am pleased to meet you also," Brian said, and, imitating the boy's gesture, put his own palms together at his forehead.

Both children broke out in spontaneous laughter.

"This is not the custom," Arunee explained. "A grown person does not greet a child with hands held so high. That is the mark of highest respect, of the kind a child gives to a grown person, or a person of inferior rank to someone much superior."

"I'll try it my way." He held out his hand to the young boy. "My friends call me Brian. I hope you will."

The young boy looked to his mother for instruction. Receiving none, he put out his hand.

"My name is Chakra, sir."

His hand disappeared up to the wrist in Brian's grasp. Ajana gave a small cry.

Arunee said, "Ajana is afraid you are hurting her brother."

Brian released Chakra's hand which reappeared intact. Ajana blushed, her cheeks turning a dusky rose. Her gaze remained shyly on Brian, while she spoke rapidly in Thai to Arunee.

"Ajana wishes to explain that she only feared because you say you are a monster."

"A reformed one."

"She doesn't understand 'reformed.' "

Brian turned to Chakra. "Will you please make this meaning clear to your sister? A reformed person is one who has begun a new and different life."

Chakra nodded proudly and spoke to Ajana in Thai. Her smile was the most delightful and charming that Brian had ever seen on a child. She parted from her mother, came to Brian and without hesitation offered her hand. Brian engulfed it in his own. She let her hand remain trustingly in his.

Brian said with grave respect, "Thank you, Ajana."

"Saowa will be here in a minute," Arunee said to her children. "You can play outside until she comes for you."

She ushered them outside. When she returned, Brian was standing at the window and staring moodily out at a barge with giant eyes painted on either side of its prow. The painted eyes seemed to be helping the barge find its way among smaller craft.

"I guess there's nothing else to do," he said. "I'll go quietly."

FIVE

The yellow Toyota stopped on a narrow street in front of a large dingy stone building. A policeman in khaki uniform was standing just inside a doorway.

"They're expecting you," Lokma said to Brian. "How do you feel?"

"Like I'm about to cross a minefield."

"It's better this way than waiting for them to issue an arrest warrant. Keep the right attitude."

"What is the right attitude?"

The policeman left the doorway to approach the car.

Lokma said, "Don't admit more than you have to. And don't let them bluff you into thinking they know more than they do."

The policeman came to the car door and spoke through the window.

Lokma interpreted. "He wants you to go with him."

Brian got out of the car.

"I'll see you soon," Lokma said.

The policeman took Brian firmly by one arm and led him inside the building. A line of men waited near a staircase that led up into invisible gloom.

Brian was taken past the line and up the stairs to where a man was stationed at a desk with an open register before him. The register was filled with hieroglyphic Thai signatures. The man pointed to an space in the register, and Brian added his name. His English writing looked strange on the page of Sanskrit.

He was taken through a small foyer that turned right into an entryway and door. The policeman knocked, and a voice answered.

The policeman opened the door into a room almost bare of furniture except for two wooden filing cabinets, a desk with a black leather high-backed chair, a similar chair facing the desk, and a standing lamp with a parchment shade.

Colonel Suvit was standing by a wide window with ornamental grilling, watering plants on the sill. The view was across a courtyard to the facade of a heavy, brown structure. Suvit continued watering plants for another minute. Then, turning abruptly away from the window, he put down the watering can and glanced at the policeman who promptly left the room.

In a harsh voice Suvit said, "You cannot deny that you are the murderer of George Denison. We have proof that you forced your way into his office and stole his attaché case. When he tried to resist you shot him. You cannot claim self defense. He was trying to protect his own property."

"Would you like to know what really happened?"

"I will listen to your explanation."

Brian repeated the story that he had agreed to tell. It was not the kind of story that would bear repetition, but Suvit was hearing it for the first time.

"When you left the office you say the victim was alive?"

"Yes."

"Who do you think killed him?"

"I understand he was in a pretty risky business. There may be hundreds of people who had a reason to."

"We do not know who these mysterious persons are. And we have no evidence to connect them to the crime. It is much different with you. His secretary testifies you went into his office without permission. He had given orders that he did not wish to see you. There was a struggle . . ."

"Did she say that?"

"You deny it?"

"It's your story. I don't mean to interrupt."

Suvit pursed his lips and was silent for a moment. "A gun was found beside his body. Did you bring it with you to his office?"

"I don't have a gun."

Suvit clearly suspected he was lying. "It will be better for you if you admit you are guilty. We know you killed George Denison, and we also know why. To steal valuable documents."

"I didn't steal anything."

"How did you get the attaché case?"

"I told you. He gave it to me. It contained my wife's personal papers."

Suvit's lidless gaze fixed on Brian with reptilian intensity. "Where is this attaché case now?"

"I told you that, too."

"Surely it is possible to invent a better story than you have told. What did you do after you discovered the attaché case was missing?"

"I decided to put an advertisement in a newspaper offering a reward for its return."

"Do you hope to find it again?"

"I don't see why not. Its contents are of no interest to anyone but me."

"You will have more time to consider changing your story."

"Am I under arrest?"

"I am merely keeping you until our investigation is complete."

"How long will that take?"

"A report is filed with the public prosecutor. Then a search warrant is obtained to search your room and the residences of others who may be in this crime. Many persons will be questioned, and some will be held for further questioning. In a murder of an important foreign person, such an investigation can take time."

"You have no legal right to keep me here."

Suvit steepled his fingers and rubbed the tips together, as though trying to remove his fingerprints.

"You are mistaken. Each metropolitan police station has a section where prisoners may be kept for a term up to one year."

"I would like to call the American Embassy."

"That is not possible."

"I'm entitled to a lawyer."

"You have not been charged with a crime."

"You can't hold me without charging me."

Suvit picked up an oblong block of wood resting on his desk and brought it down on the desktop. "You are obeying the laws of this country now. You will discover that stubbornness does not pay."

The door opened to admit the policeman who had been waiting outside.

Suvit spoke to him in Thai and then turned to Brian. "Go with him. If you wish to see me again, inform a guard at the jail of your desire."

* * *

BRIAN WAS TAKEN TO THE RECEPTION CENTER FOR NEW PRISoners, a large whitewashed room with barred windows.

The policeman removed Brian's wrist chains. A hawk-nosed, spectacled Thai ordered Brian to remove his clothes. When Brian had stripped to the skin, Hawknose examined his testicles and put on a rubber glove and prodded a finger up his anus. He removed the glove and asked Brian to open his mouth. He peered inside and tested Brian's teeth with his fingers. Only then did it occur to Brian that the examination was for concealed drugs.

Another man brought a shapeless green-black prison uniform. He held this up against Brian, frowned and shook his head.

Several other uniforms failed to provide a fit for Brian's huge frame. A lively discussion followed, and Brian was finally given back his own clothes to wear.

Next he was taken to a small adjacent room where he was posed sitting on a stool while a hooded camera took front and profile views under a harsh light.

He was fingerprinted, each finger rolled in a pad of ink and pressed down tight on a sheet of paper to leave a clear impression. At another table he was given a paraffin test—the wax put on hot and allowed to cool before being removed.

The chain handcuffs were put back on his wrists, and a uniformed guard accompanied him through a door. They went up stone steps into another large area with barred and wire-meshed windows near the ceiling. On both sides were rows of steel barred cells and a staircase of five stone steps ascended to another tier of cells.

They stopped opposite a cell where the guard unlocked the chain handcuffs, pushed Brian inside, and slammed the door.

A huskily built man was seated on one of two cots in the cell. He wore a stained, torn undershirt that revealed a blue and yellow tattoo on one shoulder.

He spoke to Brian in rapid Thai. Brian shrugged to indicate he did not understand.

"Francais?" the man asked.

"American."

"Yanqui doodle." He grinned widely. "What sign you born?" He spoke English with a heavy accent.

"I don't know."

"What month? What day?"

"April twenty-fifth."

"Taurus. I am very good astrologist. Use most modern Western method. Not Oriental."

"When it comes to astrology, I don't play favorites. I don't believe in any method."

The tattooed man stopped chewing and spat a stream of dark red betel juice at a round hole in a corner of the cell. He missed.

"My name Nguad, but everyone call me Tattoo. Nguad is Thai word for tattoo. What name of yours?"

"Buckley."

"I will work out name by numbers. I am numerologist also. Very good. You like pictured arm?"

The tattoo consisted of a crescent moon with a star between the rising horns of the crescent.

"It looks nice."

"I will give you tattoo very cheap. I am very good artist."

Brian sat down on the cot on the opposite wall.

"I am also a thief," Tattoo said. "That is my best profession."

"I'm sure you're good at it."

"Oh, yes. It is only bad luck that I am here. What is your crime, sir?"

"They're keeping me here for questioning."

Tattoo regarded him speculatively. "This is not fahrang cell block. For which kind of crime are you questioned?"

"Murder."

"Woman person or man person?"

"I didn't murder anyone." To change the subject, he asked, "What are you in jail for?"

"Mistake as astrologist."

"That can't be a crime."

"You do not understand. I am leader of *kemays*."

"Kemays?"

"Please. Your word in English for people who break in houses when persons not home or sleeping."

"Burglars."

Tattoo smiled happily. "Kemays make me leader because I tell them best time for burglar according to stars. One time I am poor astrologist, and we are catched up."

"How long have you been here?"

"One year next full moon."

"How long is your sentence?"

"No sentence. I still wait for trial."

"A year!"

"Do not concern self. If I am convicted I am move to real prison such like Bang Kwang or Chonburi or Sakhon Nakhon. Not so nice as here."

"You might not be convicted."

Tattoo looked solemn. "That would be bad carriage of justice."

In the other cells prisoners began rattling cans against the bars.

"Water time," Tattoo announced. He took a tin cup from beneath his cot and joined in the rattling din.

A stout young boy came down the corridor carrying a bucket that slopped over a little. He put the bucket down before a cell, and the occupants rushed to dip their tin cups.

"Where is yours?" Tattoo asked.

"I don't have one."

"Under cot. *Hurry!*"

Tattoo was looking anxiously at the stout young boy who had picked up his bucket to move on.

Brian found his cup just as the bucket was deposited outside their cell. Tattoo half filled a cup, drank it, and as the bucket was picked up, he quickly dipped his cup full again.

The water in the bucket was the color of stored dishwater. Scum clung to the sides of the bucket, and tiny live things crawled on its surface.

Brian did not dip his cup. The water boy moved away. Tattoo began to shout, but the water boy did not return.

Tattoo looked accusingly at Brian.

"I didn't like the look of it," Brian explained.

"You are much sorry later." Tattoo added something under his breath that sounded like swearing. "If you are camel then take for one who is not camel."

After draining his water cup Tattoo squatted over the round hole in the corner. An ammonia odor wafted through the cell.

Brian lay down on the cot. It was too short, and his feet and ankles protruded over the edge. The mattress was thin and lumpy.

"You want love maker?" Tattoo asked.

"What?" Brian thought he was getting a homosexual proposition.

Tattoo showed him a long narrow jar lined with soft greased cotton. "Love maker. I show how to use. Good as woman. Some like better."

"No, thanks."

"Cheap. Ten dollah."

"Not interested."

Brian tried to ignore Tattoo who set the jar at an angle into a slit in his mattress, kneeled in front of it, and began doing his business.

Brian wrapped himself in a cocoon of oblivion. After a while he dozed.

Images returned like a television replay. A red-jerseyed defender moved warily toward him, the only defender between him and the goal line. One on one. A battle he should win.

He faked right, shifted his weight sharply left. The red jersey floundered, hands grasping for him like a drowning man. Brian danced over the goal line and turned to look at the football field behind him. Ninety-three yards! He spiked the football in the end zone.

The image shifted with unbelievable clarity to a drizzly August afternoon, his first day of football practice after returning from Vietnam. He had the ball and was powering his way through the line. A defender blocked his way, and he tried the same move he had made more than two years before. He couldn't pivot, the leg buckled under him.

In the locker room when the others had gone, Brian stared at his reflection in the mirror on the inside of his locker door. He had passed through a barrier that left him unrecognizable to himself. He closed the door of his locker and on impulse picked up a bench and hurled it across the room.

He woke up with sweat cold on his face. His clothing was soaked.

It wasn't sweat.

In the adjoining cell the two occupants were making faces and uttering gibbering sounds. They had shinnied part way up between cell bars and were peeing on him. As Brian sat up they dropped off the bars and retreated to the middle of their cell, shrieking laughter.

Tattoo said, "They been too long time inside. New people make them crazy."

Put a sane man into a madhouse, Brian thought, and there's no hope he will cure the other inmates. *He* will go mad.

SIX

THE NEXT MORNING AFTER BREAKFAST, BRIAN HAD A VISITOR. Outside the wiremesh screen in the visitors' room was a dark-featured thin man, about fifty years old, nervously smoking a cigarette. He wore neatly pressed tropical slacks and a shirt fashioned in the distinctive Thai ikat tie-dyed weave.

"You're Buckley?"

"Yes."

"Uramadet. I'm your lawyer. Harry Lokma hired me to represent you." He spoke English with a New York accent.

"That's good news."

"I've got better. I talked to Denison's secretary, a woman named Jean Hudson. She admits she didn't hear a shot while you were there. And she left after you did. The paraffin test also proves you didn't fire a gun. That doesn't leave them with much of a case."

"When can I get out?"

"Don't misunderstand. They'll probably drop the murder charge, but they can hold you on other charges. This guy Suvit has taken a personal dislike to you."

"What other charges?"

"Stealing, resisting arrest, assaulting a police officer. Suvit is upset about an attaché case that's missing. What happened to it?"

"I lost it."

"How?"

Brian was tired of repeating the lie. "You'd better ask Harry Lokma about that."

"I will. Where are you from? The Big Apple?"

48

"Boston. But I live and work in New York."

"Greatest city in the world. I was born and bred there. Went to City College. Came back to Thailand for a visit, met a girl, and married. Here I am. But I still miss New York."

"Right now, I miss it more than anybody."

He certainly did not belong where he was. Nothing going on here was quite real to him, not a fractional part as real as a memory that just came into his head of striding along Madison Avenue and catching his reflection in a mirrored storefront. That's you. Nobody else but you.

"We haven't got much time to talk, so listen carefully. I'll plead you not guilty to any other charges. They're bailable offenses. Can you raise money for bail?"

"How much?"

"If I can get the right judge, we might get away as cheap as ten thousand."

"Dollars?"

"We're not talking funny money."

"I can't come close."

"Can you borrow it?"

"I don't have rich friends."

"I've had other clients like you. After they've spent time in a Thai prison, they find the money someplace. They borrow from their parents, from their bank, from their employer."

"There's no place I can borrow that much."

"You'd be surprised. Do you have any credit cards?"

"Yes."

"We can get a cash advance against those. Life insurance?"

"A small policy. My brother is the beneficiary. He's an invalid. If anything happens to me, he'll need it."

"Right now *you* need it. Take care of him later when you're safe at home. With a power of attorney I can borrow money on that policy. Any idea what the cash-in value is?"

"About four thousand."

"How about your airline ticket? Did you buy a round trip?"

"Yes."

"I'll get back the unused portion." He produced a pocket calculator and made a rapid addition. "You're short. How much do you have with you?"

"A few hundred. Mostly traveler's checks."

"Lokma will put up the rest. He feels he owes you."

"Don't you have bail bondsmen?"

"They all know you'll skip the country as soon as you're out."

"I won't."

"Yes, you will. It's the way things are done. The payoff is supervised by the police. An arrest is made, the people they arrest put up bail, they skip, and the police split the loot. Bail is the price of getting home."

"What if I don't pay?"

"You'll stay in jail, and they'll make it very unpleasant. Then you'll go to trial and probably be convicted. The whole justice system will be against you for cheating them out of their money."

"Can't the American Embassy do something?"

"They can't interfere with Thai sovereignty. You give it some thought, and you'll see you can't beat the system."

A guard returned to signal the end of the interview.

Brian was brought back to his cell. Tattoo presented him with a sheet of paper on which he had drawn a circle with segmented divisions and scribbled notations.

"Your horoscope. Very good auspices. You are fortunate man. Sun in Taurus and moon in Capricorn. Sun and moon form trine. This is very best aspect."

"Does it say when I'll get out of here?"

"Present difficulty caused by Saturn in fourth house. This causes trouble through lost or stolen property."

"You hit that right on the knuckle."

"Very good auspices. Keep chart. You pay when you have money."

At night lights were turned out in the corridor. Brian spent a sleepless hour, his legs protruding over the cot, his hands locked behind his head. Tiny invisible mites were dancing on his skin. He worried about what the lawyer had told him. He'd never had the knack of making money, except when he was playing football. But then it wasn't for the money, it was for the sport. That was different.

Working in a brokerage firm he became used to people who talked only of money. He thought of them running and running, holding baskets in their outstretched arms while the money rained in.

Tattoo was asleep, breathing stentoriously. Suddenly he began to groan loudly. He sat up, legs drawn up sharply beneath his chin and his head bowed.

Brian sat up also. "What's the matter?"

Tattoo shook his head. He clutched his legs tightly and began rocking back and forth.

Brian went over to sit beside him. "Are you sick? Do you need a doctor?"

Tattoo began shivering. "Nose stuff," he said faintly.

He appeared to be in a stupor, staring at Brian as though he had never seen him before. Suddenly he began to shout. Shouting, he ran to the cell door, grabbed the bars with both hands and tried to put his head between them.

The outside door to the cell block opened with a clang, and heavy footsteps came on the run. Tattoo ran back to his cot, half crouching against the wall.

Guards rushed into the cell and seized him. They hit him and yanked him from the cot. Tattoo crossed both arms over his head and howled as they dragged him across the floor.

Brian yelled at the guards, "He's sick! Leave him alone!"

They dragged Tattoo out of the cell. Brian reached the door just as it slammed in his face.

"Where are you taking him, you bastards?"

Tattoo, still howling, was dragged up the short flight of steps that led to the upper tier. More clanging, a breaking of glass, and a heavy thumping. Then a high, sharp, cracking sound. A whip.

Tattoo's howling turned into tortured shrieks.

The whip sounds went on and on, and so did Tattoo's shrieking. Prisoners in other cells banged their tin cups against the bars. Finally the whip-cracking stopped. Tattoo's shrieks subsided into a loud sobbing, then a whimpering and moaning that went on for a long time.

At five o'clock in the morning, Brian was restlessly tossing on his cot, not fully awake, not fully alert. It was hot, and he was listless. He thought he heard light footsteps in the corridor.

He turned on his stomach and put both hands over his ears, trying to re-enter the blissful blankness of sleep. Then he heard another sound, so faint it might have been an illusion. It was the clicking of a lock being disengaged.

He rolled over just as the cell door sprung open, and a bulky shadow lunged at his cot. Brian had a subliminal glimpse of a blade in the harsh light.

He moved quickly, rolling in toward the attacker. The dagger ripped into the mattress.

Brian struck out, the blow glancing off the attacker's right ear, but with enough power to twist the man's head to the side, and prevent him from pulling the dagger free. Brian seized the man by his shirt, dragging himself up as he propelled him forward. The man's fingers clawed at Brian's eyes. Brian got the palm of his hand under the man's jaw and shoved hard.

The man reeled backward, and Brian went after him. The man lashed back with his right leg, just missing Brian's kneecap and landing on his thigh. Brian drove his fist deep into the man's kidney. The man gave a muffled cry and half turned. Brian saw a face distorted with rage.

Too late Brian realized that the half-turn was a maneuver, giving momentum to a rigid forearm that crashed into his throat. Brian fell back, unable to breathe, and with astonishing quickness the man was out through the cell door and racing down the corridor.

BRIAN WAS INTERROGATED ALL MORNING BY GUARDS IN A SUF-focating, small, windowless enclosure. They seemed unwilling to accept his version of what happened. How could a killer get into the area and open the door to his cell? Brian must have been having a nightmare.

Not even his bruises convinced them. He could easily have inflicted blows on himself in a nightmare frenzy. No other prisoner in the cell block corroborated his story. Apparently they saw nothing, heard nothing.

Finally Brian was returned to his cell, to the nauseating smells, Tattoo's groaning, and the raucous voices of fellow prisoners taunting him. It happened, he told himself, no matter what anyone says.

At noon, during the brief forty-five minute rest period allowed in the courtyard, he exercised as strenuously as he could. He hoped to tire himself so that he could sleep when night came. At the end of the exercise period Brian asked for permission to make a telephone call to his lawyer. Permission was granted. Uramadet was not in his office, but his secretary took the message. Brian authorized Uramadet to start proceedings at once for bail.

He spent a sleepless night, listening for another murderous intruder. The next morning a guard came down the corridor to the prison cell. The guard unlocked the barred door and indicated that Brian should follow him. Tattoo was sitting with his back against the rear wall, staring at nothing. He roused himself to say, "I told you. Very good auspices."

The guard offered Brian a cigarette as they walked along the corridor. Brian shook his head, and the guard clapped a friendly hand on his shoulder and, smiling, said a few words in Thai meant to be reassuring. Brain would not have been surprised to hear him say, "No hard feelings, old chap."

They went downstairs to the door through which Brian had first entered the building.

Outside, the day was sunny and beautiful, with a cleansing wind that kept the humidity at a reasonable level. Outside, Brian thought, days are usually beautiful.

An ancient vintage Citroen of a faded blue color was waiting at the curb with a uniformed policeman at the wheel. The guard accompanied Brian into the rear seat.

Brian asked of no one in particular, "Where are we going?"

The guard nodded, smiled, and offered Brian another cigarette. When Brian refused, the guard lighted his own cigarette and settled back into the rear seat. He seemed to be enjoying the break from routine.

The ancient Citroen maneuvered through bicycles and motor traffic and passed through dusty streets where refuse was piled high at the curbs and skeletal dogs and crows picked through it. They stopped before a building with a large open patio fronted by two stone pillars, and the guard accompanied Brian into the building.

The courtroom had a high ceiling and several large gently whirring fans. In the spectator's section the benches were empty except for two old women, one of whom was crying.

Uramadet was seated behind a polished table facing a raised platform with a high built chair and a desk on which two incense sticks were burning in a bowl.

Uramadet got up to shake hands with Brian. He remained standing as a gong sounded faintly and the judge entered the courtroom. The judge wore a white jacket over a longyi. He sat on the high-built chair on the platform.

Uramadet leaned toward Brian. "Now you'll see how quickly justice is done when the right hands are greased. The public prosecutor prepared an indictment. Grand theft. We're going to plead not guilty. It's a bailable offense. Suvit dropped the other charges as soon as he got the attaché case."

Brian was not following this. How did Suvit get the attaché case? Harry Lokma would not have surrendered it voluntarily.

He was unable to question Uramadet further because at that

moment the judge picked up a block of wood and brought it down on his desk. Everyone in the courtroom came to attention.

The judge spoke in rapid Thai.

"He's declaring court in session," Uramadet translated.

Almost as soon as the judge finished speaking, Uramadet stood up. The judge asked him a question.

Uramadet said to Brain, "He wants to know if you understand the proceedings or need an interpreter. I'll tell him I'm your interpreter. Okay?"

"I guess so."

Uramadet spoke to the judge who seemed satisfied. The judge picked up a document and read from it at length.

Uramadet provided quick flashes of interpretation: "He's reading the indictment and bill of particulars. . . . He says you are not required to make statements that will incriminate you. . . . Now he will ask how you plead."

The judge asked a question, and Uramadet replied briefly. The judge frowned, said a few words, and brought down his block of wood on the desk.

"We can go now," Uramadet said.

Brian asked as they left the courtroom: "What happened back there?"

"You pleaded not guilty. The judge set bail at eight thousand dollars. Lokma advanced the money so I can pay bail now instead of waiting till I get it all together. You won't have to spend another night in jail."

Brian felt a pleasant chill race through his body. He was free.

WHEN HE RETURNED TO POLICE HEADQUARTERS TO PICK UP HIS belongings, he was told that Colonel Suvit wished to see him. A policeman was waiting to take him. With a sense of disquiet Brian went with him to Suvit's office.

Suvit was again standing by the window. "The attaché case has been found. It is on top of my desk. I wish you to examine it."

The attaché case was unlocked, and Brian opened it.

"Is everything as you remember it?" Suvit asked. "Nothing is missing?"

"I'm not sure I can tell. Everything was in folders, and I didn't look at them carefully."

Suvit's flutelike voice was higher pitched: "You said there were only personal papers belonging to your late wife. There are not such papers here. These deal only with business matters of no importance."

"Apparently, George Denison misled me."

"If some papers were removed, others may have been also."

"You should ask the person who found it."

"A telephone call directed us to a locker in Hualamphong Railway Station. We found the attaché case as you now see it. It is strange that it was not returned to the *Bangkok Post*, which had offered a reward for it."

Brian decided to say nothing. He did not want to repeat the absurd story of how he had lost the attaché case.

"Meestrah Buckley, I believe you know where are the missing documents." Colonel Suvit passed a hand over his shaved head. "I am forced to accept the situation for the present, but this matter is not settled. Do you plan to remain long in Bangkok?"

"I have no definite plans."

"I would be most careful to avoid trouble. The next time you will not get away so easily. *Sawat dee khrop.*"

"Good day to you," Brian said politely.

SEVEN

CONSIDERING THE LEVEL OF CORRUPTION IN BANGKOK, COL-onel Suvit regarded himself as an honest man.

He knew all about the H & D Trading Company's dealings with Khun Wanchai. The money paid out by the company in bribes was large. Although Suvit never got a share, several important government officials were receiving annual incomes that resembled their telephone numbers. Had he wished to pursue the matter he might have caused these important officials anxious moments, but his situation was delicate. At fifty-nine years of age he was only a year away from retirement. He could not incur the enmity of anyone in a position to endanger his pension.

He had learned from sad experience how vital it was to provide for one's old age. His father had been in the servant profession. When dressed in a snowy white jacket *pakima* he could perform with as much dignity as an English butler. Dishonesty proved his ruin. One night his employer picked the lock of his room and found a small treasure stored under his bed: a full bottle of twenty-year-old Scotch accumulated by emptying the bottoms of drinks left after a party, and several insignificant items of clothing that seemed unlikely to be missed.

The police were summoned, he was arrested, convicted, and served a year in prison. To single him out for such punishment was unfair. The transgression was the kind most employers would have overlooked.

On his release he had no "long paper" or reference, and so was unable to earn a living as a servant. He went downhill swiftly, became an idler, a habitual drunk, and died horribly from elephantiasis in a fly-ridden hospital ward. Remembering how his father had suffered at the hands of a white fahrang employer, Suvit vowed never to forget their cruelty. He also learned a lesson: it is crucial to protect oneself when engaged in questionable activities.

The temptation of the attaché case, however, was great enough to warrant taking an unusual risk. The contents probably dealt with secret transactions of the H & D Trading Company. With that kind of information even a person less adroit than himself could devise highly profitable schemes.

For several minutes after Brian left, Suvit sat in thoughtful silence. Finally he picked up the telephone and dialed an extension within the building.

"Has the fahrang prisoner left?"

"His personal things are now being returned to him."

"His hotel room has been searched?"

"Nothing of importance was found, sir."

"Bring here the prisoner who was with the fahrang in his cell."

As he stepped out the door of police headquarters, Brian drew in a great lungful of air. Immediately he began to feel more like himself. He was still wearing the clothes he arrived in and carrying the small package of personal items he had brought with him several days before.

His plan was to go directly to his hotel room, shower and shave, and put on fresh clothes, and treat himself to an edible meal. Then he would call Arunee and Harry Lokma and find out if anything of interest had occurred during his enforced absence.

A youth wearing a short-sleeved brown shirt and blue jeans lounged against a wall. At the corner as Brian started to cross the street, a bicycle bell rang a sharp warning. He stepped back onto the curb, and a bicyclist whizzed past without a backward look.

The youth in the brown shirt came up beside him. He spoke in an undertone without looking at Brian.

"Be at Dorn Saeng restaurant at five o'clock this afternoon. Please to make sure no one follows."

The youth hurried away without a backward glance.

Before returning to his hotel room, Brian stopped in a pharmacy. After a hot bath and shave, he washed his hair in a strong solution guaranteed to kill lice, using the solution on every part of his body. Itching symptoms in his underarms and rectum and genital organs vanished.

He lay down and slept for two hours. When he awoke he went to the closet to find something to wear. A pair of slacks was hanging more toward the center than he recalled, and the one tie he had was in the middle of the wire hanger instead of draped loosely in a corner.

On the closet floor his other pair of shoes were not precisely where they had been. He took down his suitcase from the top shelf to examine it. The lock worked more easily than it should have because it had been forced open and then reclosed.

He dressed and went downstairs. The young woman at the reception desk smiled pleasantly.

"I want to see the manager," Brian said curtly. "I have a complaint."

Her smile faded. She disappeared through a door at the rear and returned in a moment.

"Mr. Paetao will see you now, sir."

As Brian entered the office, a portly man with a tiny gray moustache rose to greet him.

"Why was my room searched?" Brian demanded.

"I am so sorry, sir. The maid informed us that the room had not been occupied for several nights. We were afraid you might have left without informing us. I gave strict orders to be most careful that nothing was disturbed."

"Please leave instructions that no one is to enter my room again without my permission."

"Do you object to the maid cleaning your room?"

"I think you know very well what I object to."

As Brian left the hotel, a taxi hovered and then moved up to greet him. Phibul was at the wheel.

"Where to, sir?"

"There are other taxis on line. Do you have a special arrangement?"

"Oh, yes, sir. Police business."

"I'm just going for a walk. Better luck next time."

He took a roundabout route, checking at each intersection to be sure Phibul was not following him. When satisfied he had eluded him, he hailed a taxi to take him to the Dorn Saeng restaurant.

He entered the restaurant and spotted the youth in the brown shirt standing beside the wall telephone near the entrance. He went over.

"The person who wishes to see you is in the last booth down the right side, sir."

Arunee was in the booth they had occupied on their previous visit to the Dorn Saeng.

"Why all this secrecy?" Brian asked.

"The first article is going to appear tomorrow morning. Mr. Lokma doesn't want anyone to know the information came from you."

He sat down opposite her. "Colonel Suvit already suspects a connection. He knows you took the important documents before giving back the attaché case."

"Were you followed here?"

"I don't think so. Anyway, it isn't Colonel Suvit I'm worried about. Something happened to me in prison that I can't believe Colonel Suvit is responsible for."

He told her about the attempt to murder him in his cell.

Her almond-colored skin had the pallor of fear. "You must leave Bangkok at once. It will not be safe for you here. Wanchai must have found out who supplied the information we are starting to publish."

"What about you and Lokma? You've both got your necks in the noose."

"That cannot be helped."

He admired her unassuming courage. "I didn't sign on to be a hero, but I came here to find out about my wife, and I'm not leaving until I do. I appreciate the advice, however."

She shook her head. "You still don't understand. The whole picture has changed. The H & D Company and Khun Wanchai weren't ordinary trading partners."

"What were they?"

"We did a lot of cross-checking during the last few days. We traced bills of lading in the attaché case and found the addresses to which material was being shipped. There were often several addresses, many of which were simple transfer points. We were able to follow the trail by comparing the description of the merchandise and the prices paid and the original suppliers. The nature of the merchandise is quite different from what it seems."

"In what way?"

"They use code words on their bills of lading. 'Typewriters' is the code for machine guns. 'Kerosene' is airplane fuel. 'Dynamite' is a plastic explosive known as C-4 that has the destructive power of a small nuclear bomb.''

She stopped speaking as the elderly waiter came to the table to take their order.

When the waiter left, Brian said, ''That stuff must be expensive. What is Wanchai up to?''

Arunee hesitated before answering softly, ''The classic route of invasion has always been from the north. Ever since the Burmese came down centuries ago to destroy the lovely city of Ayudhaya.''

''Is he really planning to invade?''

''I think so. Yes.''

''Can he get away with it?''

''It is only possible if he has the secret support of a powerful nation. A nation that does not like the present Thai government and its pro-Western sympathies.''

''Who would that be?''

''The People's Republic of China. They consider Southeast Asia to be their natural sphere of influence. Thailand would be a very rich prize, a wedge that could easily lead to an eventual takeover of all Southeast Asia.''

''The United States would never stand by and watch that happen.''

''That is why the Chinese are going to great lengths to make sure no one can connect them directly with Wanchai. They do not supply weapons or money. Wanchai arms himself entirely with Western weapons, paying with heroin. Ninety tons of heroin. Its value at the end of the line, smuggled from Central and South America and Mexico into your country, is in the hundreds of millions of dollars.''

''Then what does he need Red China for?''

''If he gains power, he will need protection against Vietnam and its allies. They would not dare to attack an ally of China. It would set off an explosion that might begin the kind of war no one dares to think about.''

The elderly waiter returned to clear away the table and present the check. Brian paid the check, she murmured ''thank you,'' and as they stood up, he again felt like an awkward giant beside her. She was so compact and gracefully proportioned that she made him feel he had a glandular problem.

Outside the restaurant a street vendor was cooking rice honeycakes over a charcoal fire.

"Smells good."

"They are good," Arunee said.

He bought two, and gave her one. The honeycakes were delicious, crumbly, and sweet. Arunee said she had to go back to the office, but they idled along the street in warm humid air.

"Would you like to visit the United States someday?"

"Oh, yes. Various aspects that I see on television impress me. My children would like to see Disneyland."

"But you wouldn't like to live there."

"Forever? No."

"It isn't all Disneyland."

"This is my home, and I never wish for another. Thais pray to the Lord Buddha that in our next life we will be reborn as a Thai."

The *Bangkok Post* building was a block ahead when Arunee stopped.

"I do not think you should come further than this."

He pointed to the shadowed side of the building where a denser darkness humped outward. "What's that?"

The hump of darkness became a man descending. At that moment a window flew open on a floor several stories above, and a woman's voice cried loudly.

"What did she say?" Brian asked.

Arunee looked at him with widening eyes. "Stop, thief!"

The man dropped to the sidewalk, landing in a crouch. He started off quickly, carrying a box under his arm.

Brian ran parallel to him along the opposite sidewalk, ducking in and out of pedestrians, and catching an occasional glimpse of his quarry through the passing cars.

They neared a park. Brian made a slanting run through traffic. Car horns blared. Brakes squealed. He pounded up onto the sidewalk a dozen strides behind the fleeing man, as he reached a low stone fence bordering the park. He vaulted over it, and Brian hurdled after him. He closed in and flung himself forward in a tackle. They crashed together to the ground.

Agile as an eel, the man twisted out of Brian's grasp and scrambled to his feet. Brian caught his ankle and brought him down again.

The man swung the metal box with great force. It cymballed against Brian's head.

For a moment Brian was dazed. He was trying to shake the

blurs out of his vision, when he saw the man leap back over the stone fence and start running along the sidewalk.

A taxi pulled up at the curb.

Brian pointed to the running man. "Get him! He's a thief!"

Phibul started to get out of the taxi.

"Damn it, *no!*" Brian shouted, pointing again. *"Kemay!"*

Phibul jumped back in behind the wheel and went racing off in pursuit.

Arunee reached Brian. "Are you hurt?"

"I'm okay."

She picked up folders that had spilled onto the ground, and began putting them back into the metal box. She glanced at a folder as she picked it up.

"I think this came from your attaché case," she said.

IN HIS OFFICE HARRY LOKMA CLOSED THE GAPING HOLE IN HIS filing cabinet by sliding the metal drawer back in place.

"Is there anything else missing?" Arunee asked.

"No. This is what the thief was after. He knew exactly where to go to get it. That means he had help from someone who works here."

"Who?"

"Someone who knew when the door would be locked, so he could come in the window and work undisturbed. I don't think it is a coincidence that my secretary was on her rest time." Lokma pressed a button on the intercom. "Let's have her in and find out."

His guess was confirmed within a few minutes of interrogating his secretary, a middle-aged Thai woman named Mrs. Phun. She claimed she had gone to the ladies room on the eighth floor to freshen up, had seen the thief and given the alarm.

"You were on the eighth floor," Lokma pointed out. "How did you see him? The eighth floor window was closed at the time. You had to open it in order to give warning. Since he was almost on the ground, you could not have seen him through the closed window."

She made a visible effort to control herself. "It all happened so quickly, and I was so nervous that I don't remember all the details."

"Mrs. Phun, I don't think you expected him to be caught. You were just trying to clear yourself of suspicion."

Her voice developed a tremor. "This isn't like you, Mr. Lokma. You're not being fair."

"Mrs. Phun, no harm will come to you if you tell the truth. We already know the thief had an accomplice inside the building. As soon as you locked the door to my office, you went to the ladies' lounge and gave him the signal. A flashing light from a ladies compact would do. The mistake was to let him take the one filing drawer that had the material he wanted. Only a person who knew where that was could have told him where to find it."

A nerve under Mrs. Phun's right eye began to jump. "I haven't done anything to deserve this." She stared at him with pleading eyes. "They were copies. I knew you had the originals in the vault." She stopped as suddenly as if she had received a hard slap across the face, and collapsed forward in her chair, sobbing.

"I wouldn't do anything to hurt you, Mr. Lokma. You've been good to me. But it didn't seem important . . . and it would save me. . . ." Her voice quivered away in tears.

"Save you from what, Mrs. Phun? What are you afraid of? What hold does Wanchai have on you?"

"It isn't Wanchai," Brian said.

Arunee and Lokma both looked at him in surprise.

"This was a police job. I recognized the thief. He was my cellmate until a short while ago. His name is Tattoo."

"Are you sure?" Arunee asked.

Brian nodded. "It makes sense. I told you Colonel Suvit wasn't satisfied with what he found in the attaché case."

There was silence in the room except for Mrs. Phun's sobbing.

MRS. PHUN HAD BEEN WORKING FOR HARRY LOKMA FOR SEVEN months. Her long paper was impeccable, thanks to Colonel Suvit, who helped her to account for the year she spent in prison for embezzling money from a previous employer. After she was released on parole, Suvit quietly arranged for her to get a position at the *Bangkok Post*. He recognized the advantages of having an informer working at an important newspaper, and he was astute enough to wait for the right opportunity. She could not refuse him, because he might revoke her parole on some excuse and send her back to prison.

"I don't think I like Colonel Suvit," Arunee said.

Brian said, "He had a similar hold on Tattoo, who has been locked up for a long time."

Brian though ruefully of how he had sent Phibul after Tattoo.

"What are you going to do about Mrs. Phun?" Arunee asked Lokma.

"We can't have a police informer working here," Lokma replied. "But I can help her to find a job elsewhere, in a business where Colonel Suvit's hold on her won't matter."

EIGHT

SEVERAL TAXIS WERE AT THE STAND OUTSIDE THE NEW THON-buri hotel, but when one pulled out and came forward, Brian guessed who would be at the wheel.

"Where you care to go, sir?" asked Phibul.

Brian leaned into the window. "How is my old friend Tattoo? The man you were chasing yesterday. The one who got away."

Phibul's cheeks turned rosy tan. "So sorry. I try very hard to catch."

"How did you happen to be there?"

"I was driving along street and saw you."

"After I left the restaurant?"

"Yes, sir. Just after . . ." Phibul stopped, realizing that he had been tricked.

"You followed me to the Dorn Saeng and waited until I came out. You're pretty good at tailing. I never saw you."

"It is Colonel Suvit's order, sir. He wishes you to be kept watch on, sir."

"The next time I see you following me, I'll get very angry."

Phibul looked unhappy. "I understand, sir. Where would you like to go now?"

"Why should I pay you to spy on me?"

Phibul said, "Because, sir, if you take other taxi I will not collect fare. And I have large family. Many children and wife." Phibul opened the rear door invitingly. "Please, sir."

Brian asked, "Where does Jean Hudson live?"

"One fifty-two Suriwongse Road, sir."

"You win a big fat cigar." Brian got in the cab. "Take me there."

The address turned out to be an ultra-modern condominium building. Phibul stopped the taxi at the entrance.

"She lives second floor, sir. Apartment numbers on right as you go in."

Brian pushed the button for Hudson, J. He waited and tried again. After a minute he returned to the taxi.

"She isn't in."

"Will you care to go where she is?"

"You *know*?"

"She is also under watch. Colonel Suvit's order."

"Why didn't you say so?"

"You only ask where she lives, sir. Not where she is. She is having lunch at Barclay Club, sir. Very exclusive. Only members and guests go in Barclay Club."

"Take me there."

They drove through dust and heat along a broad avenue of the strange flat city until they reached an area of stately homes shaded by trees where there were no pedestrians and the avenue was almost deserted.

"We are on Sathorn Street, sir, and there is Barclay Club. Very favorite of Americans and British."

The taxi drew up in front of the entrance. A doorman opened the taxi door for Brian and waited as Brian paid Phibul and added a generous tip to the meter.

"Enjoy your lunch with Mr. Calisher, sir," Phibul said before he drove away.

Inside, the club was dark-wooded and clubby. White letters on a green display board announced the day's events. A tennis tournament at two o'clock in the afternoon and cocktails on the terrace at five. At eight o'clock a lecture by the head of the Thailand Tourism Bureau, seating by invitation only.

A gentleman in a well-cut dark linen jacket and dark striped trousers approached. "May I be of service?"

Brian recalled Phibul's parting message. "Mr. Calisher is expecting me."

"He's in the dining room, sir."

Calisher was alone at a window table with a view that looked out on an Olympic-sized swimming pool. He had an almost full wine glass before him. The place settings were for two.

He did not look pleased to see Brian. "What are you doing here?"

Brian thought of a question he had been meaning to ask Calisher.

"Why did my wife call you on the day she died?"

Calisher looked both impatient and surprised.

"What makes you think she did?"

"George Denison overheard her talking to you on the telephone."

"If you don't mind my saying so, you're becoming a bit paranoid. Your wife called to find out how much protection she was entitled to as an American citizen. She also wanted to be sure her visa and passport were in order in case she decided to leave the country on very short notice."

"And you told her?"

"I reassured her about the visa and passport. On the other problem, I explained that the function of the Embassy is to help Americans stay out of trouble. There was nothing we could do if she broke the law in Thailand. We have no jurisdiction here." Calisher looked up and said, "We'll have to continue this discussion later. A young lady has arrived that I'm interviewing for a position at the Embassy."

Calisher stood up as Jean Hudson came to the table.

Brian said, "It's a pleasure to see you again. I didn't have a chance to tell you how grateful I am."

Jean Hudson looked surprised. "What for?"

"For what you told the police."

"All I told them was that I didn't hear any shooting while you were there."

"Apparently that was enough."

Calisher said briskly, "Well, goodbye, Brian. This is business. You must excuse us."

Brian said to Jean, "I'd like to buy you a drink later. I don't get many excuses to talk with a beautiful woman."

He was gambling that Jean Hudson was like most of the beautiful women he had dated, insecure, and therefore vulnerable to compliments. When Jean merely smiled and sat down, he was afraid he'd made a mistake.

Brian's head turned slightly toward Calisher, but his gaze stayed on Jean. "If you don't hire her, you're out of your wok."

Jean Hudson kept her eyes lowered. She did not seem to be paying attention.

"If you have anything more to discuss," Calisher said, "you can make an appointment with me at my office."

Jean Hudson reached across the table and took Calisher's glass of wine.

"Enjoy your lunch," Brian told Calisher.

Jean Hudson lifted the glass to her lips. Her eyes met Brian's over the rim of the glass, and one eye closed in a slow wink.

Brian left the dining room but not the Barclay Club. Instead of going toward the street, he turned and went through a door that exited into an outdoor garden. A bench well-concealed by shrubbery had a partial view of the dining room, and through concealing branches he watched Calisher in conversation with Jean Hudson at the table.

He waited patiently through lunch. A waiter brought a check, Calisher signed, patted Jean Hudson's hand, and left the table. A minute later Brian returned to the dining room.

The table was empty.

Brian found the waiter. "Has Mr. Calisher gone for the day?"

"Yes, sir."

"And the young lady?"

"I have no idea, sir."

Brian left the dining room to look for her. In the library he saw Jean pass by a multipaned window. She was wearing a dimunitive bathing suit with a short blouse over it, and she was following the path to the swimming pool.

He found her sitting on a chaise lounge beneath a large, striped umbrella. Several mature gentleman arrayed in chairs around the pool were giving her their rapt attention.

She removed her blouse and stretched out supine on the chaise. Even lying motionless, her body seemed to undulate.

Brian picked up a canvas chair and sat down beside her.

Her sunglasses looked at him.

"I'd like to buy you that drink," he said.

A hand came up to lift the sunglasses. She gave him a slow, careful appraisal.

"Vermouth cassis on the rocks."

It wasn't hard to catch a waiter's eye. In common with every other male in the vicinity, he was watching Jean.

Brian ordered a vermouth cassis and a gin sling. Jean sat up and put her blouse back on, tying the bow securely in front. The waiter got so caught up in the process that Brian had to repeat the order.

"You're the football player," she said as the waiter left. "All-American or something." She put on her sunglasses. "Is that really you under all those shoulders?"

"Be my guest."

She felt. "Jesus! What pectorals."

The waiter brought their drinks. Brian started to pay, but when he produced his wallet the waiter shook his head.

"We don't accept cash, sir. Aren't you a member?"

Jean said, "I'll sign."

"Sorry about that," Brian said.

"It's all right. Horace lets me sign."

"Horace?"

She lifted her glass mockingly. Brian clinked his glass against hers.

"I'd like to make it up to you about the drink. Have dinner with me tonight."

"I don't break bread with strangers."

They drank. "Do you give rain checks?" Brian asked.

"Sometimes."

"We're in the rainy season." When she giggled, he said, "You got something better to do?"

She dipped a finger into her nearly empty glass and outlined her lips in vermouth. "How tall are you?"

"Six five."

"Two fifty?"

"Two sixty-five."

She pursed her lips in a soundless whistle. "I like substantial men. I knew a football player in high school. He was stuck up. I had a thing for him, but he never looked at me. He was a quarterback."

"That explains it. Quarterbacks are always stuck up."

"What were you?"

"Fullback. I carried the heavy messages."

"Fullback sounds good. Quarterback sounds, well, you know, a little faggoty."

A very slender, deeply tanned woman walked out on the diving board. She paused there for everyone to see. Her white bathing suit clung to her like skin. She looked over at Brian and smiled the kind of smile that said she wouldn't mind if he was waiting when she climbed out.

She dove into the pool, cutting the green water as cleanly as a white arrow.

When Brian turned back to Jean, she was smoothing suntan lotion on to a very shapely leg, and waiting for whatever came next. He had to be exactly right, or he would lose her. It was like a moment when you are in the middle of persuading someone, and suddenly you sense that one wrong word will undo whatever progress you have made.

"Change your mind about dinner?" he asked.

"What about your friend?"

He decided the woman on the diving board didn't exist.
"What friend?"

She smiled and poured another jot of suntan oil into a cupped
palm. "Come to think of it, I don't have anything better to do."

HE ASKED HER TO NAME A PLACE AND TIME, AND SHE NAMED
La Pyramide at eight. As soon as he returned to his hotel, he
looked up the restaurant in the hotel guidebook. "La Pyramide:
Really good French food. Colorful ambiance. Expensive. Dress
code: jacket and tie."

She met him at the door of her apartment; she was a glam-
orous vision in a loose, floaty red tunic and dark blue silk slacks.
Her perfume had a languorous scent like jasmine or hyacinth.

"Out of this world," he said.

"You like?"

"You have no idea how much I like."

He leaned toward her as if she had a magnetic pull he could
not resist.

She drew back. "Don't muss me."

"Then we'd better go. I'm only mortal."

She giggled. He had been right. She licked up flattery like
ice cream.

"This is going to be a real nice evening. I can tell."

La Pyramide was quiet and luxurious. They waited in the
entranceway beneath a ceiling with a painting of a large tusked
purple elephant and a number of sinuously coiling cobras. A
five piece orchestra was playing gentle, lilting music as the
headwaiter showed them to a quiet table in a corner.

Among the diners in the main room were black-skinned Af-
ricans, white-skinned *fahrangs*, coffee-skinned Indians, yellow-
skinned Chinese, and a fair proportion of Southeast Asians:
Thais, Malaysians, and Burmese. The *lingua franca* was money.

A waiter brought a wine list covered in red velour.

"What would you like?" Brian asked.

"Champagne."

He could have predicted that.

She added, "My favorite is Taittinger."

He ordered Taittinger.

"Would you care to dance?"

"To *Ram Wong*?"

"Who's he?"

She giggled. "Silly. It isn't a he, it's music. People here are crazy about it."

Colorfully costumed dancers wearing richly embroidered robes and ornamental headdresses glided onto the dance floor. Their arms were covered with wide bracelets, and their graceful circular movements evoked a stately beauty to accompany the lilting music.

The waiter brought the champagne bottle for inspection, and opened it with a quick, expert twist of thumb and forefinger. He poured a little into Brian's glass, waited for approval, then filled Jean's glass.

Brian joined in the applause as the dancers left.

"You dig it?" Jean asked.

"Don't you?"

"Not much. I've seen and heard too much. It all sounds the same to me."

"What kind of music do you like?"

"Something with drive. Bruce Springsteen. Mick Jagger. You?"

"People have different tastes. I'm anchored back there with musical comedy and Garland and Sinatra. I like big deep voices too. Ezio Pinza."

"George never got tired of *Ram Wong*. He was a big fan."

"Denison?"

She nodded. "There was one performer he really liked. Her name is Boonsong, and she's a big star. He never missed a chance to watch her."

"She must be good."

"You can't prove it by me."

"I'd like to see her."

"You can't anymore. She's retired. Lives in a big house with bodyguards to keep out people she doesn't want bothering her."

"Garbo in Bangkok."

"Something like that. George visited her sometimes. I wouldn't go across the street." She looked around restlessly. "Let's order. I'm hungry."

The waiter brought two menus; only Brian's had prices on it, and everything else was in French. Jean ordered a paillard de Saumon Florentine, pronouncing each word clearly. Brian didn't trust his French accent, and ordered by pointing at Mignon de Boeuf Alsacienne.

The waiter filled Jean's champagne glass, and Brian switched to a double gin on the rocks. Jean emptied her glass while Brian watched. He hoped he would not have to order a second bottle.

"How well did you know George Denison?" he asked.

"I worked for him in Chicago. Came with him to Bangkok when he moved here."

He poured champagne from his glass into hers.

"George and I were having a thing. It ended when he took up with your wife."

From the moment Brian arrived in Bangkok, he had been subjected to a series of small shocks about Diane. He had no right to mind because they were well and truly separated. But a separation is not necessarily the end of a relationship.

"Did you resent her?" he asked.

"Who? Your wife?"

"Because of her taking up with Denison."

"I don't get uptight about any man. But it sure made for a lot of tension with somebody else in the office."

"Who?"

"Ellen Peterson had it bad for George. She didn't mind me because it was practically over before she showed up. But she was crazy jealous of your wife."

"How did George feel about that?"

"She was like wallpaper to him."

The waiter brought dinner, and suggested another bottle as he poured out the last of the old. Jean's eyes sparkled as she said yes. Brian ordered another double gin.

Jean sipped from her champagne glass and did that business of looking at him over the rim.

Brian said, "Those last few months at the company must have been rough."

"You have no idea. It was panic time when that stuff broke in the newspapers. I guess that's what made your wife do what she did."

"She never struck me as the type," Brian said.

"Me either. Just goes to show you can't tell much about other people."

"I guess not. How about Ellen? Is she the type?"

"For what?"

"To do what my wife did."

"I dunno. Most of the time I expect she was trying to make up her mind whether to kill your wife or George. But she wouldn't've."

"Why not?"

"She wouldn't do anything to hurt the business. They were raking it in, and she had a piece of the action."

"Ellen was a partner?"

"They had to take her in. She knows where too many skeletons are buried. Do you want to dance?"

"Best offer I've had in months."

"You're cute."

On the dance floor Jean alternated between break-away steps and moving her body in very close. When they went back to the table, she finished the Taittinger.

She looked around vacantly. "I'd like to get outa here now."

"If that's what you want."

The waiter brought a check that Brian studied in shocked silence.

"You've got enough t'pay, haven' you?"

"I'm making sure it isn't the national debt."

She grinned. "The rest of the evenin's on me."

As they were leaving the restaurant a taxi parked across the street pulled hurriedly away. Brian was sure who the driver was.

He hailed another taxi and gave the driver Jean's address. By then her gears weren't meshing.

He almost decided to say goodnight in the lobby of her apartment house. But she wouldn't hear of it."

"I wanta dance summor."

Her apartment had no hint of Thai decor; it might have been a condominium in Bayside, Queens. The basic color scheme was blond on blond. In the living room there was a glass-topped coffee table and a white sofa with squiggly cushions. Several mirrors reflected bright lamps. The most striking feature was a long colorful mural on the far wall that showed the Statue of Liberty guarding the harbor at night.

Jean said, "When I was a lil girl I wanted to grow up and be like her."

"A statue?"

"No, silly. Real American."

"She happens to be French."

"Well, history never was my strong point." She kicked off her shoes. "I wanna dance."

"Ready when you are."

She put a record on the stereo. Vic Damone began singing "Stranger in Paradise." As they were dancing she pressed against him, and her hips moved in a lazily seductive way.

When the record ended they stopped dancing. She whispered in his ear, "Let me entertain you."

They were kissing when the telephone rang.

She pretended to bite his lip. "I should have turned the damn thing off."

She walked over to the telephone and picked it up. "Oh, it's you." She listened with the surly expression of a scolded child. "I went out for dinner, that's all. . . . If it was up to you I'd never go anywhere." A long pause during which she looked at Brian and shook her head with exasperation. She blew him a kiss. "If you don't like it, you know what you can do!" she said into the phone before slamming down the receiver. "I'll count t'ten," she told Brian. "One, two, three, four . . ." She got to eight before the telephone rang again. She let it ring. "That'll teach you," she told it.

On about the twentieth ring she picked up the receiver and said crossly, "I don't wanna talk t'you anymore tonight. Call me in the morning." She put the receiver back in its cradle. Then she shifted the receiver again and left it on the table.

Standing with her back to Brian, she looked at him over her shoulder. Her hands were in front and he couldn't see what she was doing until she removed her tunic top. She wriggled out of her tight pants.

She walked toward him with a small self-satisfied smile. She wore only a transparent bra and filmy underpants. Her breasts were white and soft as angel cake. When he caressed them she said, "Oh, God." Her hands clasped behind him, forcing his body against her.

He carried her to the sofa, and she buried her face in his shoulder. She began to fondle him. "I'll bet you're big all over," she whispered. he felt her hard-pointed nipples against his chest.

When he entered her she moaned and her body began a rocking motion.

A minute later she said in a breathy tone, "Give it to me."

There was something out-of-synch, out-of-rhythm, about her reactions. She was not truly involved in what was happening. It was a performance.

Understanding that, he refused to go along. It became a contest between them. The contest became sharper and her thrusting movements almost frantic. Her breath caught and her mouth contorted. She was becoming entrapped in the coils of passion.

"I can't wait. *Please!*"

Only then did he begin making love to her in earnest. His

thrusts came hard and fast, welding their bodies. She began to shudder, and a whimper rose far back in her throat. *"Oh, no!"*

She gave a piercing cry as she went into the throes. Her head fell back, her blond hair was flung loosely over one naked shoulder. He was raving with the need for release but determined to hold out.

Her hands made uncontrollable pushing movements against his shoulders. "Come on. Come *on!*"

His surge went into her.

She lay silently shaking, her eyes tightly shut and her face crumpled like a little girl's after a crying fit. He touched her gently, as though quieting the strings of a mandolin that had finished playing.

Suddenly her eyes opened wide, glaring at him. "I hate what you did!" Tears glistened. "You had no *right* to do that!"

NINE

ARUNEE WAS WORKING IN A SMALL, COMPARTMENT-SIZED ROOM that had a copying machine and several shelves of reference books. The door was locked, and a "Do Not Disturb" sign in both Thai and English was looped over the knob.

Her typewriter was on a small reading table and spread out beside it, with additional storage on the floor next to her feet, were folders containing research material.

The folders were the reason she was not at her usual work station in the newsroom. They contained what had formerly been in the attaché case, the documentary basis for the article she was writing.

The documentary trail was hard to follow. Not only were the transactions disguised in code, but there were duplicate invoices and false bills of exchange and lading. Even the method of payment for the supplies was brambled over with entangled and confusing details. It was in the literal sense a Chinese puzzle, for Wanchai's drug payments were not sent directly to the H & D Trading Company, but were handled by the Chaozhou Chinese whose roots in drug trafficking dated back to the Opium Wars.

It was midafternoon before Arunee finished translating all this material into a form suitable for the newspaper's readers. She brought the article to Harry Lokma, along with the folders which he locked into his office safe.

Lokma settled into an armchair to read the article through. He made several small editing changes before he looked up at Arunee.

"Where do the drug shipments go after the Chaozhou Chinese take over?"

"They're shipped by couriers to Burma and Malaysia and eventually to the United States."

"Put that in."

"There's something else I didn't know whether to mention. A shipment to Wanchai was delayed recently. Some Gabriel missile launchers and 40mm Bofors guns from Singapore. He's buying more arms than he can afford, and sellers are getting worried."

"We can't prove it. Stick to the facts."

Arunee revised the article and got Lokma's final approval. She returned to the newsroom with the feeling of a job well done. The telephone was ringing at her desk. When she answered, the receptionist in the lobby told her that Mr. Buckley was waiting to see her.

"Tell him I'll be down in a few minutes."

She went to the ladies' lounge on the eighth floor to freshen up and remove the traces of several hours of hard, confining work. To her surprise her face did not need a touch of color. Her skin seemed to have a fresh supply of blood just beneath its surface.

Her mood mystified her; it was an odd mixture of pleasure and anticipation, misgiving and anxiety.

He stood up when she entered the reception room. She was struck anew by what a large man he was. He was not handsome as Thai men are handsome, but his face had solidity and ruggedness to it, as if it were fashioned from rock.

"I've made an interesting new contact," he said.

He told her about having dinner with George Denison's secretary at La Pyramide, and Ellen Peterson's infatuation with George Denison and her rivalry with his late wife.

That recalled to her an item in the morning's edition of the Thai-language newspapers. She looked through the obituary notes until she found the brief item. She translated it for Brian.

"Denison, George Charles. Years will not dim the sorrow. Private funeral service at Nine Phloenchit Road. By invitation only."

He looked amused, and that puzzled her until he explained, "I don't see how you can translate that into English. It looks so weird on the printed page. The words are all strung together to look like one word.''

"In Sanskrit lettering there is no punctuation or spaces between words except to indicate the end of a sentence or paragraph." She folded the paper and returned it to the rack. "Would you like to go to the funeral?"

He looked puzzled. "Why?"

"Wherever Ellen Peterson is, she probably knows that Denison is dead. It would be hard for her not to know. The story's been in every newspaper and on radio and television. If Ellen learns where his funeral is taking place, she might show up there.''

"I'd like to talk to that lady."

"So would I. The funeral service is today. It's by invitation only but that doesn't always apply to the press."

"Something tells me I won't pass as a Thai reporter."

"I'll think of some excuse for you."

She borrowed the yellow Toyota from the newspaper pool, and picked up Brian at the building's delivery entrance.

Phloenchit Road was a wealthy residential area, and number nine turned out to be a huge, colorful house with a wide marble verandah. A line of people waiting on the verandah were dressed in the Thai costume for funerals, the women in black and the men in white with black armbands.

She parked on a side street, and they walked around to the front of the mansion. They got on the end of the line and awaited their turn. There was not a white *fahrang* face to be seen. Brian attracted a good deal of silent curiosity.

Inside the front door they were confronted by a saffron-robed priest. Arunee produced her press credentials. The priest examined them, looked dubiously at Brian and asked a question. He received Arunee's reply solemnly, held up a hand cautioning her to wait and disappeared into the house.

Arunee told Brian, "I said you were a close friend of George Denison, and you flew here especially to attend the funeral. We'll see whether that gets us in."

The priest returned, bowed, made a *wai*, and stepped aside to allow them to enter.

In the wide entrance room they were confronted by a twelve-foot high platform covered from top to bottom in maroon cloth.

"What's behind there?" Brian asked her.

"Denison. His body is in a large ceremonial urn inside a

coffin. It will drip away into a pot until nothing is left but dry, clean bones."

Seated cross-legged on either side of the platform were four Buddhist priests. Their faces were hidden behind large ceremonial fans, and they were intoning chants in a poignant minor key.

Arunee lit a joss stick from a taper, placed it in a long double row of joss sticks, and nodded to Brian to do the same. She steepled her hands before her face and bowed toward the curtain, and Brian repeated the salutation.

Arunee said, "This must all seem strange to you. I didn't expect a Buddhist ceremony. The announcement in the newspaper of the funeral service didn't mention that."

A bullnecked Thai with short hair and a wrestler's build appeared in the archway to the next room. He signaled that they should follow him. He led the way to a large, elegantly furnished room with a giant Thai-style chandelier suspended overhead in glittering splendor. On the far wall was a beautiful mural of Buddha's son becoming a novice.

The room was crowded with people having drinks, chatting, and occasionally laughing.

"Pretty cheerful for a funeral," Brian remarked.

"We Buddhists do not believe death is the end," she explained. "There is no reason to be sad."

"Christians don't think it's the end either. Everyone goes to heaven or hell. But I guess we're sad because we don't know which way we're going." He looked around and asked, "Who is she?"

He was looking at a woman of imposing presence and statuesque beauty whose dark silky hair was piled high and held in place by a single ornamental fan. She wore a black *pasin* exquisitely crafted to fit the contours of a voluptuous figure.

Arunee recognized her. "Boonsong. Most famous of *Ram Wong* dancers." She noticed Boonsong staring at them. "I think she wants to meet us."

At closer range Boonsong's striking beauty owed something to the art of makeup. Her eyes were lengthened by dark pencilled lines, and her eyelashes were weighted with blue mascara. A layer of white powder did not quite conceal the fine wrinkling of her face.

She spoke in English, directing a question to Brian: "Who

are you? Why did you come?" Her voice was rich and full of resonance.

"I'm a friend of George Denison. From Chicago. I decided to fly over and pay my last respects."

"What is your name?"

"Buckley."

Arunee sensed an electric current of hostility flowing toward him. "Were you married to my late husband's partner?"

The question nearly took Arunee's breath away.

"Yes, I was," Brian answered.

"We mean no disrespect to your husband," Arunee said quickly, partly to confirm that Boonsong had said George Denison was her husband.

Boonsong turned to her. "You are not welcome here. You will leave at once and take your friend with you."

"Are you George Denison's widow?" She tried not to give the question any special significance.

"Go now!"

The bullnecked, muscular Thai moved forward and took her roughly by the elbow.

"That will do," Brian said. He reached out to remove the viselike hold.

Instantly, she felt the grip tighten. The Thai was watching Brian's face and smiling.

Brian took hold of the man's wrist with his hand. He did not appear to be exerting himself, but the Thai's smile slowly vanished. His lips thinned until they were white lines etched in brown parchment. He looked like someone who had just caught his hand in a closed door.

The Thai quickly released his grip on her, and then Brian let go of him.

Arunee sensed Boonsong's anger beating like an artificial heart in the room.

"Leave now, while it is safe for you to go."

Brian was standing stone still, his eyes bright with defiance. He occupies space with such authority, she thought. She wondered if he seemed as formidable to the others.

Arunee turned to Brian, "I think we ought to go."

"Not until she asks politely."

Arunee said quietly to Boonsong, "I'm sure you don't want a scene at your husband's funeral."

Boonsong replied in a clenched voice, "Please do not make me do anything for which I will be sorry."

Arunee turned to Brian. "She did say please."

He did not answer at once, and then, as though some spring of tension had uncoiled, he grinned. "I'll accept that."

They left through the coffin room where the Buddhist priests were still intoning a chant for the dead, hiding their faces behind large ceremonial fans. Their saffron robes looked yellow in the flickering light of tapers.

TEN

WHEN BRIAN RETURNED TO HIS HOTEL, HE FOUND A MESSAGE from Horace Calisher in his mail slot, asking him to call back.

Calisher answered the phone. "I've been trying to reach you. Where have you been?"

"Around and about."

"Something's come up I'd like to discuss with you. Can we have dinner this evening?"

"I guess so."

"I'll pick you up at your hotel. Six-thirty."

That gave Brian enough time to shower and dress.

For once Phibul's taxi was not at the hotel entrance. A maroon Cadillac with white leather seats swung into the driveway and stopped at the curb. Behind the wheel was a dark-featured Thai with black hair and a black moustache. Calisher was in the back seat.

Brian got in beside him. Calisher was wearing an open sports shirt and pale blue slacks. Not the kind of outfit he'd wear to a restaurant.

"Where we are we going?" Brian asked.

"My summer home. We'll have dinner there."

Brian sat back in the richly upholstered seat. "Nice car."

Calisher opened a briefcase and removed papers. "If you don't mind, I have some work to do. We'll talk later."

He put on eyeglasses and began to read.

They were driving beyond the fashionable *fahrang* district on the outskirts of Bangkok when the chauffeur turned around to say, "A taxi is following us, sir. I was not sure until we came on this road."

It was a narrow, tree-shaded road. Brian looked back through the rear window, and in a minute a pair of headlights appeared. Clearly, Phibul had an informant within the hotel.

"That's my shadow. He works for Colonel Suvit."

"Are the police following you?" Calisher asked.

"For some time."

"Why?"

"It has to do with certain documents from the H & D Trading Company. Colonel Suvit doesn't believe I lost them."

"Did you?"

Brian did not answer directly. "Did you hear about the burglary at the *Bangkok Post*? Someone broke in and tried to steal documents relating to the H & D Trading Company."

"Were the police informed?"

"They didn't have to be. Colonel Suvit ordered the break-in."

Brian told him about his violent encounter with Nguad, otherwise known as Tattoo.

Calisher listened with a slight smile. "Why would Colonel Suvit go to such lengths?"

"It's possible he thinks he can use the documents for extortion."

Calisher shrugged.

"You don't seem surprised," Brian observed.

"What you must keep in mind is that persons in government service here are paid poorly. They often make arrangements to supplement their income. Corruption in Bangkok is a way of life. It is also a very efficient way of doing business. You can't change the way people live."

"Is that the official position of our government?"

"Hardly. Ten years ago a virtuous America president had the notion that he could impose his version of morality on Thailand. He thought the country should present a bright shining picture of honesty, to contrast with the Communists—who happen to be, for the most part, the only honest politicians around. They don't want filthy lucre, just power, and they live like monks."

"Did he get anywhere?"

"Of course not. The whole idea was impractical. Bowing to his pressure the Thai government finally agreed to declare bribery illegal—but only if it exceeded 200,000 bahts." A taut smile barely moved his lips. "The Thais are a wonderful people. Sometimes I think the more virtuous the people, the more corrupt their government." He glanced out the window. "We're almost there."

The Cadillac stopped in a white gravel courtyard. A large cantilevered structure of Eurasian design looked out across a sandy beach to the gulf. In the deep-blue evening sky, stars were glowing softly.

The living room of the house was furnished with slingback chairs on a tile floor, a free-form teakwood table, a sofa and an expensive-looking lacquered cabinet before which Calisher paused.

"Care for a drink?"

"Martini. Very dry."

"When in Thailand, do as the Americans do," Calisher replied.

Brian sat in a sling-back chair and sipped his drink. The chauffeur disappeared in the direction of what Brian assumed was the kitchen. There was no sign of anyone else in the house.

"Is he the cook?"

Calisher nodded. "An excellent one. Technically, Thainin is my servant. The truth is, Thainin is master of the house, and I am his guest on occasion."

Brian recognized the sort of remark his father might have made: the aristocrat's tribute to egalitarianism, signifying nothing.

"How did you meet him?"

"My wife and I frequented a small restaurant where he was the chef. She particularly liked his cooking, so I hired him. Since then he's been invaluable to me. He's a very interesting fellow. Used to work on a *durian* plantation in the Muang district."

"What's *durian*?"

"Every culture has at least one inedible food. *Haggis* in Scotland, *vegemite* in Australia, *fish maw* in China. In this country it's *durian*. It's a fruit with short sharp spikes, an ugly greenish yellow color, and a taste that's somewhere between rotting broccoli, over-aged onions, and putrid cheese."

"Sounds irresistible."

"Most Thais love it, usually cooked with sticky rice in coconut milk and a bit of palm sugar."

"Where's your wife now?"

"At home with the children in Vermont. That's where she prefers to live. If you wish to infer from this that we are not happily joined in matrimony, you are free to do so."

Brian did not want to hear why Calisher's marriage was unhappy. "Do you come here often?"

"It's my sanctum sanctorum. I come whenever I have private business to conduct. These walls have heard a great many secrets." Calisher finished his drink. "Would you care for a tour?"

The house was laid out in a formal plan, traditional and charmless. There were no surprises, nothing to break the line. The floors were tile, the bedrooms were spacious, the bathrooms were small. The master bedroom opened on a terrace with a fine view of the water.

A few paintings were hung together in a clump in a dimly lighted hallway. Brian was looking at these when Thainin appeared to announce that dinner was served.

The table was set on a wide wood-planked terrace with a view of the gulf. Dinner was so delicious that Brian half expected the food to rise off the plates and take a bow. Crisp rice noodles and shrimp were sauteed in a delightful plum sauce and served with beansprouts, the fish egg soup blended exotic spices in a lime juice broth. The main entree of roasted crab claws was seasoned to perfection and served with garlic butter. Two bottles of Thai wine accompanied dinner, one brilliantly dry, the other sensuously soft and sweet.

Calisher slowly sank into a depressed mood as he returned to the subject of his marriage. He stared into his glass as if he were reading tea leaves in it, and Brian braced himself to play the role of confessor.

Calisher began by saying that his wife never spent any time at the beach house because the sun was bad for her complexion. She suffered from an ailment that caused her skin to flake off in shiny patches. She had been a handsome woman in her youth but had not aged well. It had not been a love match to begin with, and after she bore two children their sex life virtually ceased. The two boys adored her and paid no attention to Horace. He would have sent them away to military school, but she would not allow it.

"She wanted the boys with her. Now they're both in their late teens, and they prefer to live in Vermont, too. Sooner or later they'll probably live there permanently. I'll be the odd man out. I'll have no one." Calisher swallowed as though he had gulped an olive from his martini glass. He asked suddenly, "Do you care for her at all?"

"Who?"

"You know. You were in her apartment last night."

"Was I?"

Calisher's voice took on a sharp accusing edge: "I was there, waiting in my car. I saw you go in. You didn't come out until two o'clock on the morning.'

Rain had been falling heavily as Brian waited for a taxi in the entrance to Jean's apartment building. He remembered a car's headlights that brightened down the block. At first he had been sure it was Phibul, but then the car made a U-turn and drove away.

Calisher said, "She's the only person in the world who matters a damn to me. I won't let you take her away."

"I didn't know you had a claim."

"I'm in love with her. I'd marry her if there was any way I could. It would mean an expensive divorce and would probably ruin my career, but I'd do it if she wanted me to."

Brian was about to offer reassurance when Calisher said, "I warn you. Don't try to see her again. I can be a very good friend but a very bad enemy."

Instead of saying what he had meant to, Brian answered, "I don't think what I do is any of your business."

Calisher's fingers tightened on his glass. Hostility was rising in him like sediment from a shaken wine bottle. Before he could reply, Thainin appeared in the doorway. There seemed to pass between Thainin and his employer an unspoken message.

"Perhaps Mr. Buckley will be interested in seeing my pets."

Calisher roused himself to his duties as a host. "A good idea. Thainin has an unusual hobby. Let him show you."

Calisher returned to the liquor bar, while Thainin led Brian toward a screened area on the terrace. They went inside and Thainin proudly showed him several large glass-enclosed cases in which colorful pieces of rope appeared to move. It was a miniature snake farm.

"Aren't they beautiful?" Thainin asked. "I am never lonely while I have my pets."

Brian watched the long slender shapes sliding and slithering. "Are they dangerous?"

"Oh, yes. The Asian cobra there probably kills more humans than any other snake species. Its venom is five times more deadly than the black widow spider."

The cobra raised itself, weaving back and forth as though sensing a nearby prey. It had a monocle-shaped marking on the back of its head.

"Would you examine it more closely?" Thainin asked.

"No, thanks."

Thainin introduced him to his other pets, the dabois, the pit viper, the krait. He brought out trays of insects, frogs, and a bowl of little fish to feed his collection. He gave Brian a small frog, and indicated he should put it into a glassed-in cage. Brian declined the honor. He gave the frog back, and did not watch what followed.

When they returned to the living room, Calisher was leaning back in his chair with his eyes closed. A wine bottle, half empty, was on the table before him.

"I think I'd better be leaving," Brian said.

Calisher opened his eyes. "Sit down."

Because Brian did not wish to provoke him further, he sat down. From the side Calisher looked thinner and his nose was elongated. It had been hard at first for Brian to feel sympathy for a man so stuporous with self pity, but he was beginning to regret not having made allowances for an aging, unattractive man skewered by his passion for a young attractive woman.

Brian said, "If you'd like to know, nothing happened in Jean's apartment. I was interested in her only as a possible source of information. And she wasn't interested in me at all."

"Is that the truth?"

"I'd have no reason to lie," Brian lied.

A tremulous motion started in Calisher's mouth. "Here in Thailand, you know, this kind of thing is pretty well accepted. Thai men take what they call secondary wives, set them up with houses and cars, have children with them, and sometimes even acknowledge they are the fathers. It's perfectly respectable."

Brian felt he ought to do more to help Calisher subdue his anxieties.

"Now that I know how you feel, I won't see her again."

Calisher made an effort to steady himself. "It's for your own good, too. If you kept seeing her you'd fall in love with her, and you admit yourself that she doesn't have any interest in . . ."

Calisher's eyes widened. His expression changed to horror.

"In God's name, don't move!"

Brian froze. He glimpsed a whiplike shape coiling on the back of his chair, almost parallel with his shoulder.

"Thainin!" Calisher called.

The snake slithered slowly down Brian's arm. Within inches of his hand, its pink forked tongue twitched in and out of an angular head.

Thainin came swiftly. Approaching Brian's chair cautiously,

he seized the snake's head from behind and held it firmly between his thumb and forefinger. The small wriggling body flailed the air.

Thainin pointed the snake's head down and exerted pressure until the jaws opened wide and a spurt of venom gushed. Still holding the snake's head in a firm grip, Thainin brought it out to the terrace.

Calisher said shakily, "I don't understand how the damn thing got loose."

Brian's voice was steady, although that was not how he felt. "It was pretty careless."

Thainin returned to the living room. "So sorry, sir."

"It was nearly a bad accident," Calisher said. "What happened?"

"It must have escaped during the feeding."

"This must never happen again," Calisher said sternly. "If you can't look after your pets better than this, I won't allow them in the house."

Thainin bowed slightly. "I understand, sir. I will be most careful."

Brian's suspicions were at work in a different direction. "The snake seemed to be moving directly toward my hand. Is there any reason for that?"

"None, sir. A snake's instinct is to find a place to hide."

Calisher said, "I think we can both use another drink."

"I certainly can," Brian agreed. He was remembering the small frog that Thainin induced him to handle. The odor might still be on his hand. "I'd like to know what kind of snake it was. Poisonous?"

"It is called a pit viper, sir," Thainin replied. "Not as sluggish or as heavy as the Malay. It's also called the *hyappoda* or hundred pace snake because that is how far a person, once bitten, can walk before collapsing."

Brian emptied the martini that Calisher poured for him.

"It's been an interesting evening. But I think I'll go home now if you don't mind."

"I quite understand. Thainin will drive you."

"It won't be necessary. My police shadow is probably somewhere nearby. I ought to let him earn a fare for his night's work."

As they stepped outside into the gravel courtyard, Brian put two fingers to his lips and blew a shrill whistle. A hundred yards down the road a car's headlights came on and an engine started.

"You must come again," Calisher said. "I'm so glad we're still friends."

That was pushing the definition of friendship a bit far, Brian thought.

With a triumphant honk of the taxi horn, Phibul arrived.

ELEVEN

DURING THE LONG RIDE HOME, BRIAN REFLECTED ON THE events of the evening. He felt like a man invited for a swim who suddenly found himself in shark-infested waters.

It was hard to believe Horace Calisher could be responsible for attempted murder, but he recalled the look of understanding between Calisher and his servant shortly before the encounter with the deadly snake. And he reminded himself that Calisher was in the grip of a sexual obsession.

Early the next morning, as he was about to leave the hotel, he saw a folded paper in light blue computer print stuck into his mail slot. His hotel bill. Brian studied it with detachment, thinking of the inroads already made on his slender resources. He would have to move to cheaper living quarters.

He put the bill in his pocket and nodded reassuringly to the clerk.

Phibul's taxi was not among those at the stand outside the hotel. Brian consulted a small guide book and tourist map, then walked off rapidly, following the New Road along the Chao Prya's winding course. A ferry was leaving its dock, and a water taxi raced past with its nose out of the water. A slow-moving teakwood barge was pushing up river like a great tortoise.

As Brian neared his destination, he saw a policeman in khaki uniform standing in a canopied hut and manually operating a traffic signal. Brian did not ask him for further directions. If the policeman did not understand English he could not be helpful, and if he did understand he would try to be overly helpful, which was worse.

Brian preferred to trust to his maps, instincts, and luck, and with these aids he stood a few minutes later in front of the house he was looking for. It was small, with a slanted tile roof and walls of plastered white stucco, and fronted by low-lying neatly trimmed bushes that resembled guardian munchkins.

This was where Ellen Peterson lived.

The ornamental door knocker sent a hollow summons through the house. As he expected, there was no answer. He waited a minute, blinking in the sunlight's white glare, then went around the house to the back. A wide lawn was cut with almost military precision, and at the rear was a tiny frame house that he guessed was a servant's quarters.

This time his knock was answered by a singsong cadence in Thai.

"Do you speak English?" he asked of the closed door. "I'm a friend of Ellen Peterson."

The door opened to reveal an aged woman with the kind of high, balding forehead that often results from hair being pulled into a tight knot. She wore a *pakima* that her body rendered shapeless.

"May I come in?"

She stepped back to allow him to enter. He had to stoop to fit under a ceiling a foot shorter than he was. Furniture was scanty in the dim, unpainted living room, and the air was moist and warm.

The woman sat on the very edge of a worn rattan chair so that her feet could reach the floor. There was no other chair, so Brian remained standing, hunched beneath the low ceiling.

"Do you know Ellen Peterson?" he asked politely.

"I am her *amah*." Her voice had a whispery huskiness.

"I'm looking for her because she has come into a great deal of money, an inheritance." He thought her attention sharpened at the mention of money. "Can you tell me where I can find her?"

"She is not home."

There was an interruption. An elegant, regally slender Siamese cat came over to deposit a dying mouse on Brian's shoe. Brian tactfully ignored it.

"If you can help, I'm sure she will be very grateful. It's important that I get in touch with her." He was not sure how much she understood, so to add authority he said, "I'm her lawyer. Do you know where she went?"

She lifted narrow shoulders in a shrug. The Siamese loped over to the woman and leapt into her lap. She began to stroke it. The cat watched with unwavering emerald eyes as Brian removed his shoe from beneath the extinguished rodent.

"Police come," she said.

"The police? What did they want?"

She made a quick downswipe at something round and ugly on the arm of her chair. She had excellent reflexes. The round ugly thing became oblong and flat.

"What did you tell them?" he asked.

Up went the shoulders again.

The police were probably on a routine visit to ask routine questions about the bombing at the Royal Palace. There was no reason for them to search for evidence.

"Do you have a key to her house?"

"*Tham reim.*" She saw that he did not understand. "It is custom," she added.

"I would like to look in the house. She might have left a message."

She shook her head. "I can not give key."

"I want to help her get money that is coming to her. There may be a reward. Money for you." He sensed her resistance continuing. "You can come with me and watch."

That seemed to satisfy her. She pushed the cat off her lap and got up. She went through a beaded curtain divider to a small area with a pallet that served as her bedroom. She removed a key from inside a pillow.

They crossed the lawn to the rear of Ellen Peterson's home, and she used the key to open the back door.

The kitchen was gloomy because the blinds were drawn. The air was stale. He opened the refrigerator. The shelves were bare except for a half-empty milk bottle. The milk had a sour odor. He opened the freezer compartment. It was empty.

He said, "There's no food. She must have been planning to leave."

She shook her head.

"Then what happened to it?"

Her sorrowful brown eyes were hooded. "She not leave money to pay."

Brian got the point. Because the *amah* had not been paid, she felt entitled to take the food.

"Has she ever done that before? Not paid you?"

She shook her head.

In the living room there were touches of Thai decor. Woven bamboo mats served for carpeting, and the room was walled in teak panels. Sliding doors were partly drawn to close off the living room from a rather stark study.

In a wall niche of the study there was a startling Christ figure, gaunt and agonized, arms twisted back painfully and hands nailed to the cross. The figure loomed over a prayer stool that held a large Holy Bible in white leather resting on a cushion.

The ribbon marker in the Bible was at Psalm Seventy: "Make haste, O God, to deliver me; make haste to help me, O Lord. Let them be ashamed and confounded that seek after my soul; let them be turned backward, and put to confusion, that desire my hurt."

In a somewhat chastened mood he continued the search. In the bathroom a sparse array of cosmetics was lined up on the top shelves of the cabinet. Jars of cold cream and nonallergenic makeup, and several short cylinder lipsticks resembling the blunt end of bullets. Evidently, Ellen Peterson did not go in much for cosmetics.

On the lower shelves were tubes and bottles of medicines, for coughs, for asthma, for athlete's foot, for headaches. There was also a jar of Valium tablets. A green toothbrush was in a plastic wall holder, and an almost full tube of toothpaste rested on the edge of the washbasin.

She didn't even come home to pack, Brian thought. She left in a hurry, possibly as soon as she heard of the bombing.

Brian's chief impression was of a lonely person. There is a difference between living alone and being lonely. The bedroom seemed to crackle dryly. The radio, silent beside the bed, must have rarely played a lively tune.

Hanging in the closet were several dresses of summer fabrics but sober hue. Unfrilly blouses and plain skirts drooped beside them. Two pairs of light sturdy shoes, in a style best described as sensible, rested neatly beside a pair of brown leather slippers on the floor.

A low dresser occupied part of the closet. A handbag, scarf, and some scattered costume jewelry were in the topmost drawer, bras, slips, panties and stocking in the next. The underclothes were white, the stockings were brown.

The bottom drawer yielded a photograph album: "Graduation Day, June 25, 1971, Morrisville High School." While the *amah* carefully observed, Brian examined a thin sheaf of stapled newspaper clippings and letters tied with a rubber band. The letters were from friends in the United States, the latest had a two-year-old postmark. The newspaper clippings were all about one person: "George Denison Forms New Trading Company," "Denison Appointed to Board of Trade," "Denison Acquires New Partner," "Denison Company Renamed." The only clipping not about Denison consisted of a few lines announcing that Ellen Peterson was appointed treasurer of the H & D Trading Company. That item was dated a few months ago.

Inside a large manila envelope Brian found a black-and-white studio photograph of a younger, smiling George Denison. There was also a framed color photograph of a serious-looking young woman with direct, level, gray eyes.

Brian was aware of the *amah* watching as he turned the album pages with photographs of the graduating class at Morrisville High School. Beside each photograph was the graduate's name and a few lines of rhyme supplied by the class poet. Ellen Peterson's photograph was a black-and-white reproduction of her large color photograph. Without the aid of color her serious look was almost grim, her direct, level gaze more unsettling.

The class poet had written:

> *She'll be a missionary if she can*
> *Unless she marries the right man.*

Brian felt a touch on his arm.

"We go," the *amah* said.

"In a minute."

He leafed through the letters. As far as he could tell, almost all were from hometown friends. One was from the Good Samaritan Church saying that her application "to work in God's vineyard in the mission field has been given consideration, but no appointment is possible in the near future."

The *amah* yanked impatiently at his sleeves. Brian nodded and picked up the framed color photograph of Ellen Peterson. He removed it from the frame.

"I'd like to keep this."

The *amah* shook her head. Brian took out his wallet and offered a hundred baht note.

"*Khob khun krop,*" she said, smiling. There were gaps in her betel-stained teeth.

They left the house, and she locked the back door carefully. The Siamese ambled casually toward them across the lawn.

"Is the cat yours?"

She shook her head. "B'long mistess. I feed until she come, or no food left."

The fine-featured Siamese, doubtless one of the four pure extant varieties, was living on borrowed time. The *amah* did not appear to have any mystical or sentimental attachment to it.

Brian opened his wallet again and gave her some of his colorful Thai money.

"For the cat," he specified. "Don't let it go hungry."

She nodded expressionlessly. As Brian returned the wallet to his pocket, he was struck by an idea.

"How did she pay you? In cash?"

"Once she write a check."

"Do you remember the name of the bank the check was drawn on?"

She shook her head, but her gaze was calculating.

Brian took out a fifty baht note from his dwindling wallet. "The bank might help me find her."

She found the offer persuasive. "Thailand-America."

"Far from here?"

"Not much walk."

AT THE THAILAND-AMERICAN BANK BRIAN TOLD THE SAME story he had told the *amah*: he was trying to find Ellen Peterson because she had inherited a good deal of money.

The manager, Warren Hack, was an American. He had a short haircut, a poor complexion, and colorless lips.

"What would you like me to do for you?"

A Hoosier accent.

"She left no forwarding address. I thought you might know where to find her."

"Did you try her place of business?"

"They're not in business any longer. I was hoping you might have some communication from her."

"Not to my knowledge."

"Where she is, she will need money. Perhaps she's paid for something with a check from your bank."

"We do not give out information about our depositors."

"If you can just tell me when you last heard from her."

"Sorry."

Hack had the smug condescending air of someone who knows he is in the right. Brian was reminded of his brother of Martin, whose moral attitudes were as clearly defined as an Aesop's fable.

He thought of a way to disconcert Mr. Hack.

"Have the police been here?"

Hack was startled. "Of course not."

"They will be soon."

"I can't imagine why."

"We're dealing with a person who has disappeared. I'm going to tell the police that you have valuable information about the missing person's whereabouts but are unwilling to release it. You may find it harder to refuse them."

"I'll handle that problem when I have to." Warren Hack put both hands on his desk, and was about to stand up to end the interview.

Brian said, "The police may decide to look into your possible connection with drug smuggling."

"What!"

"Ellen Peterson was a partner in the H & D Trading Company. There are serious charges about the company's involvement with drug smuggling."

"The company was never a depositor at this bank."

"Ellen Peterson was. As she was the company's treasurer, her personal bank account will certainly be of interest. And there's no telling where the investigation may end once it gets started."

"We have nothing to fear. Our business is completely aboveboard."

"At the very least, there will be a lot of unfavorable publicity. Your superiors won't be too pleased about that."

"That's my concern, not yours."

"You may not realize how a thing like this can mushroom. A murder investigation is also underway. Ellen Peterson's disappearance may be connected with it. It's even possible she's met with foul play. This whole affair can go on for months and be no end of trouble for you."

"I'm sure you're very concerned about that."

"Oh, I am. Especially when your superiors find out how easily it could have been avoided."

Hack sat for a moment, staring at him. "Exactly what do you want?"

"When did you last hear from her?"

Hack turned to his intercom and gave an order. A few moments later, a woman entered to put a bank statement on his desk. Across the front of the statement large red letters were stamped.

Warren Hack was barely able to conceal his satisfaction. "It seems you're wasting your time. She isn't a depositor here any longer. She withdrew her money and canceled the account.''

"When?"

"A week ago.''

"She must have intended to leave the country.''

"I'm a banker, not Sherlock Holmes. You'll have to work that out for yourself.'' This time when Hack put his hands on his desk, he did stand up. "Good day to you, Mr. Buckley.''

TWELVE

BRIAN CALLED THE *Bangkok Post* FROM A PUBLIC TELEPHONE in his hotel lobby. He was told that Arunee was working at home. He got her home number and called her.

"I thought you should know what's happened since the last time we talked."

She said, "I have some things of interest to tell you also. Would you like to come here?"

"Now?"

"In about an hour. I've got some work to finish."

As Brian was about to leave the hotel, he stopped at the reception desk to ask if there was a way out other than the front entrance. There was a small tradesman's entrance that let out onto a side street. He left that way and saw no sign of Phibul.

Consulting the map in his guidebook, he found his way to Arunee's home. The door was open and he heard her talking on the telephone in another room. Thai was a soothing language, with gentle cadences and rhythms.

"Is that you, Brian?"

"Yes."

"I'll be a minute. I'm just calling in a story."

He sat in the living room. With the windows and door open, it was almost like being outdoors. Heavy, warm air wafted in, and lay on him as comfortably as a familiar garment on his shoulders.

He admired the view from the window. A boat was pulling a string of barges that rode so low in the water, they appeared to be sinking. Delicate, golden temple spires reached skyward in the middle distance.

"There, that's done," Arunee announced, returning to the living room. "Water's boiling. We will have tea."

She made a ceremony of pouring and serving, working with unobtrusive efficiency. She placed the tray with cups and saucers on the banquette between them.

"This is very nice," Brian said. "Did you always have tea? I mean, with your husband?"

"I was happy with him and fortunate to be his wife."

At first he thought she had not understood his question, then he wondered if she understood too well.

"He had no faults?"

She hesitated. "I do not know your word for small oddnesses."

"Eccentricities."

"Every morning Aelbert had the same breakfast. A glass of mango juice, toast, and herbal tea. He wore a suit and tie on the hottest days. And he had melancholies. It was his," again she searched for the right word, "disposition."

"Was he a good father?"

"Oh, yes. Chakra and Ajana adored him."

"He gave them Thai names?"

She smiled at his question. "We named them Charles and Angela, but agreed they would choose when they went to school. They chose Thai names."

"Fair enough."

"Aelbert was always fair. It was his world I was not fond of."

"What was the problem?"

"The men spoke only of business and money. I saw them go off to work with briefcases and papers and well-pressed clothes, and their eyes were full of worry. I wanted to go up to each of them and say, 'Do not go to work today. Walk with your wife in a garden. Laugh and make love.' But they did not. So their wives drank and gossiped and talked about clothes, and spent most of their time trying to seduce their friends' husbands." She added in a low, bemused tone: "That part of my life seems to have taken place in a different time, a different world."

"And now?" he asked gently.

"I have my children, my work, my home. That is more than enough." In a far high corner a clock made a low burbling sound, and a bird startled to the ceiling. "My children will be home from school soon, and I won't have much time to talk. Shall I begin or will you?"

"I'd rather listen."

"I will begin with minor news. Boonsong really is married to Denison. The registrar of marriages in the town of Patchburi entered her name on the marriage certificate as *B. Srisouta* so no one would recognize it. *Srisouta* is her last name. No one would recognize it."

"Why is that?"

"Last names are not important here. There were none for centuries until a king ordered us to have them. My grandmother was the first in our family to be given a last name at birth."

"Come to think of it, I don't know yours."

She smiled. "It's long and complicated, and you would soon forget if I told you. I'll write it out for you sometime."

"Why would they want their marriage kept secret?"

"Thais are very proud, very prejudiced, and would not like their most celebrated *Ram Wong* dancer to marry a *fahrang*. Boonsong probably wanted to wait until after she retired, when there would be less unfavorable reaction." She sipped her tea and put her cup and saucer down carefully on the tray. "Now for more important news. I heard from Saowa, my baby warden, that the wives of the government ministers are filling their *klong* jars."

"What's a *klong* jar?"

"They are used to carry water from the canals when there is no other source of water supply. Public utilities are always the first to shut down when a coup is in the making."

"That doesn't seem an infallible way of forecasting a government crisis."

She managed a smile that didn't quite hold. "I trust it. When the wives of important men, those with inside knowledge of the situation, order their servants to fill the *klong* jars, it means trouble will begin almost any time."

She put away her teacup, and turned to him expectantly. "Now tell me what news you have. I will be glad to hear."

He told her about his visit to Ellen Peterson's house and his conversation with the *amah*. He showed her the photograph of Ellen Peterson he had acquired.

She nodded with approval. "This is a good likeness. All we have is a snapshot."

"I also visited her bank. She closed her account a week ago."

"How much money did she keep there?"

"I don't know. I have an impression not much."

"She probably had a way of getting larger sums out of the country. It does seem she was planning to leave Bangkok."

The asthmatic school bus stopped outside, and Chakra and Ajana flew in like birds released from a cage.

Ajana saw Brian and ran to him. "It's the monster," she cried happily.

Her eyes widened with surprise as Brian swung her off the ground. He began slowly lifting her to the ceiling. She looked down at him uncertainly, and Brian grinned at her. As fear dropped away, her exhilaration was wonderful to see. She broke into musical laughter.

Up, up she went, approaching a ceiling as remote to her as the peak of Kilimanjaro, until she reached it and put one small hand palm flat against it.

When Brian brought her down, she clapped her hands and, dancing from one foot to another, held up her arms for another trip into the stratosphere.

Chakra stepped forward, his gravely handsome face betraying a childlike willingness. Brian lifted him by very slow stages to the ceiling. Chakra put both his hands flat against it, his fingers splayed, claiming it for his own. When he returned safely to ground level, he looked at Brian as a climber might look at a mountain he has conquered.

Ajana was doing an odd little jigging dance, waiting to be transported again.

"No more," Arunee said. "It's almost time for Saowa. And she has a surprise for you today, Ajana. Her dog had puppies."

Ajana clapped her hands and laughed in delighted anticipation. She ran into her bedroom.

"Ajana promised the new mother a present," Arunee explained. "Something she's made herself."

"I'm sure the new mother will be pleased."

"You have a way of making friends with children. You must like them."

"I'm a former child myself."

Chakra was standing by patiently, waiting for his chance to speak. Now he asked, "Are you from America, Mr. Bucka-lee?"

"Yes, I am."

"Are you acquaint with Clint Eastwood?"

"Not personally."

"He is very exact with a gun, is he not?"

"Very exact."

"I know this is in movies only. It is not what really happens. Men who fall only pretend to be wounded."

"That's true."

"Do you see many Clint Eastwood movies?"

"A few."

"I will be pleased to hear what happens in them. Ajana would also be pleased to hear about Disneyland and Niagara Falls."

"They are quite different," Brian said.

"Which is the popular?"

"I think Disneyland. People usually prefer the one that is not real."

Arunee interrupted: "You can talk to Mr. Buckley some other time. Saowa is here now."

Ajana turned in the doorway to wave at Brian. Her smile opened wide in a glowing face.

Chakra regarded him with the challenging scrutiny of youth. "Do you think Michael Jackson is a serious musician?" he asked.

"I'm quite sure he thinks so."

Chakra left, apparently satisfied.

Arunee said, "Would you care to stay for dinner?"

"I was hoping you'd ask," Brian said.

JEAN HUDSON WAS ANGRY. THE HOTEL OPERATOR HAD JUST told her again that Mr. Buckley had not returned, and, yes, her previous messages were in his callbox.

She had been going to suggest that they meet so she could clearly set forth the terms on which she would continue to see him. At their last meeting he had shown too little regard for her feelings. She was accustomed to a man wanting her so badly that he could not restrain himself, and she could forgive that. What she could not forgive was that Brian had deliberately caused *her* to lose control.

She had known how to handle men since she was barely a teenager, living in Morston, Pennsylvania, where her four brothers and father worked in the coal mine. In those days her hair was brown, and she wore homemade dresses and sandals with flat heels.

Ed Tilton was her boy friend, and she was thirteen when she got into the rear of a Valiant with him one night and gave him what he wanted. The radio was playing, and Barbra Streisand singing "The Way We Were."

She did not come close to orgasm, but she had plenty of opportunity to watch the effect that making love to her had on Ed. His face turned as red as her fingernails, and his breath became a strangle in his throat.

Afterward he stammered fevered words of love, while she thought, I've done it and I'm going to keep on doing it. She had found a contest in which she would always emerge the victor.

When she left Morston four years later, she had perfected a technique of counterfeiting passion, with gyrations, maddening whispers, loud cries. A lover never knew she was shamming until he looked into her cool eyes. It didn't matter then if he was dissatisfied or resentful; he would come back to try to prove his potency.

She met George Denison when she went to work as a receptionist in his office in Chicago. Seducing him was easy; in the bathroom of his apartment afterward, she winked at herself in the mirrored cabinet. You did it again, kid. Her reflection winked back at her knowingly.

Somehow, though, she never got him in her power. He was different from any man she had known. It was the first time her technique failed her. He took her body without any need to possess her. He did not seem to particularly care.

An older woman in the office, who'd had her own brief fling with Denison, told her about him. He had been a campus Lothario who majored in women. Good looking, a fluent talker, and a free spender, he expected no resistance and found none. The woman added, not without bitterness, that his bedroom door ought to have a turnstile in it.

Jean had no regrets when their affair was over. Denison was not an experience she would file away under miscellaneous. She admired his smoothness and sophistication. She had learned from him how to modify her style of dress, how to speak menu-French, and how to order champagne instead of beer or whiskey. These lessons would be valuable to her in the future.

Before Denison left Chicago he offered her a chance to work for him in Bangkok. Because there was no other man in prospect, she accepted. Travel to a distant exotic city was intriguing, and she hoped to meet a man who could afford to give her the kind of life she craved.

She met Horace Calisher.

Money talked, but with Calisher she heard it shouting. His father had made a small fortune in textiles, and compound interest did the rest.

There were problems: he was married and had kids, he was not attractive, and he was so tight that a dollar squeaked coming out of his wallet. But he thought her the most beautiful and desirable woman in the world, and she needed that after Denison, who at times had made her feel like a soggy roll of toilet paper.

She used her sexual power to overcome Horace's penny-pinching. Asking him for money was a one way conversation, like talking to a Trappist monk, but she persuaded him to buy her an apartment and furnish it. He balked at paying for a full-time servant, explaining that a servant would pry and find out things that should be kept secret, and, because he had an important position in the diplomatic corps, he was vulnerable to blackmail. She had to settle for a cleaning *amah* once a week.

Finally, he proposed a new arrangement. "How much do you know about the company you're working for?" he asked one evening during dinner at his beach home. "Would you like to send weekly reports on what's going on there to the U.S. Government?"

"What kind of reports?"

"Names of persons and companies they do business with. Important letters. Invoices. You've got a copying machine in the office."

"How would I know what letters are important?"

"Just copy anything that doesn't arrive by ordinary mail."

"Why is the government so interested?"

"I won't go into too much explanation. But this is what it comes down to. Our government is backing the present Thai government. We're fairly sure the H & D Company is doing business with a rival leader, one who might try to take over. If so, we'd like to know about it."

He was confusing her, and she was glad when he cut to the heart of the matter. "You'll be paid double your present salary. And you can still collect what you're being paid at work."

"I'd be spying, right?"

"You'll be working for the United States Government. On their payroll. Well, the CIA's payroll anyhow."

"They have to do with spies."

She knew he was pushing the arrangement because she would become less of a financial burden for him, but there were ways around that. She wouldn't let him off the hook.

He said, "They're the only protection our country has against enemies who are spying on us. You'd be doing a patriotic thing."

"Well, if you put it that way."

When the telephone rang, she was certain Brian was calling her back, and was disappointed to hear the voice of Peter Judds, her CIA contact. He had the kind of hard heavy voice that left her ears feeling bruised.

She listened to him in sullen silence until suddenly she was wide awake, ears wide open, hearing every word.

"Are you telling me I'm fired?"

"Your job disappeared when the H & D Company went out of business. There's nothing for you to report on anymore. We can't pay for services that aren't being performed."

With another man the remark might have a sexual undertone, but not with Peter. Despite his seemingly strong male presence, he was not interested in women.

"This is a fine way to treat somebody."

"I don't make these decisions, Jean. If I did, things might be different."

"It isn't fair. I've done everything you wanted. I was taking chances. Anybody could have caught me."

She nearly had been caught. She was going through the files in Diane Hollings' office when Diane came back unexpectedly. Diane had left for lunch but came back to pick up papers she forgot to take with her. It was just luck that Jean heard her coming up the stairs.

"I think you owe me a little consideration. Am I getting another check, or am I fired retroactive?"

"I'll see what I can do."

"Thanks a hundred. Next time get somebody else to do your dirty work."

HORACE WAS WAITING WHEN SHE ARRIVED AT KHAO DIN PARK. A heavy shower had left the lawn beside the lake green and wet, and brimmed the pond at the base of the man-made waterfall. A shroud of mist remained.

She told him about Peter Judd's phone call. "I hope you realize what a situation this puts me in. I don't have a job, and they've cut off my only income."

"You won't have any trouble getting another job. I'll call a few people tomorrow."

"I'm not going back to being a receptionist or a secretary. I've got used to better."

"Everything will be all right. You mustn't be so upset."

"You'd better do something. You've had a pretty easy time of it for too long."

Nearby the waterfall flowed strongly in separate rivulets that poured over the edge and exploded into a spray like white smoke. The noise made it hard for her to hear his muttered reply.

"I don't think you've done all that badly."

"If you expect me to be grateful, think again. Plenty of men would like to be in your place."

With one shoe he pushed up a small barricade of dirt against water encroaching from the pond.

"I'm sorry I can't give you all the things you want. I'd hate to think you only care about how much I give you."

"I didn't say that."

"You do like me, don't you?"

Whenever she talked to him seriously about money, he put on this doglike approach, sitting up on his hind legs and begging for a bone.

"I like you a lot, Horace," she said, aware that the truth would not solve her problem. "I guess I've proved it by sticking around like I have, and you a married man with children. What kind of future do I have?"

"I've asked you to marry me."

"I would never do that to you. Your career is too important. All I want is a little money. That isn't too much to ask from someone who says that he loves me."

"Why don't we got to your place and talk this over? We'll come up with some good ideas."

"I know the kind of ideas you'll come with."

"We'll stop and get a bottle of champagne. Taittinger. And some cold cuts."

Just like him. Cheaper than having dinner out at a nice restaurant.

"I've got a headache, and champagne would make it worse."

"I'd really like to be with you."

With chest heaving and tongue panting and imprecations to the Almighty when he started to cave in too quickly. She had no interest in going through that again.

"I think I'm coming down with something. It may be the flu."

"Have you taken your temperature?"

"Not yet. I will when I get home."

He drove her home and parked on a side street, safely away from the front entrance. He suggested coming up "just for a minute." She firmly refused. He began to beg, playing Fido again.

"Please don't pester me. I don't feel well."

"If there's anything you need . . ."

"You know what I need. I'm relying on you."

She watched him drive away. In her apartment she had two martinis and a head of lettuce and turned on the telly. The bad news from Peter Judd had shaken her confidence, but she was recovering quickly. If the U.S. Government wasn't willing to pick up her tab, there were others ready and waiting. The kind of information Peter Judd wanted should interest the other side. Things might fall into place better than ever. The bottom line is looking after yourself, because no one is going to do it for you.

She made a few telephone calls. At eleven-thirty, as she was about to take a sleeping pill, the telephone rang. She smiled when she heard Brian's voice.

"I got your messages. Anything important?"

"I've been wondering why you didn't call."

"I got the impression you didn't want me to."

She was unwilling to lecture him over the telephone. "Maybe I was a little annoyed, but you shouldn't take it so seriously. I thought your were smarter than that."

After a pause he replied, "I wouldn't feel right complicating your life. You're involved with someone else.

"Has Horace been talking to you?"

"He cares a lot for you."

"I don't care about him at all."

"He's not such a bad fellow. You could do worse."

What kind of game was he playing? Did he expect her to come right out and say she didn't want Horace, she wanted him? She would never do that.

"Thank you very much, but I pick my own company. I don't need any advice from you!"

She slammed down the telephone receiver. She didn't mind letting him know how angry she was.

When he called to apologize everything would straighten out. She would greet him with tears, recriminations, then tenderness and a sweet reconciliation.

After ten minutes she realized he was not going to call.

How could he behave like that?

Her anger found a new target: how dared Horace butt into her private life? He didn't own her. No one owned her. No one ever would.

She undressed and got into bed. Her need for love was like an ache in her body. She felt like a pair of hands reaching out in the air, to anyone. Well, not quite anyone. Not Horace.

She was not going to sleep, not even with a pill. She got out of bed, looked up a telephone number and called it.

Half an hour later she was waiting in bed, wearing an almost transparent baby blue nightgown, when she heard a discreet knock at the front door.

She called out, "It's open. Come in!"

The front door opened and closed. Footsteps approached the bedroom, then hesitated.

"I'm in here," she said.

John Nixon entered the bedroom.

THIRTEEN

BRIAN WAS WORKING WITH TWO EMBASSY CLERKS IN AN EMPTY storage room down the hall from Calisher's office. Calisher was at a reception at the Belgian Embassy. He had left instructions with his secretary to give Brian whatever cooperation he asked for.

After three hours Brian was getting nowhere in his effort to discover how and when Ellen Peterson left Bangkok. Calls to both international and domestic airlines did not turn up her name on any passenger list. Travel agencies returned the same message, so did car rental agencies and train and bus lines.

Ellen's own car was in a garage where she had brought it after failing the new emissions test for vehicles. The car was ready but she had not picked it up.

An Embassy clerk found a copy of Ellen's work permit. It was due to expire in two weeks, and Ellen had not applied for a renewal.

"That might indicate she planned to leave the country," the clerk said. "But she would need her passport. She couldn't cross a border without presenting it."

"There should be a record of that."

"We haven't found it. Of course, she may not have used her own name. There are a lot of forged passports and visas around. So many Cambodian and other refugees need them to get into this country."

Brian dined alone that evening at a small inexpensive cafe. The waiter did not speak English, so Brian ordered what a man near him at the counter was eating. It turned out to be a red chili chicken curry with a sauce hot enough for a fire-eater. He needed several Singha beers to wash it down.

In his tourist's guide he looked up modestly priced accomodations. The choice came down to a hotel on Yaoara Street that the guide book said was "clean and reasonable."

When he returned to the New Thonburi hotel, he gave notice that he would be leaving the next day.

In his room he packed his few belongings. He was feeling tired and downcast. He studied the photograph of young Ellen Peterson on her graduation day.

Where the hell are you?

He slept poorly. He had a disturbing dream in which he was in jail when fire broke out. He was locked in his cell and could not escape.

He awoke to find the room full of smoke.

Thick, oily, suffocating smoke, the kind that quickly induces unconsciousness and death.

A coughing attack bent him double. He staggered into the nearby bathroom, soaked a towel under the shower and wrapped it around his nose and mouth, knotting it awkwardly behind his neck. By then the bathroom was filling up with a black mist. He pushed open the shutters on the window.

Outside the air was clear. Only a few hazy tendrils escaped to stain the early morning light.

A narrow ledge, no wider than six inches, ran the length of the building's facade.

Behind him the bathroom was filling up with dense blinding poisonous smoke.

He had no choice.

He stepped up onto the window sill, got a firm grip on the window frame and put his right foot sidewise onto the ledge. Turning his body sharply toward the building, he planted his left hand flat against the wall and brought his left foot across to rest on the ledge.

Leaning in to keep a precarious balance, he took a sliding step along the ledge. Sweat rolled down from under his arms. Harsh smoke billowing out the window began to penetrate his wet towel. He fought down a racking compulsion to cough.

The muscles in his forearms gave a quick jerky movement, then the muscles in his legs began quivering. He plastered himself against the wall, unable to move.

He risked a glance ahead. The distance to the next window was a continent away.

He clung to the wall until the trembling fit passed.

Try again.

His foot fumbled for another place on the ledge, and slipped on a bird dropping or a place worn smooth by weathering.

At that moment he almost felt relief. He wouldn't have to struggle anymore.

It was over.

He regained his balance and dizzily leaned his forehead against the wall.

He risked a shallow breath, and to his surprise did not inhale smoke. He was beyond the smothering cloud still curling out of the windows. A breeze was moving it in the other direction.

"Just a little further. You've almost made it."

The voice was so startling that he froze, carefully poised, on the narrow ledge above empty space.

"Come on. It's easy."

A hand appeared, stretching toward him from the window ahead. A man's face appeared behind it.

Brian took a slightly longer step and reached toward the outstretched hand. He grabbed it.

"Take this!"

A short knotted sheet dangled almost beside him. He took it with his free hand. Then he released his grip on the man's hand and seized the sheet rope with both hands.

He swung off the ledge in order to plant both feet against the wall, and began to climb.

At window level other hands pulled him over the sill.

The room was almost a duplicate of his own. The bed was pulled almost over to the window, and the other end of the sheet was tied to one of the legs.

Two men were in the room, one wearing white pajamas with short sleeves that showed honey-brown brawny arms, and the other a thin, spectacled Thai who worked at the hotel reception desk.

The brawny man said, "Glad you made it."

"So am I." Brian turned to the Thai. "Is anything being done about the fire in my room?"

"No fire," the Thai replied. "Just smoke. Fire department come anyway. Very soon now."

"You look pretty shook up," the brawny man said. "You could probably use a drink, and I've got a bottle in my room." He put out his hand. "My name is Peter Judd."

Brian felt better after having a drink. Judd was a relaxing man to be with. He told Brian that he had smelled smoke and had gone out into the corridor.

"When I saw the smoke was coming from your room, I banged on the door, but there was no answer. The door was locked. So I called the hotel desk.

"They called the fire department and sent up someone with a key to your room. We went in just long enough to be sure there was no fire and no one was in there. Luckily the man they sent up had a key to the adjoining room, too. From there we saw you out on the ledge."

"If it wasn't a fire, what was it?"

"Damned if I know. I hear firemen in the corridor. You want to ask them?"

Brian nodded.

The Thai fire chief was five feet tall, and could not have weighed more than a hundred pounds with his helmet and boots on. He smelled of smoke.

He told Brian, "Oily rags causing smokiness. Someone throws them over transom into room. You know of someone who will do this?"

Brian had had a rough time, and he was tired. If he admitted that what happened might be an attempt to kill him, the police would question him as well as the other guests and employees in the hotel. The hotel management would not be happy about that, and neither would he.

"It was probably an accident," he said.

Shortly afterward, the hotel manager, Mr. Paetao, came to the room. Peter Judd excused himself to shower and change his clothes.

Mr. Paetao apologized for the difficulties that Brian had endured and assured him that his belongings had been removed from his room to be deodorized and defumigated. If any permanent loss was incurred, the hotel would gladly make restitution.

"Naturally you will be moved to another, more satisfactory room at no extra expense. I hope this sufficiently expresses our regret in this unfortunate incident."

"Not quite," Brian said. "I've been put to a lot of trouble. My life was endangered."

Paetao sighed. "What do you suggest, sir?"

"Someone tossed that bundle of oily rags over the transom into my room. We have to assume it was an employee of the hotel."

"I do not think one can assume that, sir."

"If it was not carelessness, then it was a deliberate attempt on my life. The police will investigate. There will be considerable publicity. The media do not usually demand proof when a good story is at stake. On the other hand, a small accidental fire in a hotel room, quickly put out, isn't likely to be reported. Which would you prefer?"

Paetao touched his moustache with his forefinger. "I assume that you do not intend to bring a legal action against the hotel."

"That can be part of an agreement."

"On what shall we agree, Mr. Buckley?"

"That I am your guest for the rest of my stay in Bangkok. Whatever I owe you will be forgotten, and there will be no charge for my new improved accommodations."

"Do you intend to stay long?"

"Not very. Certainly less than a month."

"We shall be very pleased to have you as our guest, Mr. Buckley."

BRIAN WAS BARELY INSTALLED IN HIS NEW, MORE SPACIOUS ROOM when the telephone rang. He sat in a comfortable armchair to answer it.

A woman's voice full of timbre and resonance answered: "Am I speaking with Meestrah Buckley?"

"Who is this?"

"You came to my husband's funeral."

Boonsong!

"I must see you at once. I require your assistance."

She had her nerve, expecting him to jump at her summons.

"Sorry. I have no intention of going anywh—"

He was speaking into a dead phone. She had broken the connection.

He did not owe her any courtesy. Quite the opposite. It would serve her right if he simply ignored her call.

He was too curious.

He called the clerk at the reception desk who told him that the valet service would not open for another hour. His clothes, however, had been put in the valet's room marked for immediate attention.

Brian told the clerk to go into the room and reclaim certain items of clothing.

"I need these right away. Is there someone who can wash and press and spray them with deodorant?"

"The maid, sir. But that will not remove . . ."

"I know," Brian said.

His skin was saturated with unpleasant smoky odor. He showered and shampooed his hair and scrubbed his body for ten minutes. When the maid brought his clothes, he put on a bath towel to greet her and gave her his pajamas with instructions to burn them if necessary.

Deodorizing his clothes had succeeded only in adding a strong lemony undersmell. Brian went through the hotel lobby leaving a scent trail.

The weather was no help. There was hardly any breeze, and the air was close and muggy.

Phibul's taxi pulled up to the entrance.

Phibul sniffed. "You catch fire?"

"You can drive me to the waterfront, if you don't mind having me in your cab."

"I will open all windows."

Brian rode in malodorous comfort through the morning rush hour. The streets were filled with autos, mopeds, three-wheel motorized samlars, bicycles, and overweighted buses. On the sidewalks crowds flowed through each other with a radarlike precision of avoidance.

Whenever the taxi stopped, they were assailed by children selling rice sweets and cold drinks, and others repeatedly calling *"Olian, Olian!"* Olian was a popular, inexpensive drink sold in plastic bags. The bag was half filled with ice, and black coffee was poured over it.

Brian had not had breakfast, so he bought one. The top of the bag was tied together tightly leaving room only for a sipping straw. But the cold coffee was restorative.

At the waterfront several streets intersected in chaos. The taxi came to a halt in gridlock.

Brian handed Phibul the empty bag of *olian*. "I'll get off here."

Ignoring Phibul's protest, he dropped money for the fare on the front seat. He got out and walked back two blocks before taking a circuitous route to Boonsong's house.

There were no mourners waiting on line this early in the day. The door was opened by the muscular Thai with whom Brian had tangled on his previous visit. He led Brian past the maroon curtains concealing the coffin. The smell of incense mingled peculiarly with Brian's own redolence.

Beyond the large living room was a smaller room where Boonsong was seated, surrounded by vividly colored pillows on a plump, white couch. Twin lamps enclosed her in refulgent light; she wore a gown of Thai silk, and her eyes were as carefully made up as those of an exotic silent film star.

She would have suited that era, Brian thought, living in a large Beverly Hills mansion with statues and totem poles on the lawn, rainbow-colored fountains in the garden, a Rolls Royce in the garage, and white Russian wolfhounds breakfasting beside her table on the terrace.

She indicated a chair near her. "I am grateful to you for coming at such short notice. I hope the early hour was not too inconvenient."

As he sat down, her nose wrinkled slightly.

"I'm sorry," he said. "There was a fire at my hotel. A lot of smoke."

"I must apologize for what happened at our last meeting."

"I'm willing to forget it if you are."

"I cannot forget how well you handled yourself. That is why I sent for you. I must leave on a dangerous journey, and I would like you to accompany me as my bodyguard. The journey will not take long. And you will be very well paid."

"I appreciate the offer, but I'm not for hire."

"Everyone is for hire. The only question is price. How much do you want?"

He considered his reply, while an enormous black fan circled silently overhead. She was George Denison's widow. There might be something to learn from her.

"I'll need to know where you're going and why you need a bodyguard."

The skin tightened around her artfully made-up eyes. "I am leaving the country for a day or two. And I am afraid of someone. That is all I can tell you."

"That isn't good enough. If I risk my neck, I have to know why I'm doing it."

After a moment she said, "Very well, then. I hope I can rely on your discretion. Perhaps you know the business my late husband was engaged in was immensely profitable. He could not risk keeping money here. Even bank vaults are not safe from the *force majeure* of a government, and explanations would prove difficult. He had to deposit the money outside the country."

"Where?"

"Kuala Lumpur. In Malaysia. That is where I am going."

"You said you were afraid of someone." It seemed to him that fear surrounded her like a ghost image.

"A person who knows of my husband's fortune, and who is clever enough to devise a way to claim it."

"Who is it?"

"You don't know her. She's the treasurer of my husband's company."

"Ellen Peterson?"

"You have heard of her?"

"Yes." For Brian, this put an entirely different light on her offer.

"George always said she is extremely clever in financial matters."

"Why do you think she's after your late husband's money?"

"As the company treasurer she would know where it's hidden. I believe she's already left Bangkok, and is on her way to get it. I cannot delay. If I don't go quickly, I'll arrive to find everything gone." She gave him a pleading look. "Will you come with me?"

"Why not choose someone on your personal staff?"

"I cannot trust them. I believe I can trust you."

He looked at her thoughtfully. "There's someone I've got to talk to first. I'll give you my answer by noon today."

Boonsong smiled. "I look forward to our traveling together. I will feel much safer if you are with me."

FOURTEEN

BRIAN TOOK A *SAMLAR* TO THE *BANGKOK POST* BUILDING. The open carriage and fresh air helped to eradicate all but a whiff of the fusty odor in his clothes.

In the lobby of the *Bangkok Post* building, Brian asked the receptionist to call Arunee. She was not in, so he asked for Harry Lokma.

Lokma listened with interest while Brian told him of his meeting with Boonsong.

"Are you going with her?"

"I'm thinking about it."

"That's where Ellen Peterson may have gone. The partners needed a place to hide their money, and Kuala Lumpur is a good choice."

"But they could have picked another spot."

"Jean Hudson might have a clue."

"There are problems about that."

"Oh? She's a valuable contact. I was hoping you'd remain on friendly terms."

As Brian was about to reply, he felt a strong tremor, followed instantly by a distant booming, as though a very heavy object had fallen from a window. Lokma's chair lifted a few inches off the floor and slid into the wall. Brian's heavier bulk kept his own chair in place.

Lokma pulled himself out of his chair and grabbed the phone at his desk. "What was that?" he demanded of the mouthpiece. He waited, his expression intent, as a high-pitched, unintelligible babble came from the other end of the phone.

"Is anyone hurt?" Lokma asked, adding quickly, "I'll be right down."

"What happened?" Brian asked.

"An explosion in the basement."

They took the staircase down. The whole basement area was a wreck. A powerful plastic bomb had destroyed the giant Miehle printing press. There was one casualty, a security guard on duty when the bomb went off. He was pinned down beneath part of the casing of the press, and several men were trying to free him. Brian lent a hand, and the heavy metal casing was quickly removed.

An ambulance arrived minutes later. A preliminary examination revealed that both the man's legs were broken, and he had suffered an internal hemorrhage. He was removed on a stretcher, and the ambulance raced him to a hospital.

"We're lucky there were not others injured," Lokma said. "A few hours ago there would have been. The press had not finished running off the morning edition, and the workers were still here."

At the entrance to the newsroom Lokma and Brian met Colonel Suvit arriving.

Harry Lokma said, "I'm counting on you, Colonel, to conduct a thorough investigation. I want to know who's responsible."

"I will do my best. Your newspaper has many enemies. This is not a case where one searches for a suspect. There are many such."

Brian left Lokma and Colonel Suvit and made his way down to the lobby. The lobby was crowded with people, and the woman in the reception cubicle was trying to cope with a demanding switchboard. Several policeman were blocking anyone from going upstairs, announcing alternately in Thai and English that the building was being evacuated so the bomb squad could search for more explosives.

Brian saw Arunee near the lobby doors.

"I heard what happened," she said. "Do they have any idea who did it?"

"Colonel Suvit is in charge of the investigation. I don't know how much you can expect from him."

More and more people were entering the lobby from the upper floors. There was hardly room to stand.

Brian said, "We can't talk here. Let's go somewhere else."

Police cars were parked in front of the *Bangkok Post* building with their signal lights flashing, and policemen were keeping curious bystanders from approaching too near the building. They passed through.

He said, "I had word about Ellen Peterson. She's left Bangkok."

"I know. She left yesterday on a river barge."

"How did you find out?"

"A sailor named Manit was working on the barge and saw her come aboard. He recognized her from the circular we printed asking for information about her and offering a reward. He called us. I went to the dock today, hoping to meet him, but no one seemed to know anything about a sailor named Manit."

"This might be a trick to throw us off her trail."

"Why do you think so?"

Brian thought of the time he had spent at the American Embassy checking out air and ground transportation. "Ellen wouldn't have waited two days to leave. And she shouldn't be on a barge traveling north. She should be en route to Kuala Lumpur."

"Why would she go there?"

"Because that's where the money is."

He brought Arunee up to date on his meeting with Boonsong and what she had told him about the money cache in Kuala Lumpur.

"Boonsong is certain that Ellen Peterson is headed there to get her hands on the money."

"I'll have to do some further checking on this Manit story."

When they returned to the *Bangkok Post* building the last police car was pulling away. Inside the lobby, people were lined up waiting for elevators and others were going up the stairs. A policeman stationed in the lobby told them that the bomb squad had finished its work and given an all clear.

Arunee went directly to her desk in the newsroom. Brian stopped at Lokma's office.

"Here are a few things we've discovered," Lokma told him. "Two Buddhist monks were in the news room early this morning. They were making the rounds with their begging bowls, but they apparently became fascinated with how the printing press worked. When the workers left at the end of the press run, the monks were still here. The security guard had no reason to suspect they intended harm."

"Did he give a description?"

"Pretty vague. He's in considerable pain and under sedation.

But he says one monk had a scar below his left eye. We've asked Colonel Suvit to check at monasteries and temples, but I don't think those men really are monks. A monk's costume is not only a good disguise, it's a good way to get into places without causing suspicion."

"Who were they and what did they hope to accomplish?"

"My guess is that they're in league with Wanchai. They're trying to stop us from printing any more stories about the shipment of military supplies to him."

"Can you keep publishing?"

Lokma nodded. "We've made temporary arrangements with the *Bangkok World* to use their presses until we get a replacement press from Hong Kong."

Brian found Arunee on the telephone in the newsroom. When she hung up she said, "I got some pretty quick answers. There *is* a sailor named Manit who was employed on a barge operated by the Orient Shipping Company."

"Was?"

"He was fired just before the barge left Bangkok."

"Where'd you get the information?"

"I persuaded the clerk at the Seamen's Mercantile Association to look up his employment status. They'd just got word of his discharge."

"Why did the others tell you they never heard of him?"

"They were probably protecting him from debt collectors. Birds of prey descend pretty quick when they hear someone's lost a job."

"Where is Manit now?"

"Where would you go if you had no money and had just been fired?"

"I'd probably go home to bed and pull the sheets up over my head."

"I don't know what he did after he got home. But you're right. That's where he went. I suppose he didn't believe he had much chance of collecting a reward."

"What I can't figure out is why Ellen Peterson is on a barge traveling north? It's the wrong direction. Like traveling east into a sunset."

"She's looking for help from Khun Wanchai."

AT A FEW MINUTES PAST NOON, BRIAN KEPT HIS PROMISE TO call Boonsong. He made the call from Arunee's desk.

"Mistess not here," a woman's lilting voice informed him. "She leave this morning."

"Who are you?"

"Work for mistess."

"She was expecting me to call. My name is Buckley."

"Mistess leaves message for you." A long moment of silence, then a rustle of paper: "It say, 'Please come Patchburi express train. I will meet you at station.' "

"Will you hear from her?"

"Mistess calls tonight."

"Tell her I'm sorry, but I had to keep a previous appointment. Wish her a safe and pleasant journey."

He hung up and turned to Arunee seated nearby.

"I hope you've made the right choice," she said.

"The main thing is Manit actually saw Ellen Peterson. Boonsong is just acting on a hunch."

The sun had passed its zenith when they set out for Chonburi and the small adjacent hamlet where Manit lived. Arunee was driving the battered yellow Toyota.

For almost two days there had been no rain, a welcome but unusual event during the monsoon season. Arunee said that the provincial roads they were driving on were impassable after a monsoon. Then the only connection between villages were footpaths and tracks.

Brian said, "I hope the break in the weather means other things are turning our way."

He observed her covertly. She could have been almost any age, with her petite figure, dark eyes, olive skin, and small features perfectly arranged on her face. The ink-black hair that fell loosely to her shoulders was caught in back by a red ribbon.

He said, "I know so little about you. I'd like to know more."

"What would you wish to know?"

"Start at the beginning. Tell me about your parents."

"They are both dead. Drowned in a ferry crossing. Along with my younger brother, and two hundred others."

"I'm so sorry."

"It happened a long time ago. When I was eleven years."

"Who looked after you?"

"I looked after myself. I have an older brother, some years older, but he's married, and has a family and no money. I could not impose myself on him."

"How did you manage?"

"It was not easy. But I survived. I lived in the streets. When

I was thirteen, I moved in with a man. He was old, a widower, and very kind. It was because of him I began going to school. After he died, I was not willing to give up my studies. I earned money the only way I could."

"I didn't mean to pry."

She looked at him with an amused expression, and to his surprise he found himself flushing.

"I am not ashamed of anything. There are thousands who live now as I did. They are called the butterflies of Bangkok."

There was no air conditioning in the Toyota, and the afternoon heat made him feel as if his blood were frying in his veins. He opened the car windows wide, so the breeze cooled his cheeks.

At that moment he remembered Diane and how she looked in a striped jersey and tennis shorts.

After awhile Arunee said, "You have gone away behind your eyes. But your thoughts are pleasant. You are smiling."

"It may seem silly, but I was remembering how Diane played tennis. She was very good. I used to win from her occasionally until she found out I had a weak backhand and played to it."

"And won?"

"And won."

Diane wanted to win so badly. He never understood what drove her with its incessant: *I want. I must have.* Even winning did not assuage her unrest. When he asked her why, she answered: *No one but me knows how much I need, and no one but me knows how disappointed I'll be if I don't get it.*

He said, "I suppose we all have some of that desire to win."

"Lord Buddha teaches that one must be at peace with oneself. What is most important is to maintain a cool heart."

"A cool heart. I like that."

When Diane wanted something, she went for it. "You have to lock your eyes tight on what you're after and keep heading for it. Don't let anything stand in your way." Money was her goal and prize, the sacred blood and the flesh, the Holy Grail. "Sure, a lot of rich people lead incredibly empty lives, but being poor doesn't exactly fill your life to the brim, either."

They left the road to Chonburi and followed a narrow dirt road jammed with oxcarts and bicycles. A single row of huts propped up on stilts with thatched roofs and straw walls appeared on one side of the dirt road. Children and dogs ran beside the car. The children wore ragged clothes, the dogs were skeletal and had open sores on their bodies.

A woman was drawing up water from a well enclosed by a low circular wall of mud and brick. Arunee stopped to ask directions, and the woman made a gesture with one arm and muttered briefly.

Arunee drove on to a thatched hut. A middle-aged man with a grizzled beard was sitting on the porch, his *rattan* chair tipped back against the wall. As they approached he spat a long stream of betel juice over the porch railing.

Arunee got out of the car and called up to him. He answered in what sounded like a grunt.

Arunee said to Brian, "This is Manit, the sailor. He knows few words in English, and I must talk to him in our language. You will please excuse us."

Brian removed a taped manila envelope he had put into the glove compartment of the Toyota. "You might try this on him."

He opened the Manila envelope and removed the graduation photograph of Ellen Peterson. She took it up to the porch. Manit did not move the position of his chair. Arunee showed him the "wanted" circular and the photograph of Ellen Peterson. Brian watched for a reaction. The grizzled sailor looked puzzled for a few moments, then nodded.

Brian waited until Arunee and Manit stopped talking before he joined them on the porch. Through the open door he glimpsed a wooden bed covered with a mat, a straight unpainted chair, and a small cupboard that appeared to contain only a drinking glass, and a small radio. Dishes and cooking pots were piled on the floor near a charcoal burner. The entire house was the size of a motel room.

Arunee reported, "He says it is the same woman, but younger than the one in the circular. She is the one who got him fired."

"How?"

"It is not easy to explain."

"Try."

"He had been warned that he would come to harm if a white *fahrang* woman was above his head. A *phi* was placed on him."

"What is a *phi*?"

"A spirit curse. Thai people are superstitious about anything concerning their heads. Children do not even like their heads to be touched."

"Why is that?"

"Each person has a *khwan*, a spirit which resides in the head. If the *khwan* should leave a person and not be able to get back for any reason the person will become very ill or die. And the *khwan* is very timid. An unexpected touch may frighten it away."

"You believe there's a spirit in your head?"

"What you Westerners believe is not so much different. We do not fear black cats crossing our path, walking under ladders, breaking mirrors, or knocking wood to keep bad things from happening. And we do not believe there is any special power in the number thirteen."

"You win. Go on."

"He was loading the barge. He refused to continue because she was sitting on the deck above his head. The sole of her foot was also pointing at him. This is very bad manners—as bad as sticking out your tongue or thumbing your nose would be to your people. He suspected she was the white *fahrang* woman who would bring the curse on him. So he refused to continue loading, and the barge captain fired him."

"I see. Does he know where she was going?"

"I asked him. He doesn't have any idea. He suggests that I talk to the owner of the barge."

She spoke to Manit, who rose from his chair, bowed slightly, and made a *wai* at forehead level.

"I told him that he will definitely get the reward," Arunee explained, "and more if she is found."

They started back toward the city. Under a banyan tree off the road, hidden by its branches and broad leaves, a man watched them go. Without hurrying, he lit a cigarette. In the light of the flaring match, a jagged scar beneath his left eye was visible.

EN ROUTE BRIAN BEGAN TO FEEL HUNGRY. "CAN WE STOP somewhere for lunch?"

"I have a better idea."

She parked the Toyota outside a dusty grocery store and emerged some minutes later carrying a wicker basket covered by a large paper napkin. A bottle peeked out of the napkin at a forty-five degree angle, its neck resting lightly against the basket's side.

"We'll *bai tiaw*," she announced. "I know just the spot."

"Is that your word for picnic?"

"To *bai tiaw* means many things, from a picnic to just relaxing."

A mile further on she turned off the road onto a flat grassy expanse surrounding a small *wat*. The *wat* was covered with thousands of pieces of colored glass and contained a serene Buddha.

She parked near a lone coconut palm tree. She spread the large paper napkin on the ground and opened the basket. Grilled sliced beef was rolled around bamboo sticks to form small cylinder shapes. The bread was home made, rough, crusty, gray, and satisfying. The bottle of cold white wine was exactly the right complement for the spiciness of the dry chili peanut sauce.

"Fit for King Rama," Brian said, dipping a beef slice in the sauce. His glance fell on the nearby palm tree. The tree had many colored ribbons tied around its base. "What are those for? The decorations?"

"It's a lucky tree. Once a tree is known to be lucky, people come and tie a ribbon around its base. Then they make a wish."

"Have you ever done it?"

"With another lucky tree. Just before I was married."

"Did your wish come true?"

"Oh, yes."

Arunee wrapped the last few crumbs in a napkin and put it back into the basket.

Brian was still looking at the palm tree and its decorations. "Charming custom. If I had a ribbon I'd try it."

Arunee untied the red ribbon from her dark hair which flowed out loose and bounteous. She gave him the ribbon.

"Shall I wish for something general or something in particular?"

She looked at him uncertainly. "That is up to you."

He tied the ribbon carefully on the tree trunk, apart from the others.

"What did you wish for?" Arunee asked.

"I can't tell you. That's a Western superstition. If you wish for something, you won't get it if you tell anyone."

He had wished for a cool heart.

IN THE EVENING, AFTER THE TRIP TO CHONBURI, BRIAN HAD dinner at her house. While she prepared a meal of mussels and clams and stewed eel with ginger, he read a story to her children from Chakra's learn-English book. Chakra sat crosslegged, following the words raptly, his lips moving as though he were memorizing. Ajana did not understand all the English words, but she listened with unwavering attention, hypnotized by the sounds.

Near the ceiling, a red-throated bird hopped from one rafter to another. Through the open window a mild breeze sent in warm quavering waves of air.

When Brian finished reading, Chakra gave a little sigh, and Ajana clapped her hands and wanted Brian to start over again.

He didn't, because Arunee was ready to serve dinner.

"Are you interested in sport, Mr. Buckalee?" Chakra asked at the table.

"Yes. I used to play football."

"I do not understand how it is played. But I know that it is popular in the United States of America."

"I'll be glad to show you sometime."

"I hope this should be very soon."

"So do I."

The dinner, with its mixture of unusual ingredients, was a delicious experience. Afterward Chakra shook hands gravely and said good night. As though this were a signal, Ajana ran to Brian and held up her arms. Brian lifted her, and she kissed him on the cheek. He held her a moment before reluctantly putting her down.

Arunee left to put the children to bed. She promised to return shortly and make tea.

The sun had set long before, but seemed to have left behind innumerable pale fires from houses where cooking was taking place on outdoor grills. Dogs barked at a passing boat that was piled high with netting, crates, and pigs in conical wire baskets.

Brian was filled with an inexplicable contentment. He wanted to cling to the feeling, and to prolong it, he allowed himself to indulge in a fancy. How would he live in this country? The projection of himself into an imagined world was a deception, rather like a child pretending to believe in a fairy tale.

He would need to earn a living. He might go into business for himself, perhaps open a store that sold sports equipment. When the store was a success (in his imagining, failure was not possible), he would franchise other stores while maintaining quality controls over the merchandise offered for sale.

Arunee returned, put water on the stove to heat, and made her customary ceremony of pouring tea.

"I've been thinking about your idea of keeping a cool heart," he said. "Do you think it's possible?"

She paused before replying, "I have known many who achieved it. But I have not mastered the secret. There is too much in the world that disturbs me."

Speaking softly and haltingly, with pauses for reflection, she told him she had studied Buddhism with a very wise teacher who taught that the universe has neither a beginning nor an end, but moves forever from growth to equilibrium, from equilibrium to decline, to dissolution and to renewed growth. Its purpose is to serve as a stage for the transmigration of souls, and for the punishment and reward of deeds committed in earlier incarnations. The immortal soul occupies many transient bodies on its journey to *Nirvana*.

"Something like the Christian idea of heaven."

"It is not the same. *Nirvana* is the end of the cycle of rebirth, a state of being where suffering is unknown. The soul returns like a drop of water into the great ocean of the Absolute."

He smiled at her with his eyes. "Do I have to wait that long for a cool heart?"

She smiled back at him. "That may come much earlier, even in a present existence. Buddha taught that unhappiness and suffering are caused by such things as greed, hatred, and ignorance. We must rid ourselves of our wants—the want to gain, not to lose what we have, even the desire to hold on to life itself. Only then will we have true freedom, and hearts free of strife."

"That's a pretty tall order."

"I am still an apprentice, but my teacher assured me that the only way to wisdom is by meditation. One must turn inward, transform oneself from the inside. In this way the surface peels off and the true face emerges. When you see your true face, you accept who you are without resentment, and are no longer troubled. Above all, my teacher taught, one cannot be the hating type."

He was quite sure at that moment that she was looking straight through him. "Is that how you see me?"

"You are one who has suffered losses and wishes to find a quick remedy."

The words of denial were on his lips when, suddenly, he found himself unable to speak. He had suffered losses, had been hurt for no valid reason. His father's suicide, his mother's death, Martin's dreadful fate, his own career brutally cut off before he could achieve success. And then, of course, Diane.

"Did this teacher of yours tell you how to stop being a hating type?"

"The Theravada sect of Buddhism, to which he and I belong, believes that each person must find his own liberation, as a snake must cast off its own skin."

"That isn't too helpful."

She said, "Perhaps this is more clear. A person should look at himself as an image in water, a reflection that could not be there unless he was, but which does not in any way affect him. He can move away from it, and the reflection is gone."

"The image isn't always separate from the person. It may be part of him."

Her eyes fixed on him with the curiously intent gaze of a birdwatcher. "I do not think the heart can find peace until one learns to listen not with ears, but with an inner receptor."

"I've still got a lot to learn."

She looked at him. "The hour is late, and we have had a long day. The car is parked outside. You may drive it to your hotel, but be certain to return it to the newspaper in the morning."

Driving the yellow Toyota through the rainy night, Brian wondered: Am I a hating type? He was far from having a cool heart. Perhaps that goal was easier for Buddhists, because they believed each life was merely a stepping stone to further advancement.

Suddenly he thought of Denison sequestered behind a crimson cloth, dripping away his flesh.

The power of the vision shook him.

I don't want to die in Bangkok, he told himself.

FIFTEEN

COLONEL SUVIT FOUND THE SITUATION MOST ANNOYING. Mostly he blamed the *fahrang* Buckley and the *Bangkok Post*'s editor. The documents not returned to him with the attaché case were surely the basis for the articles now appearing in the newspaper. Everyone in the city was talking about the weapons shipments to Wanchai, the drug trafficking, and the corruption within the Thai government.

With each new revelation the value of the information to him diminished. When all was published, nothing would have value.

Suvit sat behind the desk in his office with a sheaf of arrest records before him that he was supposed to be going through. His mind was occupied by bitter thoughts.

This very morning his ten-year-old granddaughter had been knocked off her bicycle by a hit-and-run motorist. Her injuries were painful but not serious. Nevertheless the bills for hospital and medical care would be considerable.

He would have to pay because the child's parents were too poor. They owned a small stand in a market where they sold spices and cooking sauces and varieties of peppers. His daughter had not made an advantageous marriage, but he could not allow her or her children to suffer for that.

Suvit believed in the importance of family ties. Why else would he have put so many relatives on the police payroll?

Phibul was announced and appeared in the doorway shortly afterward.

"You wish to see me, sir?"

Suvit regarded him with irritation. "I have been waiting for a report on the *fahrang* Buckley."

Phibul blinked. "I have been filing reports every day, sir."

"Not the one I have been waiting for. I still do not know where to find the documents that were taken from the *fahrang* Denison's office."

"But you have the attaché case, sir. It was returned to you."

Suvit answered with the exaggerated patience of someone who has long since run out of it. "Not necessarily with everything it originally contained."

Phibul flushed. "I am not sure my poor head understands all this," he said nervously.

"I mean that Mr. Lokma and the *fahrang* Buckley are still withholding evidence."

"Then why do we not arrest them?"

"Because we need proof."

"How shall I provide this, sir?"

"Use your eyes to more advantage. Note carefully when the *fahrang* Buckley meets with Lokma. Buckley may still be supplying him with information."

"I will do my best, sir."

Suvit thought sadly: If only your best was good enough. Phibul was not well-equipped with intelligence, but he had been his mother's favorite. In a drawer in his desk Suvit kept a portrait of his late wife. She looked almost beautiful in the portrait, the sharp lines of her face softened by a recent pregnancy, her "floating eye" not visible, her bust still firm and supple. The birth of nine children had drained her breasts and left them flaccid and limp as pancakes.

She had been a good wife to the end. Never complained, was economical, cooked well, and raised their children to be obedient and reverent. He hoped she was happy in her new incarnation. She deserved to be.

His next visitor was an unlicensed food vendor with whom Suvit had done business before. The vendor paid a fine and a small remuneration to Suvit for not ordering his merchandise confiscated. By never soliciting a bribe, taking only what was freely offered in gratitude, Suvit avoided creating resentment or inclinations toward revenge. But now he wondered if he had been too cautious.

While he was pondering this, one of his officers called in with a report of a student demonstration on Patchburi Road. In these troubled times, there seemed no end of student protests. Suvit had no doubt the students were led by Communists intent on overthrowing the government.

He issued orders for more police to be sent to the site of the demonstration. Undoubtedly the students would march up Ayuthaya Road to the Victory Monument. He had to deploy his forces to cut off their route and scatter them. He needed more manpower for that. He called paramilitary headquarters for help. Then he got into his police chief's car and drove to the scene.

When he arrived, the main body of students was on the march. A few stragglers were slitting open garbage bags and emptying their contents into the street. A young man was waving a placard with a portrait of King Rama on which a death's head had been pasted over the royal countenance.

Such insolence had to be punished. Buddha, the King, and the national flag were enduring national symbols, above criticism.

Suvit leaned out of the car window, lifted a whistle to his lips and blew one short and one long blast. The shrill signal drew the attention of youthful stragglers who turned toward his car with clearly hostile intent.

Suvit quietly removed his pistol from its holster and placed it in his lap.

A police car, responding to his signal, streaked up with sirens blaring. Two policemen jumped out with teak nightsticks at the ready. The youths turned and fled.

"Are you all right, Phan Eg?" one policeman asked.

Suvit returned his pistol to its holster. "Are the police cordons in place?"

"Yes, Phan Eg. An official of the American Embassy is trapped in his car by marchers on Ayuthaya Road."

"Get him out quickly."

"He is surrounded. That will require more police."

Colonel Suvit was not a coward, and he had a good deal of experience with unruly crowds. "Show me the way."

He followed the police car. From a block away he saw police and demonstrators milling in battle. Stalled in the center, unable to move, was a Cadillac limousine with a small American flag flying from its antenna.

Suvit drove over a brilliant glitter of broken glass strewn everywhere in bits, needles and shards, and stopped the car only a few yards away. He moved forward confidently. The secret was to put everything out-of-mind except where you wanted to go, and act as if you were willing to do anything to get there.

A young man lunged at him. A policeman clubbed the young

man down almost at Suvit's feet. A young woman grabbed Suvit's arm. She received a sharp blow from another policeman's short heavy nightstick.

Suvit pushed through until he was beside the stalled Cadillac. The driver, alone and cowering down on the leather seat, was Horace Calisher.

Suvit signaled Calisher to let him in the other side. The door unlocked, and he slipped into the passenger seat.

Calisher said faintly, "I was on my way back from the airport. Suddenly they were all around me."

Someone broke off the antenna with its American flag. The flag flashed briefly among struggling bodies, shot up triumphantly for a moment, then disappeared.

A heavy object clattered on the car roof. Calisher jumped. A bloody face floated up to the window beside Suvit and cried something unintelligible. Puffed lips drew together and spat saliva on the window.

Suvit rolled down the window and spoke sharply in Thai: "Move on or I will order your arrest."

A bottle crashed with a splintering impact on the hood. Something struck the door with a deep thumping bass sound. Then the rear window shattered with a noise like a gunshot.

Calisher whimpered. "They're trying to kill me."

Suddenly the crowd swelled outward as from an explosion. The demonstrators began running wildly in every direction as men on horseback charged through. The paramilitary had arrived. An upsurge of cries and shouts escalated into a roar of fury as screaming demonstrators fell beneath horses' hooves.

Suvit had a sudden inspiration. At any moment the uproar would subside as the combined force of police and paramilitary took control. The battle would break into isolated skirmishes and the main body of student demonstrators would retreat.

"I think you should try to leave now," he told Calisher. "As long as you're in an American Embassy car, you're in danger. You must abandon it."

Calisher's voice teetered on hysteria: "I *can't* go out there!"

"It will be worse if you stay. I can't guarantee your safety if you don't go quickly."

Suvit signaled a policeman nearby.

"An important person from the American Embassy is here. Take him in your police car wherever he wishes to go."

"Are you sure it will be safe?" Calisher asked.

"Yes! But hurry!"

Close by, someone shrieked horribly. That decided Calisher. He scrambled out and went with the policeman.

Minutes later the street was almost deserted. The defeated students had abandoned their march to the Victory Monument. The demonstration was over.

Suvit moved into the driver's seat, turned the key in the ignition, and started the engine of the Cadillac. In the police garage there would be time for a thorough search of the vehicle, including any secret hiding places.

Suvit felt like a diver exploring in unknown darkness who suddenly comes upon a glittering treasure hoard.

SIXTEEN

HORACE CALISHER WAS HALF AWAKE WHEN THAININ ENTERED the bedroom at nine o'clock in the morning, carrying a breakfast tray.

"Good morning, sir."

Horace sat up while Thainin put down the tray to arrange a bedseat behind his back.

"Did you sleep well, sir?"

He had slept fitfully after his harrowing experience the night before. He had asked the policeman to drive him to his beach house. If the rioting spread, the Embassy might become a target, and in his city house he would be defenseless.

Breakfast was tomato juice, a poached egg with pork strips, and a pot of steaming coffee filtered to his taste with a dash of cinnamon. He glanced at the newspapers on the tray: the *Bangkok Post*, *Bangkok World*, and *The Nation* were English-language daily newspapers published locally. Airmailed copies of the *New York Times* and *Washington Post* offered two-day-old news from home.

Thainin rolled up the bamboo blinds. "Rain will come from the northwest today, sir. Not too strong, but steady."

"That was quite a disturbance I was involved in yesterday."

"I understand a number of persons were taken to hospitals. Some have serious injuries. The story is in the *Bangkok Post*, sir. Page two."

"Thank you."

The reports of police brutality would influence American public opinion. Horace believed that the United States should observe a strict policy of neutrality between the present Thai

134

government and Khun Wanchai. His report to the State Department had put forward a strong case, pointing out that Khun Wanchai was not a mere native warlord, but a graduate of very good English schools and a grandson of Prince Bowaradet. A man of such breeding, background, and intelligence would certainly be no worse than the present corrupt rulers. It was not possible to believe the rumors that Wanchai might be in league with the People's Republic of China. The rulers of China were, after all, Communists.

The State Department's reply had been delivered to him personally by courier at the airport last nigh—

Horace sat up straight against the bedseat. *"Thainin!"*

His servant appeared.

"Has there been a telephone call this morning?"

"There have been several, sir."

"Any from the police?"

"No, sir."

Horace decided not to mention that an important communication from the State Department was still in the diplomatic pouch in the Embassy car.

"My car was left behind last night. Find out when we can pick it up, will you?"

He went in to shower and shave. When he returned, wearing his bathrobe, Thainin informed him that the Embassy car was in the police garage and that Colonel Suvit was on the telephone and would like to speak to him in person.

Horace's anxiety vanished while talking with Colonel Suvit, who promised to return the Embassy car at once.

"I would like to call on you to present my apologies for the inconvenience," Suvit added.

"That really is not necessary."

Suvit was politely insistent, however, and Horace scheduled a meeting in his office for eleven o'clock in the morning.

Promptly at eleven o'clock Suvit arrived and Horace came out of his office to greet him. They shook hands and Suvit began his apology. Horace waved it away. Suvit preceded him into the office which gave Horace a chance to flash five fingers at his secretary. She nodded that she understood. He had told her to interrupt with an excuse if the meeting with Suvit took longer than five minutes.

Horace closed the door. "All in all it was quite an evening," he said. "Almost like the start of a revolution."

Suvit's lidless stare was disconcerting. "Apparently you

would not find that unwelcome. That is how I must interpret the message found in your Embassy car.''

Horace felt his knees weaken; he went to his desk and sat down. "I'm afraid I don't know what you are talking about.''

"A letter from your government's Undersecretary for Asian Affairs. It was in the diplomatic pouch from your State Department, carefully concealed beneath the floorboard in a small compartment.''

Horace wanted to take a cigar from the humidor on his desk, but he was not sure that he could trust himself to light it with a steady hand.

"That car is the property of the United States. You had no right to search it.''

"We did so only for security reasons. During the rioting last night, someone might have planted an explosive.''

"Diplomatic correspondence is privileged. You must have noticed its 'Top Secret' classification.''

"I found the Undersecretary's comments on our government most interesting. This was in reply to information you apparently supplied to the Undersecretary.''

Horace tried to remember exactly what the Undersecretary had replied.

"Where is the letter now?''

"Returned to its hiding place. No one but myself has read it. I assume you do not wish anyone else to read it.'' Spiderlike, Suvit's long, thin fingers advanced a few inches across the desk. "I have, of course, made a copy.''

The intercom buzzed on the desk. His secretary said, "I'm sorry, sir, but you have an appointment with the Ambassador in a few minutes.''

"I can't be interrupted now. Please give him my regrets and inform him that I will be late.''

Horace flicked off the intercom. He would not dare put off an appointment with the Ambassador, a man of thin patience and rotund wrath whose dignity was far too easily offended. But the moment of counterfeit bravado proved invigorating.

L'audace. Toujours l'audace.

"What do you intend to do with your copy?'' Horace asked in a challenging tone.

Suvit said, "It is my duty to turn over such important information to the Prime Minister. I am only a police officer and not fit to deal with such high matters.''

"This will not improve relations between our countries.''

"I regret the embarrassment to your government."

Horace drew on a dependable inner resource, his conviction that in a confrontation with someone from an alien culture—a confrontation excluding actual physical violence—he would inevitably prevail.

"Embarrassment? Not at all. I will accept the blame and resign, and the matter will be forgotten."

"What a sad end to your brilliant career."

"I have an independent income, and I'm not really too fond of the diplomatic service. I'm afraid you will suffer the most."

"I, sir?" Suvit seemed nonplussed.

"As you have pointed out, this important matter must be dealt with at the highest levels. I shall report the theft of the document immediately to my State Department and to your Prime Minister. I shall, of course, also report the use you tried to make of this document."

"What use, sir? I have asked nothing of you."

"I don't think our superiors will have any trouble recognizing your clumsy attempt at extortion."

Suvit's stare no longer made Horace uncomfortable.

"Nothing like that has entered my mind."

"Then why did you make a copy of the document? For your private enjoyment?" Horace was feeling better. He chose a cigar from the humidor. "No, my dear Colonel, you are the loser. My government will certainly demand your resignation. It is quite possible that you will be prosecuted for theft and extortion."

Suvit's fingers began a slow retreat across the desk.

"We are both gentlemen, sir, and patriots. What do you consider a fair solution?"

Horace's fingers were steady as he lighted his cigar. He was quite sure now he was going to win this contest of wits.

"Let's be honest, Colonel, and speak plainly. You don't want a fair solution. You want a fair price."

"I have no wish to make trouble. I am prepared to be most reasonable."

"What do you call reasonable?"

"I must retire soon on a most inadequate pension."

"I am sorry to hear that."

"I have great medical bills because of an accident to my ten-year-old granddaughter."

"We have an excellent American hospital here in Bangkok. I

will arrange for her to be treated there, and for the bills to be sent to me."

"That is most helpful. You are most generous."

"Is there something more?"

"Several persons in the Thai government are presently on the payroll of your Embassy."

"You are mistaken. There is no such arrangement with any persons in the Thai government."

"I would be ungracious to contradict you."

This was the first detectable sign that the balance of power was shifting back. Colonel Suvit would not make such a bold accusation unless he was prepared to back it up.

Horace tilted back in his chair and blew out a plume of cigar smoke. It occurred to him that Suvit was nearing the age when he would be forced to retire.

He said, "If we make such an arrangement with you it will be reviewed every year."

"That is acceptable. Provided what I receive in the first year is equal to what you give a cabinet minister."

Horace's instinct for combative interplay had been finely honed by years of service in the diplomatic corps. It was time to exact further poundage.

"I will need your written confession."

"A confession to what, sir?"

"To the theft of a top secret report from an American Embassy car. If a copy of that should appear after we have made our agreement, I will need some way to punish you."

Suvit looked troubled. "I give you my word as a gentleman that you have nothing to fear."

Suvit was hanging over a spit, and Horace was quite prepared to let him sizzle.

"I am pleased to have your word. However, a gentleman who is sufficiently tempted often behaves like any other man. I need the confession. Without it we have no deal."

Suvit's thin fingers curved like mandibles, but he answered with grave politeness: "It is not possible for me to agree to these terms."

"Perhaps you need more time to consider."

"Time will not change my opinion." Colonel Suvit rose, then said almost casually, "I believe you are well acquainted with a Miss Jean Hudson."

Horace felt as though he were looking at a barometer that foretold an unpromising shift in the weather.

"I wouldn't say well acquainted."

"This is not my concern. Recently, however, it reaches my attention that she is offering to sell information to enemies of our government."

He felt an odd tingling at the back of his neck. "I do not believe that." The tingling spread quickly down into his arms, and through his body. "Miss Hudson has no interest in politics, and no information that anyone would think worth buying."

"We have enough proof to bring her in for questioning. I would not be surprised if we were able to get a confession."

Horace's head throbbed. "I don't put much faith in confessions," he said quietly. "Most people are weak and will say anything out of fear. It is better to deal on trust."

Colonel Suvit slightly inclined his shaved head. "We agree on that, sir. This is a topic we should discuss further, in our mutual interest."

An hour later their business was done, and Suvit rose to leave. "I have a duty to tell you, sir. The persons Miss Hudson is selling information to are very bad people. Very dangerous people. It is most unwise for her to continue to deal with them."

Horace had a sour churning in his stomach from their negotiations. There had been no written confession.

"Why tell me?"

"Perhaps you will care to give her warning."

"I'm sure you're wrong. But I'll pass on your message."

Colonel Suvit bowed and departed.

LATE AFTERNOON SUNLIGHT CAME IN THROUGH THE OPEN WIN-dow of his hotel room. Brian opened his eyes. Earlier in the day the air conditioner had not functioned, because at the peak heat there was not enough electricity to meet the demand. He had lain down for a nap, and in his sleep a faucet of memory had opened.

DONG LAI!

Mud sucked at his boots. Sun baked his helmet.

A young girl was running across a field, carrying on her shoulders a long bamboo pole with baskets balanced at each end. She wore the Vietnamese peasant's uniform of black tunic, black pants, and a floppy straw hat.

DONG LAI! Sergeant McNeil shouted again.

It was the command to halt in Vietnamese. The girl did not halt. She kept running.

McNeil fired off a long burst with his M-16. The bullets went into the ground behind the running girl, then caught up. She wavered and fell.

McNeil examined the baskets she was carrying. They contained nothing but merchandise bought at the market.

McNeil said, "We're in gook country. She could've been carrying grenades. You can't tell a good gook from a bad gook, so treat 'em all alike."

Brian stood mute, looking down at the bloodied corpse. The girl was no more than twelve years old.

HE FELT A BUZZING INSIDE HIS HEAD AS OTHER IMAGES WERE waiting to pour through, images that he could not afford to let enter his mind because they were too powerful and would overwhelm him.

NO!

Brian forced himself to close off the faucet of memory. His brain was empty and silent; the stillness inside him was frightening, almost like death.

He needed a drink. He knew that he drank too much, but at times it was the only remedy.

Brian met only an occasional passerby until he reached a street alive with people, color, and sound. Very drunk, and grinning foolishly, a Thai soldier weaved by and called out a greeting.

Bars and discos abounded in the area. Through a curtained doorway he caught a glimpse of an exotic dancer in a fringed bikini. Her movements were provocative. She moved her hands slowly, caressingly over her bare breasts.

Next door was a video shop ablaze with light. Two large monitor screens inside a window faced the street, showing pornographic images to a small crowd. A family of hill people in their traditional dress squatted on the sidewalk, watching the screens with astonishment.

A man holding a thin cigarette in one hand lounged in a doorway. "Fi' American dollar. See real live action."

Brian shook his head and went on. He stopped at a bar where

liquor prices were listed on a plastic yellow sheet attached to the inside of the window.

He went in and ordered a Mekong whiskey. The music from an old jukebox thundered with heavy metal rock. The vibrations made him feel defocused and vulnerable.

After his third Mekong, the noise became bearable. But at the first opportunity he put in a coin and chose another record. As he listened to the wail of a rural love song, he ordered another Mekong.

The bartender poured the drink. "You want girl?" He handed Brian a business card. "Go here. Treat you good."

Brian stuffed the card into his pocket and left the bar. Fresh air made a volatile mix with Mekong. His balance was unsteady as he walked down a narrow, cobblestoned street between narrow houses lined up in an unbroken row.

Women sat in seductively lighted first floor rooms. They smiled and made inviting gestures.

"Speak English," one called out. "Make nice show."

He crossed the street, looking for the address on the card he had been given. In front of the house he was welcomed by a doorman wearing an embroidered silk blouse, tight-fitting fancy breeches, and white gloves.

Brian stumbled up the staircase inside. In a large, open parlor on the first floor, three divans were positioned against the walls and pillows were scattered about on the floor. On the divans men were embracing partially disrobed women. In the center of the room a European man was talking with an attractive Oriental woman in a diaphanous costume.

A slender Eurasian woman walked toward him, smiling, and introduced herself. She wore a very tight skirt that was made with a tuck under the rump.

She led him to an empty divan, lighted a thin cigarette from a bowl, and passed it to him. Brian took a shallow puff. She placed her fingers between her breasts and inhaled, indicating that he should take a deep lungful. After a few puffs a pleasant listlessness came over him.

He looked around the room. On another divan an older white woman was having a low-toned conversation with a young Chinese man whose slender figure in a black, form-fitting outfit made him look like a bullfighter. The older woman's mouth was crumbling, and her makeup looked as if it were about to melt and run down her chin.

Brian leaned back and let the Eurasian woman remove his

jacket and unbutton his shirt. She caressed him beneath his chin and down his throat, then reached inside his shirt to fondle his nipples with the palm of her hand. She made small murmurings and kissed him with ripe, full lips. He tasted her astringent mouthwash.

"What's your name?" he asked. "Who are you?"

The Eurasian woman helped him off the divan. She led him up carpeted steps into a long corridor with doors on either side. They entered a room just large enough for a bed and a wash-basin.

She finished undressing him. He stretched out nude on the bed, and she began to massage his body with a sweet-smelling herbal ointment. She knew just how to touch and where to press or make gentle circular rubbing movements.

She stood up and removed her clothes. The sight of her na-kedness, her small pink-tipped breasts, gave him an instant erec-tion. She leaned close to him, letting the lower part of her body touch his. His pulse beat with a rapid alternating motion as she fit her soft yielding over him. He tried to think of something other than what she was doing to him but the sensation of himself deep inside her body was too much. He could not hold out. He could not.

For just a moment he thought of Arunee.

And suddenly he knew it was her he wanted.

SEVENTEEN

THE TELEPHONE RANG AT ARUNEE'S DESK IN THE NEWSROOM. She recognized the caller's voice.

"What is it, Saowa? Is anything wrong?"

"I am so sorry to call where you work. But children did not come home on bus."

"They're probably still at school playing with friends."

"They not in playground, mistess. I go there when they not come."

"Then they're probably in a classroom. Sometimes children are punished by having to stay after class."

"They are good children."

"Of course. But I'm sure they're all right."

She thought uneasily, one child might possibly be kept after class, but not both.

"When is the next bus coming?"

"No more, mistess."

"Wait there, Saowa. If they don't show up in the next half hour call me back."

A few minutes later when the telephone rang, Arunee answered immediately.

A man's voice said in Thai: "What happened to the sailor can happen to your children."

"Who is this?"

"Write no more for the newspaper. Remember Manit."

The receiver clicked. The line was dead.

She walked quickly down the hall to Lokma's office. He was sitting with both feet up on his desk, reading the article she had finished a short time before.

The moment he saw her expression he asked, "What's happened?"

She told him about the telephone call.

He said, "It might be a hoax. The children might be home now. What's the number?" He called and spoke to Saowa. Then he put down the pages he'd been reading. "I'm going with you."

A few minutes later they were driving along the New Road. Lokma was pushing the yellow Toyota as fast as it would go. She kept her eyes closed in the foolish hope that the trip would go more quickly. Then she was forced to open them again to banish the frightening inward visions she was having of what might be happening to her children.

When they arrived at the house, Saowa came out to greet them. Chakra and Ajana were not there. Arunee told Saowa to go home and tend to the other children for whom she was acting as baby warden. The children might be starting to worry at her absence.

Lokma suggested they call the police.

"Not yet. I'll make some other calls first."

Once the police were called, the story would be in the newspapers. She did not know how the kidnappers would react. She would do nothing to endanger her children.

She called Chakra's and Ajana's teachers and several parents at their homes. She tried not to sound too concerned. During a call to an American couple whose daughter, Emily, was Ajana's close friend, she got her first eyewitness report. Emily had seen Chakra and Ajana with a man who was a stranger to her. Emily said she called to say that the last bus was leaving, but they all got into a van and drove away.

"What kind of van?" Emily was almost sure the color was gray.

"Would they go with strangers?" Lokma asked when she told him.

"I've told them not to but they might. They've never had a reason to distrust strangers."

They would believe anything a grownup told them because grownups had always been good to them.

"We still don't have anything definite," Lokma said. He meant the remark to be consoling.

"I know," she said, thinking that what the man said to her on the phone sounded pretty definite.

Remember Manit.

She wished she had a swift-acting anodyne that would deaden pain by compelling her not to think. But she had to think.

"Try to find Manit," she told Lokma.

He understood. "I'll send a reporter at once. If Manit is there, we'll get the police to put him in protective custody. I don't want to leave you alone here. Would you like to come back to the office?"

The dear man. Anywhere she went, her children's absence would create the same frightening aloneness.

Where are they? What are they doing to them?

What happened to the sailor will happen to your children.

Before he left Lokma said, "Nothing more you've written will appear in print. Not until this is settled."

"Thank you."

Her children were being used in a primitive but effective form of censorship, but she couldn't worry about that. She had one obliterating concern, and if she tried to add another she would disintegrate into fragments.

Remember Manit.

Sitting quietly in the living room of her house, she forced herself to think purposefully. The man spoke Thai perfectly but with an undertone, a mere suggestion that he spoke another language with equal fluency. Thai might not be his native tongue.

Where had she heard that sort of nasal sibilance before?

There came into her mind a picture of a crowded, busy district southeast of the Royal Palace. Low-rise buildings painted a bright yellow were streaked with rain and grime. The Sampeng area of Bangkok was the center of the Chinese community. Vertical signs hanging above modest shops were written not only in Thai and English, but in Chinese.

That reminded her. Manit worked for the Orient Shipping Company and Ellen Peterson had escaped from Bangkok aboard one of their barges.

There *was* a Chinese connection. Chinese secret agents in Thailand were aiding in the transportation of munitions destined for Khun Wanchai. Ellen Peterson had used this same method of transportation to escape from Bangkok.

She called Brian at his hotel, but he was not in. She left a message for him. Then she called a taxi.

"The Orient Shipping Company," she told the driver. "On Sampeng Lane."

* * *

As THEY DROVE THROUGH THE CENTRAL CHINESE DISTRICT, past the large movie houses on Maha Chai Road, rain begin to fall in heavy sheets. Traffic was moving at a water buffalo's pace.

Arunee paid the driver. She got out and ran. In a moment she was soaked, her face wet and streaming. She passed shops selling herbs and joss sticks and caged birds. Through the torrent she saw a ramshackle, two-story building with a brightly colored sign proclaiming in Thai, English, and Chinese that this was the Orient Shipping Company.

A rickety staircase led up to a second-floor landing where a plump Chinaman sat behind a desk fanning himself. He was wearing a green silk shirt, pegtop trousers, and a heavy red tie adorned by a brass stickpin.

"Yes, please?"

She stopped in confusion. She had replayed that voice in her mind too many times not to recognize it.

"I'm looking for the owner."

"This is person. Chang Tsu."

She held herself tight, not registering that she knew who he was.

"I'm a reporter for the *Bangkok Post*. I'm inquiring about a woman passenger who left on one of your barges a few days ago."

Chang Tsu fanned himself, smiling in a puzzled manner.

"Some mistake. Barges not carry passengers."

He had altered the tone of his voice. So he knew who she was, too.

"The woman's name is Ellen Peterson. She's wanted by the police. You must have read about the H & D Trading Company in the newspapers. She's the treasurer of the company."

"I know nothing of this person."

She had an idea that she might somehow use Ellen Peterson as a bargaining chip, imply a threat of police intervening, and then offer to let it all go if he would only be reasonable and return his children. But her swiftly rising tension could no longer be suppressed.

"Listen to me," she said, not trying to conceal the desperation she felt. "I don't really care about this woman. I don't want to make trouble." There was only one thing she cared about; everything else was unimportant. The burning in her womb was the physical reaction of a mother whose children have been wrenched from her. "All I want is my children. I know you have them, and I'm willing to give you anything you want."

In her mind their names kept repeating themselves in the slow muffled rhythm of a drum: Chakra, Ajana, as if this were an incantation that would somehow produce them unharmed. She felt her eyelids swelling with unshed tears, but she was determined to shed no tears in front of him.

"I won't write any more for the newspaper. I'll give you the documents in the attaché case. Anything you ask." She kept her face averted because she was not able to look at him. "Have mercy, please. Give me back my children."

Deep inside, in a silent place where no relief could reach, she was screaming: Chakra! Ajana!

Chang Tsu continued fanning himself, but his hand movements were slower. "You have made a serious mistake in coming here," he said with measured deliberation and in perfect English. "It is the kind of mistake for which there is no remedy."

BRIAN SPREAD THE COLORFUL THAI MONEY ON THE BEDSHEET in his hotel room. He had just returned from cashing his last traveler's check at the bank. Looking at the money Brian realized that there was not enough for him to stay much longer in Bangkok. He would have to say goodbye to the land of *klongs* and temples and palaces.

He picked up the money from the bedsheet, and as he was stuffing it into his wallet, the phone rang. The clerk at the reception desk said, "A telephone message came while you were out, sir. Shall I read it to you?"

"I'll come down and get it."

He read the message while standing in the lobby near the hotel cashier's grill.

> Brian: *I'm going to the Orient Shipping Company. Join me if you can.*
>
>   *Arunee.*

The clerk had written the time the message was received: *4:24.* Above the reception desk, the round-faced clock showed 4:38.

Phibul's taxi met him at the entrance. Ten minutes later they were driving through pouring rain along the New Road. A monsoon rain doesn't rain cats and dogs, Brian thought. It rains tigers and elephants.

Brian knew from his tourist map that the New Road crossed Yawarat Road on the southeast bend of the river.

When the taxi stopped at a red light, he said, "I'll get off here."

Phibul turned around. "Please, sir, do not do so again. It is most embarrassing."

His protest grew into a faint wail as Brian ran through the downpour.

Brian's wet shoes made sloshing sounds as he climbed the narrow staircase inside the Orient Shipping Company building. A fat, pudgy-faced Chinaman was emerging from a back room. He looked startled, and turned quickly to close the door behind him.

"What may I do for you, sir?"

"I'm meeting someone here."

"No one has come."

"Then she'll be here any minute."

"You may be in wrong place."

"Orient Shipping Company. This is the right place."

The Chinaman's face twitched as though a fly had touched his cheek. He sat down and began to fan himself.

"May I ask your business, sir?"

Brian thought he knew why Arunee was coming here. "I'm interested in finding out about a woman who booked passage on one of your barges. I'd like to know where she was going."

"Some mistake. Our barges do not carry passengers."

"I've already spoken with a sailor who saw her on board."

The Chinaman shook his head. "Not happen. Manit make up story." He smacked thick rubbery lips. "Lazy good-for-nothing. Tells many lies."

Brian said quietly, "I didn't mention his name."

"He is fired for bad work. Now he tries to make trouble."

"This woman has disappeared. She may have booked passage on your barge without your knowing it. She is wanted for questioning by the police."

Underneath his green shirt, the Chinaman was sweating. The sweat stain partly revealed the shape of what might be a knife scabbard or a gun holster. Brian's suspicious were mounting.

"We are a legitimate business, sir. We are not involved in police matters."

Brian said forcefully, "The woman's name is Ellen Peterson. She's involved in smuggling military supplies to Khun Wanchai. If I tell the police she escaped on one of your barges they'll begin an investigation. They will subpoena all your records, even the lists of cargoes that your barges have carried.

A smile crept over the Chinaman's fat sleepy countenance. "Then they find out who is liar."

"They will arrest you for aiding a fugitive from justice. You might even be accused of treason."

The Chinaman's smile did not falter.

"You nice man. You not take word of lying sailor."

A loud thumping came from the back room. The Chinaman's smile vanished, his face settled deeper into a fleshy neck.

"What was that?" Brian asked. He was sure the man was hiding something.

"Move crates in storeroom."

Brian surmised that contraband goods were being smuggled out in those crates.

"We close now. You go," the Chinaman said.

"Not until the woman I'm meeting gets here."

Another fainter thumping, then a rustling, as of something being dragged across a floor. Brian, listening closely, thought he heard a muffled cry.

"Let's have a look in there."

He moved toward the door, but the Chinaman got up quickly to block his way.

"Step aside," Brian said.

Small eyes encased in fat showed defiance.

Brian lifted the Chinaman from the floor and put him aside so he could try the doorknob. The door was locked.

"The key," Brian said.

As he turned, the man was wriggling one hand beneath his shirt. Brian jammed him against the wall and pressed his arm like a steel bar into his throat.

The Chinaman gasped.

"Well?" Brian asked.

The Chinaman beat his fist against Brian's chest. Then his eyes rolled up to show the whites, and he slid slowly down the wall until he sat on the floor with one short fat leg doubled up beneath him. His head lolled.

Brian searched through the pockets of the peg-top trousers until he found a key ring.

The third key opened the locked door.

Inside the storeroom, crates were piled on the dusty floor. There was a narrow, grimy window and a trap door in a corner. The dust on the floor was disturbed around the edges of the trap door. The disturbance was from footprints, not a crate being moved.

Outside, a car engine whined.

From the narrow window, Brian saw a gray van moving out of an empty lot. The lot was hemmed in by buildings and there was no exit except to the street.

He raced down the stairs as Phibul was entering the building. Brian brushed past him into the street.

The gray van came out of an alleyway and stopped, looking for an opening in traffic.

When the driver saw Brian coming, he stepped hard on the gas pedal. The van shot forward and collided with a passing bus. Metal tore, heat shimmered, glass tinkled. The bus crushed the van's hood and fender into metal ridges.

The van backed up. Brian reached through the door window, and whipped the driver's head against the metal frame. When he pulled the door open, the driver slid bonelessly out.

A man leapt out from the rear of the van with a gun in his hand.

Brian ducked behind the open van door. Metal rang against metal, and the door sprouted a white gash.

Then silence.

The gunman was moving into position for a clear shot.

Brian hoisted the driver's limp body. The gunman appeared barely a dozen feet away. Using the driver's body as a shield, Brian ran at the gunman. He fired and the driver's body gave an odd jerking motion.

Brian lifted the body and flung it. A loosely flapping arm hit the gunman's shoulder, and the next shot went wide.

Then Brian was on him. He seized the gun with his left hand and swung his right fist hard into the man's jaw. There was a satisfying, crunching sound. The man fell forward, and his forehead struck the sidewalk.

Brian went to the back of the van. Arunee and her two children were inside, gagged and bound with rope.

Arunee's eyes were wide with terror.

"It's all right," he said. "You're safe."

Too late he realized her terror was for him.

A roughness circled his throat, and his head was pulled sharply back. Above him, he saw the Chinaman's face grimacing as the garrote pulled tight.

He tried to jerk his head upward and ram the Chinaman under the chin. No use.

The rope bit deeper. Blood vessels in his head felt as if they were bursting through his skull. All the strength drained out of him.

He heard a shot. Surprisingly the strangling grip eased, and a little air came back into his starving lungs. Rockets stopped exploding behind his eyes.

He was on his hands and knees, gulping for breath.

An image appeared, repeated in a hundred tiny images, as though in the facets of a cut glass bowl.

Phibul.

Phibul's hand was pressed tight against his shoulder. A knife haft protruded between his middle and index finger, and blood crisscrossed on the back of his hand.

"Damn man put knife in me. I fix him good."

The Chinaman lay supine on the sidewalk, his eyes staring blankly at nothing. His green silk shirt was slowly turning purple.

EIGHTEEN

Boonsong booked passage on what the State Railway of Thailand called an ordinary train, the equivalent of third class travel. To confuse anyone who might be trying to discover what route she was taking, she also purchased a ticket on Thai Airways to Phuket Island, the "pearl of the South." She told everyone that she was going to rest and relax on the white sand beaches of the island's magnificent coastline. She even reserved a suite at a luxury hotel.

In the morning, shortly after Brian came to see her, she changed into a peasant costume and shawl. She waited at a municipal bus station until the yellow-black bus arrived that would take her to the railroad station. Sitting with a woolen carpet in her lap, she looked like an ordinary peasant woman.

Her other luggage, consisting of eight suitcases and a small trunk, was checked on to the Thai Airways flight to Phuket Island.

She left the bus near the entrance to Hualamphong, the central railway station where a shouting horde of boys descended upon passengers disembarking from taxis, pleading to carry their luggage. No one bothered with an awkward peasant woman struggling with a large, ragged carpet bag.

She passed between tall lotus-headed pillars to the interior of the station. A train was just disgorging its passengers and she made her way with difficulty against the incoming tide.

She padded along toward a third class coach and clambered aboard clumsily—she who had enchanted royalty with her gracious movements and gestures. She wedged herself in between passengers on a long, yellow, varnished wood bench. The woman on her right was drinking beer and eating a spicy sausage. The man on her left smelled of goat and garlic.

The narrow aisle bulged with wicker baskets, cloth bundles, and cardboard suitcases. A man with an unbuttoned shirt and loosened boots sprawled on a pile of luggage, snoring loudly.

She huddled into her shawl and drew it further about her face. The odors, the oppressive heat, the coarse belching were making her nauseous.

After an hour she left the train at a town that had a name and a location on a map, but was actually no more than a single street of stores surrounded by a colony of raw teakwood houses.

In the small shack that served as a restroom, she opened her carpet bag and took out a change of clothing, including a large handbag. She emerged in twenty minutes looking like herself. Her peasant costume was in a garbage container behind the shack.

The express train roared in, deigning to stop only because there was a passenger for Patchburi. The rest of her journey was more pleasant. From her private compartment, she amused herself with sights along the way: children playing soccer, a parade of ducklings marching single-file out of an over-brimming *klong*, a plodding bullock cart, a speeding car racing the train across a landscape of rich meadows and orchards. She nibbled on *lamyai*, a small fruit with a firm skin and sweet pulp resembling a Chinese lychee nut.

The train sped in to Patchburi, stirring up steam vapors that became dancing wraiths in the dim light of the station lamps.

Her friends were waiting. They were friends from the theater. Thanol had conducted the *ungkaloong* orchestra for many of her performances. She had known his wife Narinwi since they were young students at a classical school of dance that featured ornate costumes, fierce demon masks, and frolicking monkey gods.

Boonsong had become famous. Narinwi had married.

Thanol embraced her. Narinwi sniffled. She was a small, part-Malay woman who wore four-inch heels and a Medusa hairdo. A sweet-natured, sentimental creature. "We are so sorry. Until we got your letter we did not know you were married. He must have been a fine man." She barely got out the last words, stringing them along on a sob.

"Where is your luggage?" Thanol asked.

She displayed her large handbag. "I'm afraid this is all I have with me."

She gave the explanation she had prepared. Her luggage had

been delivered by mistake to Thai Airways and was now en route to Phuket Island. An incredible mix-up, not unfamiliar to travelers in Thailand.

Narinwi said, "We will find something for you to wear. Your own clothes will catch up in a few days."

"I'm taking the boat to Songlka tomorrow."

"Oh, please stay longer. There is so much to talk about."

"I'm afraid I can't."

Narinwi looked to her husband for help, but none was forthcoming.

Thanol said, "We are honored to have you in our house for a day, a week, or a month. I hope your journey here was not too tiring."

She thought how puzzled they would be if they had seen her in her peasant costume on the ordinary train.

She accompanied them to their car, a well-groomed Mitsubishi. On the way she had a misadventure. She accidentally killed a tiny *gecko* by stepping on it. Narinwi's reaction to the demise of the baby lizard was startling. The poor woman was close to tears.

"Whatever is the matter with you?" Boonsong asked, smiling.

Narinwi shook her head and said it was nothing, but then her tears began to spill, and finally she admitted an astrologer had told her that harm always resulted from the death of an innocent creature.

Boonsong's laugh had a hard brightness. "The astrologer was right. Its blood has stained the bottom of my shoe."

Thanol moved swiftly, using his expensive pocket-handkerchief to wipe off Boonsong's shoe.

"That was a very foolish thing to say," he scolded his wife. "Intelligent people do not believe such things. You have upset our guest."

Narinwi did not try to defend herself. "My husband is right. I am a silly person. Please forgive."

"There is nothing to forgive," Boonsong said. "I know you are my good friend. And your husband is a lovely person."

The hour before dinner was spent reminiscing, with drinks and an appetizer of blushing shrimp in spicy sour salad. Twilight quickly plunged into moonless dark. A chorus of night insects complained.

Narinwi's reminiscences turned predictably to nostalgia. She recalled Boonsong as a frightened youngster whose voice failed the first time she stepped onto a stage. Thanol refused to believe this.

"For me, you have always been a star of the very first magnitude. And a woman of much dignity," he added, flashing a look of annoyance at his wife.

Boonsong came to Narinwi's rescue. "What she says is true. I was very frightened. I acquired dignity to hide how timid I was."

Dinner was tasty meat curries and leaf-wrapped sweets. Thanol poured from an exquisitely cold bottle of Graves. After dinner Boonsong's favorite rice-based liqueur was served. She was having a pleasant evening.

"Will you sing for us?" Narinwi pleaded. "Thanol will be happy to accompany you."

"First I must make a telephone call."

She called her home and spoke to Leah, her personal maid, the only one in the household she trusted. Others gossiped or sold information, for every Thai servant is a born spy.

Leah assured her that everyone believed she had gone to Phuket Island. Then she read a message from a Mr. Buckley, who said that he could not join her but wished her a pleasant trip.

Boonsong did not sing that evening. Neither Thanol nor Narinwi inquired into the reason for her abrupt change of mood. Boonsong excused herself early and went upstairs to her bedroom.

Before retiring she placed a small framed photograph of her husband on the night table beneath the lamp. She had wanted nothing more than for the rhythm of their lives to carry on through the years, but now he was gone.

Kharma.

THE SMART-LOOKING DORY AT THE PIER WAS FLYING GAILY COL-ored pennants at its masthead. Boonsong had asked Thanol to hire the boat, assuring her anonymity to the last possible moment. She was being careful in the smallest details. As it turned out, this precaution was not needed. The Malay pilot did not have any idea who she was.

She stepped over the out-flaring side of the narrow, flat-bottomed craft. Seated comfortably in a deck chair aft, she waved goodby to Thanol and Narinwi at the pier. Narinwi was crying.

She had deliberately chosen the longer journey by water, although the Thai railway would have taken her by a shorter route to the Malaysian frontier, where it connected with the main line that went via Butterworth to Ipoh and Kuala Lumpur. But passengers on the train might have recognized her. She was safer this way.

Overhead a gull with outstretched wings glided and circled, repeating its lamenting cries as it wheeled in the bright blue sky like a lost soul searching for its mate.

She thought: My fellow creature, you must find something else valuable to replace what you have lost. Life must go on, following its predestined course, even though you and your mate no longer travel together in it.

She saw the lonely gull as a bad omen, and was relieved when the bird deserted the dory during its journey down the coast to Songlka.

AN OFFICER WEARING MILITARY FATIGUES WAS WAITING TO greet her on the dock. He was a young man, quite good looking, with cheeks burnished red from the sun.

He spoke with a slight lisp: "General Prapha is most impatient to see you."

"What is your name?"

"Mahidol. I am General Prapha's adjutant."

Mahidol paid the boatman, and she got into his motorcar. He acted as the chauffeur. They drove for about ten minutes and stopped before a modest white frame guest house.

General Prapha was waiting on the verandah. She scarcely recognized him. He had grown older, and had a henna-dyed beard.

He assisted her from the motorcar and kissed her hand.

"It is a pleasure to discover that you are as lovely as I remember."

She withdrew her fingers gently. "The years have not changed me a little?"

"Only to make you more beautiful."

The ritual flirtation recalled to her the handsome young officer who had caught her fancy at a time in her life when she was readily available for the pleasures of the bedchamber. She had enjoyed their liaison while it lasted.

"I am very pleased to renew our acquaintance," she said, choosing the Thai word that meant friendship without implications of romance.

He understood, and accepted with more equanimity than she

expected. "Perhaps you will have time for a drink with me before we dine."

"That would be most pleasant."

She sat with Prapha on the verandah, sipping champagne. She noted with approval that his military bearing, his most attractive feature, had not vanished with maturity.

After a few minutes of conversation it was clear that Prapha did not know she had married and was a widow. She decided not to tell him, for this was an opportunity to practice anew her art with a man.

At dinner she enjoyed the intimate undertones of sexual maneuver. It was all so pleasantly familiar, and recalled their good times together. He had always complimented her on her flashing eyes and glossy black hair, always admired her well-rounded figure. He had also been a jealous lover, who preferred her to dress in the Thai manner and not expose any part of her body in front or back. Their relationship was not without tension.

She teased him now about his henna-dyed beard: "Did you decide to wear it to look more like a general?"

In a moment she realized she had made a mistake.

"You are not a Moslem," he said, "and so you do not know this signifies one who has made a pilgrimage to Mecca."

She had forgotten that Prapha was a Moslem. She felt as if she had been issued an order to which she must respond.

"I apologize for my ignorance. I know so little about your religion. Please tell me more."

Unwittingly she had found a topic that elicited his enthusiasm. The word *sanuk* in Thai describes a quality that all wish to find in themselves and look for in others. It is a simple yet complex word that can mean joy or pleasure, and an all-pervasive sense of well-being. In talking boout his trip to Mecca, and its spiritual meaning to him, Prapha was indeed *sanuk*.

He contrasted the high moral standards of the Moslem people with what he perceived to be the depravity of the rest of Thailand.

"I am told that over a million young women are working in the sex trade," he said rapping his knuckles angrily on the arm of his wicker chair. "Bangkok is full of massage parlors and brothels. You can order prostitutes like room service in hotels, and in restaurants the waitresses are numbered like the sandwiches on the menu. Very young girls are offered to tourists as 'virgin prostitutes,' and command a higher price." His eyes narrowed. "This is not to be tolerated. We need a spiritual renewal of the kind that took place in Iran under the Ayatollah."

She was about to remark—being in an acerbic mood—that in her experience sexual morality increased in direct proportion to the decline of sexual power. However, Prapha continued on another line, the less interesting area of politics.

"Most Thai-Malays here in the south have been stirred up by the Islamic movement. The government in Bangkok does not understand the situation here. It is very serious."

"Is there any connection with Khun Wanchai?"

Prapha blinked. "What do you know of him?"

"I have friends, many friends, who talk much of Khun Wanchai these days."

"What do they say?"

"That he plans to invade our country."

A flush on Prapha's cheeks almost matched the color of his beard.

"Hardly that. Khun Wanchai is a grandson of the noble Prince Bowaradet. He may be called a revolutionary, but not an invader."

"I have heard some people say that the People's Republic of China is supporting Wanchai."

"In turbulent times there are many such stories. They are usually exposed as lies."

"If there is a revolution, will it succeed?"

"I cannot speculate."

"I am asking for your opinion as a soldier."

"Much will depend on the Navy. Some naval chiefs openly support Khun Wanchai. If there is a revolution and they choose his side, they can bottle up the Gulf of Thailand so no supplies come in that way. They can also open the river route to Bangkok from the northeast, allowing Khun Wanchai and his troops free passage."

At that moment Boonsong decided that when she had the money from Bank of Bhumipitra, she would not return to Thailand. She would go to the United States. George had told her about his hometown of Chicago, and going there would be her pilgrimage. She would return to Thailand when the situation returned to normal.

"I still do not understand why you chose this unusual way to travel, dear lady."

She was a bit vexed by his return to a topic she had thought settled. When she first called him from Bangkok, he had been surprised at her request, but in the end he had told her there was a military convoy heading south to the Malaysian border, and she could travel with it.

She took a sip of an after-dinner liqueur that was not her favorite. "Perhaps I merely wanted an excuse to renew an old acquaintance."

She was disappointed that he did not rise to the bait.

"You have chosen a most difficult method to do so. A military convoy has no special facilities. Our trucks are designed for hard traveling, not for sightseeing."

She thought his persistence inexcusable. "I am not as fragile as I look."

She was instantly sorry for the rebuke, which would make Prapha aware she was heavier than when he had been her lover.

She added quickly, "When I called you I only hoped that you would extend me the courtesy of a safe escort."

Disbelief hovered in his eyes. "Do you consider yourself in danger? Why?"

She leaned toward him, offering her radiant luminous attention. "A woman traveling alone is always at some risk. But I have nothing to fear with you as my escort."

He said, "I cannot accompany you. My adjutant Mahidol will go with you and try to make you as comfortable as possible in the circumstances."

The conversation ended abruptly soon afterward.

She said formally, "I have enjoyed your hospitality. I will be ready in the morning."

He rose, bowed, and kissed her hand. "At six. The convoy will leave promptly on the hour."

THE TRUCK IN WHICH BOONSONG WAS RIDING WAS AT THE REAR of a convoy of sixteen trucks, Czech Skodas and American GMCs, stretched out along a dirt road that was undermined by recent rains. The thin surface broke and formed potholes under the heavy weight of the passing vehicles.

None of the soldiers riding in the truck with her looked more than twenty years old. They assumed a serious professional air as they cleaned their rifles, but they kept stealing covert looks at her.

Mahidol, the General's adjutant, ignored her. He was not wearing his officer's cap, and his clipped short hair gave the impression that his scalp was pressed flat against his skull.

"Do you have a cigarette?" she asked.

"I am sorry, madam. I do not smoke."

She shrugged and searched through her purse to find her cigarette case. She took a cigarette and held it near her mouth.

"Do you have a match?"

"I am sorry, madam."

She found her cigarette lighter and extended it to him. He stood above her, swaying with the truck's movement as he lighted her cigarette.

With a grinding terrible jolt the truck settled down. Mahidol was thrown against her. She guarded herself with her arms protectively about her.

He flicked out the lighter and returned it to her. Their fingers touched briefly.

"We're not moving. I will find out what has happened."

He made his way to the rear of the truck, let down the loading platform and jumped out. The soldiers kept cleaning their rifles as though nothing had happened.

In a few minutes Mahidol was back. "The driver tells me we cannot go farther in this vehicle." He turned to bark a command at the soldiers. "Move up to another truck. The convoy is waiting."

The soldiers rose obediently, formed a single file, and departed the truck.

Boonsong began to gather her things.

"Not you, madam. They will send someone back for us as soon as the convoy reaches the next village."

"Why can't we move to another truck?"

"There is no room."

Boonsong finished smoking her cigarette. Time passed slowly. Silence thickened between them.

"Stand up. We are leaving now."

"Leaving? Has someone come?"

"No one is coming."

"I don't understand."

He pulled her roughly to her feet. "You don't need to understand."

Holding her arm in a tight grip, he led her to the rear of the truck. She was furious, but too afraid to protest. She sensed danger, and wished she had the American with her as a bodyguard.

They descended to ground softened from the passage of many vehicles before them. Her shoes sank deeply into muck. He dragged her along the road until they reached a trail that led off into the woods.

"Where are we going?"

He did not reply but pulled her after him on the trail. What would he do if she refused to go? Beat her? She might as well find out now.

She stumbled and fell to her knees.

"Please," she said. "I can't go on. I can't."

He removed a gun from his holster and pointed it.

At her!

"At the count of five I will put a bullet through your head."

A thrill of terror went through her. Was he serious? No, he could not be. He was trying to humiliate her into obeying him. She bent forward and put her hands over her face.

"One."

"I don't know what you want from me."

"Two."

She was unable to open her hands to look at him, for then he would know how much she feared him.

"Three."

He was sadistic. He was an animal. It was useless to appeal to him.

"Four." The safety catch of the gun pulled back.

She got to her feet, smudged with dirt. He put the gun back in his holster and grabbed her arm more roughly than before.

No resistance was left in her. She was sodden with defeat as he pulled her along the trail. Her veneer of self-assurance had cracked to expose the little girl who had once sung and danced for coins on street corners.

He was not bluffing, she thought incredulously, he would have killed me. He would have left me dead on this trail. She thought of her bones picked clean and scattered, and someone coming upon them in years to come and not knowing whose bones they were.

Exhausted, her steps became shorter and strayed a little. How much farther? she wondered. Where is he taking me?

How did he know about this trail?

The accident to the truck might have occurred at any point along the road. How could he have predicted where?

Unless it was not an accident.

The driver might have been his confederate. The truck might not have been badly damaged. Everything could have been staged to get rid of the others.

To what purpose?

They came to a clearing in the woods. A helicopter was waiting with two armed men on guard around it.

She kept her voice steady by an effort of will. "General Prapha will be very angry if anything happens to me. He will have you shot."

She sensed his amusement.

"For obeying his orders?"

Mahidol laughed.

NINETEEN

BRIAN WAS IN A PRIVATE ROOM AT THE AMERICAN HOSPITAL. He was sitting up in bed while a pretty Thai nurse spoon-fed warm tea to him. Each swallow made his throat feel as if it were being scraped with a potato peeler.

He indicated that he wanted to communicate. She put down the teacup and handed him a pad and pencil.

He wrote: *I'd like to see what it looks like.*

"When I take off the bandage you will see."

After he finished the tea she unwrapped the bandage and brought him a small hand mirror. From his chin to his clavicle he was a long, purple, yellow bruise. Circling his neck was a quarter-inch ribbon of raw red flesh.

"It will look so for a week," the nurse told him. "Then will start to fade."

She applied liniment before rebandaging his throat. Her lightest touch was painful.

She brought him a pill to swallow with a glass of water. *"Yah dee, dee kah,"* she said. "Medicine is very good."

She always said that in the same way, as if she thought that telling him in two languages made the message more persuasive.

This time he had prepared a surprise. He wrote on his pad, *Yah mai dee, chep mock.* That meant the medicine was no good, because it hurt too much. He had asked the daytime nurse to spell out the message for him.

She smiled. "You learn Siamese. Very good." She busied herself straightening out the bedcovers. "A pretty lady is wishing to see you. Her name Arunee."

He nodded vigorously to tell her that the visitor was welcome, but not until she finished with the bedcovers did she say, "She only stay few minutes. Do not use voice."

He nodded, accepting the terms.

When Arunee came in, he picked up his pad and scribbled, *Can't talk.*

"I know. The nurse told me."

Glad to see you. Tell me everything.

She explained how Chakra and Ajana had been kidnapped and taken to the Orient Shipping Company.

"They were put into crates used for shipping small animals. The crates would have been loaded into the cargo hold of a river barge. It would be very easy at night to drop the crates over the side and let the children drown."

The enormity of that thought made her pause. The picture was so vivid in her mind that tears shone in her eyes. He wanted to console her, to stroke her long, dark, silky hair and put his arms around her and tell her he understood how she felt.

And you? he wrote.

"I would have been killed, too. No one would know what happened, so they would continue saying we were hostages and threatening the newspaper."

Who told you this?

"The one survivor wrote a long rambling confession. He can't talk. You struck him very hard. They had to wire his jaw shut."

Brian nodded with satisfaction. He wrote on his pad, *How are the children?*

"Very grateful to you. Chakra wrote you a note. Would you care to read it?"

> *Deer Mr. Buckalee, My mother tole me of yur saveng of her and my sistir and me. Yur estreem currage is much like Clint Eastwood, of whom we are both admireng. I am writen to say how much we apreciate it. Hopeng to see you when yur well.*
>
> > *Sincereness,*
> > *Chakra*

> *P.S. Ajana does not have meny words in Inglish yet. She will sing for you wen you come. She has most pleesing voice.*

Brian was reluctant to put the note down. He read it a second time, then sat holding it in his hand.

After a minute he wrote on his pad, *You have great kids.*

"I didn't correct his spelling. Chakra wanted the letter to be all his."

I wouldn't change a word, Brian wrote. He added, *How is Phibul?*

"Recovering nicely. He was knifed when he tried to stop Chang Tsu when he came down the stairs after you. It took him a minute to get over the shock. Then he went out, saw Chang trying to garrote you, and shot him."

The nurse came to the door to announce another visitor.

Brian shook his head.

"Police," the nurse said.

Arunee told the nurse, "Say that Mr. Buckley can't see anyone just now. Doctor's orders."

Colonel Suvit pushed past the nurse into the room. He put down a manila envelope on a side table near the door.

"I will speak to Meestrah Buckley," he declared with the air of a man determined to have his way.

Arunee said calmly, "He can't speak. He has lost his voice."

"A police officer is badly injured," Suvit replied. "It is fortunate he was not killed." He turned his bleak gaze to Brian. "You are a cause of much trouble. I will arrange for you to leave Bangkok as soon as possible."

"If he does not wish to leave?"

"Police have right to deport undesirable persons."

Arunee said, "He is not an undesirable person. Mr. Buckley saved my children and me from being kidnapped and probably killed."

"He is free on bail, awaiting trial on a criminal charge."

"He can't be considered undesirable unless he is convicted."

"It will not be difficult for an error to be discovered in an alien's documents."

"My newspaper will fight any attempt to deport him. And we will inform our readers that you harass innocent people to cover up your inability to find guilty ones."

Brian settled back against his pillow. The liniment was cool and soothing on his throat, and he was enjoying himself.

Suvit turned to Brian. "When you are released from hospital you will report at once to police headquarters. Otherwise I will put out warrant for your arrest."

Arunee said, "I think he deserves a medal. The Rajaniyom Medal is usually given for lifesaving."

"I have given warning. You may rely that I will do as I say."

Arunee said scornfully, "If you find a judge to issue a warrant, my newspaper will start an investigation to find out if the judge is taking bribes. Then we'll start another investigation of your department. We won't have to look far to find corruption there."

Not by the flicker of an eyelid did Suvit acknowledge defeat. But when Suvit turned his attention to Brian, he no longer seemed to be memorizing him for a description in a WANTED poster.

"I would like you to identify a photograph."

He retrieved the manila envelope from the side table, removed a large glossy photograph, and crossed to the bed to show the photograph to Brian. It was a morgue shot, looking straight down at a bloated face with tangled hair on a slab.

"Can you identify?" Suvit asked.

Brian nodded.

Suvit showed the photograph to Arunee who looked at it quickly and turned away.

"It's the sailor. The one we talked to."

"He was strangled, and his body put down a well. A village woman found him."

"Do you know who did it?"

"We have description of a man seen near village not long before sailor disappears. Asiatic male, probably Chinese, between twenty-five and thirty years. Scar under left eye."

Arunee stared. "That's the man who posed as a monk. The one who was near the printing press just before the bombing."

SINCE THEIR ONE PASSIONATE INTERLUDE JEAN HUDSON HAD not heard from Brian.

She fought down an impulse to call him. He might guess the compulsion that made her do it. Men were so cruel when they were in power.

She put on her robe and tuned in to the English-speaking station on TV. She lit a cigarette, and after two puffs she put it down. Everything bored her.

Her heart gave a great throb as the telephone rang.

At last.

"I have to talk to you," Horace said.

Her mouth formed a silent mew of disappointment.

"I've heard rumors that I hope aren't true."

That piqued her curiosity. "What rumors?"

"I'd rather tell you in person."

Another ploy, she thought.

"Sorry. Not tonight."

"Please listen to me, darling. This is serious. You don't know the kind of people you're dealing with. Whatever you're being paid, it isn't worth the risk."

She smiled to herself. "Some people are willing to pay more than petty cash and a lot of talk about God, country, and flag."

"These people will stop at nothing. They are ruthless killers."

Politics didn't matter to her, but she disliked and feared violence.

"I'm not doing anything wrong. Just making the best deal I can for myself. I think you're a bastard for trying to frighten me."

She hung up and took the phone off the hook. If Horace called, he would get a busy signal. She didn't want to hear any more from him.

A few nights ago she had been at an intimate dinner party given by the owner of a sugar mill in Suphan Buri province. He did business with H & D Trading Company, and they had a friendly joking informal relationship, but the invitation to dinner came completely out-of-the-blue.

After dinner he asked for a private word with her. They sat in a quiet corner, and he spoke in low tones although there was no need to; the servants were cleaning up in the dining room, and the subdued clatter and jingle of dishes and silverware made anything he said inaudible to anyone else. His wife maintained a lively conversation with the other guests. When he brought up the subject of paying for information, she knew that she had found a Prince Charming who was about to fit a glass slipper to her foot.

He described the kind of information he was interested in: where H & D Trading Company bought the military supplies they shipped to the northeast, how much they paid the suppliers, and who in the Thai government was being paid not to interfere. This would ordinarily have been available in the firm's business records but, unfortunately, vital documents were missing.

She called him the next day to describe the kind of information she had. She was only a secretary, but she had learned what kind of documents were worth copying. Peter Judd was a very good teacher.

He asked her to name a price, and she set a figure several times higher than Peter Judd had been paying. He did not bargain.

Later that day, following his instructions, she put the documents in an envelope and placed it in her mailbox after the postman had left. An hour later, when she checked, the envelope was gone, and there was another envelope in her mailbox. This contained mint-fresh American currency.

The next time he called, she named a much higher price. He told her politely that he would have to see what information she had before he paid such a large sum. She told him that she didn't do business that way, and he promised to meet her terms. He would send someone directly to her apartment to complete the transaction.

On the English-language channel the news announcer was now telling about the wounding of a Thai policeman, the deaths of two kidnappers, and an injury to an American visitor. She heard the name B.T.B. Buckley. He was at the American hospital for observation, but his injuries were not considered serious.

She felt the impact in her nerves before she translated it to her brain; then she was overwhelmed with forgiveness. This was why he had not called. The poor darling.

She dressed and drove to the hospital in her car. She got his room number at the lobby information desk.

When she got off in the corridor, she had no trouble locating his room because angry voices were coming from it. Through the partly open door she had a narrow angle view of Brian sitting up in bed, his huge frame seeming to dominate it. He had a bandage around his neck.

Nearer the door she saw Colonel Suvit, whom she recognized. She moved to the other side of the corridor to get a view of the rest of the room. A slender Thai woman was arguing with Suvit.

The argument was conducted in English with raised voices, but she could not have cared less what it was about. Her real interest was the attitude of the young Thai woman. This little Thai nobody was defending Brian with the fierce protectiveness of a woman defending her mate, and he was watching her with approval, as if she had a right to act that way.

Unthinkable.

A nurse left a room farther down the corridor and turned in Jean's direction. The nurse did not see her, and Jean decided not to let her presence be known. There was nothing to be gained by staying to hear more of the confrontation in Brian's room.

By the time she arrived home she had gained a better perspective, and had even reached a conclusion. There was nothing important between Brian and the little Thai creature. He had nothing in common with her.

She had her nightly bath and made her ritual appearance nude before the full length mirror. The view was reassuring. What could a frail Thai woman with lime-sized breasts offer to compare?

She put on her robe and called the hospital. She asked to be connected to Mr. Buckley's room.

EARLIER IN THE DAY A HOSPITAL ATTENDANT HAD BROUGHT A wheeled wagon of books for Brian to choose from. He picked a slim volume that a Buddhist philosopher had written for those who wanted to know more about the faith. Halfway through the book he found himself being drawn slowly toward comprehension, his imagination expanding, his intelligence tuning in. The diffuse and otherworldly concepts were revealing truths that were somehow familiar to him, that he felt he already knew.

In a short time he was so caught up that he resented the nurse because she brought tea and he had to stop reading.

At the end of visiting hours, however, when Arunee and Colonel Suvit left, he did not pick up the book again. His mind was too busy with the startling exchange that had taken place in this room a short while ago.

The nurse opened the door. "I'll be back in half an hour. You must be asleep by then."

A moment after the nurse left, the telephone rang on his night table.

"Brian? This is Jean."

"Can't talk," he said in a husky whisper. His throat felt coated with ground glass.

"Poor baby. I just heard about what happened, or I'd have called you earlier. How long are you going to be in the hospital?"

He made a small humming sound to indicate that he was on the line, even if not replying.

"I'll come to see you tomorrow. That's a promise. Is there anything you'd like me to bring you?"

He was wondering if it was worth the effort to answer when her heard a faint buzzing on the line.

"Can you hold for a minute, darling? There's someone at the door."

He heard the receiver put down. Her receding footsteps made padding sounds as though she were wearing slippers.

A quickly stifled scream was swallowed in silence.

"Jean!" he cried in a raucous croak.

Footsteps approached again, definite, hard-edged. The receiver clicked.

The nurse returned. "Lights out. You have to sleep. I told you—"

She backed away, startled, as Brian flung himself out of bed. He grabbed his clothes from hangers in the shallow wall recess that served as a closet.

The nurse said, "You can't leave. I'll call the security guard."

He dressed quickly and ran out of the room.

In the lobby a guard sat reading a newspaper with his chair tilted back against the wall. The wall telephone near him began to ring.

Brian ran past him to the street. He knew how to get from the hospital to the American sector. He ran all the way.

The second floor window of Jean's apartment was alight.

Downstairs in the vestibule he pushed the button opposite her apartment number. An answering ring was needed to open the vestibule door.

No answer.

With the palm of his hand he pressed all the buttons on the board.

At the first ring he pushed through the door into the lobby. The ringing followed him as he raced up the stairs.

A sliver of light showed from the ajar door to her apartment. Something was blocking the door and he had to force it open.

Jean was lying on the floor in her bathrobe, one bare knee lifted slightly, one hand resting laxly on the carpet. Her hair was wrapped in a towel from which blond strands of hair protruded and a small circle of blood beneath her head was reddening the towel in back.

He felt the artery in her neck. No pulse.

The living room looked as if a threshing machine had been run through it. Tossed cushions, pictures pulled from walls, a bookcase emptied of books, the large photograph of the Statue of Liberty at night turned askew. Drawers were pulled out of side tables and chairs overturned with their bottoms knifed open. The innards of a sofa were ripped apart to reveal the springs.

Someone had done a hasty but thorough job of searching.

The bedroom was also in chaos. Bureau drawers were pulled out onto the floor and their contents scattered. Clothes taken from the closet were shredded with a knife.

But the bottles on a dressing table had not been disturbed and the bed was untouched.

A curious omission, unless . . .

The bathroom door exploded open, and a burly figure leapt out. Brian had a quick glimpse of a swarthy, snarling face with a vivid white scar beneath the left eye. A dagger flashed. Brian brought his hand down sharply on the burly man's wrist and sent the dagger flying. The next instant he felt a paralyzing burst of agony in his groin.

He sank to his knees and a piercing spasm made him throw up. He forced himself to stand up, and lurched weakly into a wall.

Scarface was gone.

Brian staggered to the window and saw him descending to the side of the building. He made a final jump to the sidewalk and ran down the street beneath over-branching trees, visible only as a moving part of the darkness.

A motorbike was parked in a misty penumbra of light near a street lamp. The man leapt onto it, the engine rasped, the bike surged forward.

There was no chance of overtaking him.

Brian heard voices outside the apartment. As he went out the door, several frightened-looking people were milling in the corridor. They drew away from him. He went down the stairs, carefully holding onto the banister.

He emerged onto the street. It was raining again. At Lanluang Road he hailed a motorized samlar that had a small canopy to protect its passengers from the rain.

TWENTY

HARRY LOKMA RODE HIS MOPED UP TO THE ENTRANCE OF THE *Bangkok Post* building.

He dismounted, carried the moped with him into the building, and gave it to a security guard to put into the room where employees' bicycles were kept.

A printout of the latest news stories was on the desk in his office. He was reading it when Chamnan, the news editor, came in. Chamnan was fifty years old but looked ten years older because his hair was snow white. He had worked for the newspaper most of his life.

"Have you seen the printout about the murder last night?" he asked.

"Yes. Is there any more on it?"

"The police say the *fahrang* Buckley did it. They have a number of witnesses who give an excellent description."

"I thought he was in the hospital."

"He left suddenly last night to go to the house of the American woman."

"It doesn't make sense that Buckley would do it. It sounds to me like Colonel Suvit is allowing his personal feelings to affect his judgment."

Chamnan seemed uneasy. "Colonel Suvit asks if we know where the *fahrang* is to be found. He also gives a warning. Anyone who assists the *fahrang* in any way will be arrested."

The telephone jangled on Lokma's desk.

"Are you free to talk?" Arunee asked.

"Yes," he said guardedly. "In a minute."

172

He nodded permission for Chamnan to go and waited until the office door closed.

"What is it?" he asked.

"Brian's here. He came last night after he left Jean Hudson's apartment."

"What was he doing there?"

She explained that Brian was in the hospital talking on the telephone with Jean when the killer arrived at her apartment. Brian got there in time to interrupt the killer in his search. There was a struggle, and the killer escaped.

"He was able to identify him, though. It's the same man, the one with the scar under his eye. The one who dressed like a monk, and who killed Manit."

"Why didn't Brian wait there and tell the police what happened?"

"No one saw the other man. Brian would have been the chief suspect."

"You can't keep him at your place. Suvit's given warning. Anyone who helps him will be in almost as much trouble as he is."

"You know what will happen if Suvit gets his hands on him. He'll keep him in jail indefinitely. He won't even try to find out if anyone else did it."

"Where is Brian now? This minute?"

"Asleep. He's exhausted."

"Stay with him. I'll call you back as soon as I think of something."

He failed to elicit interest in Buckley's case at the American Embassy, or even an expression of concern that an American citizen might be falsely accused of murder. The senior consul, Horace Calisher, told him that the Embassy would not exert itself in any way to help Buckley.

Meanwhile, the reporter at police headquarters called in with the preliminary autopsy report. Jean Hudson was killed by a dagger wound to the back of the neck, which neatly severed a band of nerve fibers in the brain that connected the lobes of the cerebellum to the medulla and the cerebrum. The killer was someone trained to strike at the most vulnerable part of the human anatomy.

In Lokma's view, that helped to confirm Brian's innocence, but he doubted that Colonel Suvit would agree. Nor would Suvit be impressed by the havoc wreaked in a search of the dead woman's apartment. The newspaper's reporter on the scene said the destruction was hasty but systematic, not the work of someone in a murderous rage. This fit Buckley's account, relayed by Arunee, that he was ambushed by a killer who was searching her apartment.

Chamnan interrupted with an unrelated development. A researcher working with Arunee on the investigation of H & D Trading Company had produced a puzzling lead. The company had made large contributions to a charity whose only purpose was to operate a leper village eighty miles north of Bangkok on the Chao Prya river.

This was unusual because funds for the care of the half a million lepers in Thailand were supplied by the government, the American Leprosy mission, or religious groups. Why would a trading company contribute heavily to a charity that operated a leper village?

Lokma asked Chamnan to get more information from the researcher.

An hour later Chamnan reported back that the funds were spent mainly for docking and storage facilities at the village. These were now so greatly improved that some barges traveling north stopped there en route to Lampang.

"Why would barges stop at a leper village?" Lokma asked.

Chamnan, more gifted with diligence than imagination, had not thought of that. "Shall I ask him?"

"Never mind."

A researcher wouldn't know. The barges probably carried an illegal cargo that would attract attention if unloaded at a large river port. The village must be a transfer point for unloading cargo onto smaller craft, which could then deliver it at any of hundreds of small inlets or bays to be picked up and carried overland to a final destination.

Lokma placed a call to the Defense Ministry and spoke to a deputy minister. After listening to Lokma's theory, the minister said a Navy patrol boat would be sent to investigate the leper village.

Lokma said, "I want the exclusive story. I'll assign a reporter to accompany your patrol boat."

"He won't be allowed to file a report until the mission is completed."

"I understand."

"If the leper village really is a transfer point for smugglers, they won't welcome visitors. There may be trouble."

"I'll send someone who can handle himself in a situation like that."

BRIAN AWOKE TO THE SOUND OF GIGGLING. HE WAS LOOKING at a window bathed in clear, yellow sunshine. A small bird flew by outside, and its wings were briefly touched with golden light.

More giggling.

Arunee was shepherding her children out the door. They were carrying schoolbooks and departing reluctantly. They kept looking back at Brian.

Suddenly a honking came from outside, and they ran.

"What was so funny?" Brian asked. His voice was so husky he could not force it above a whisper.

"I'm sorry if they woke you. It's the blanket."

He felt a slight breeze on his bare skin. The blanket had pulled away, and his behind was protruding. Quickly he pulled the blanket over to cover himself.

"May I use the bathroom?"

"Your clothes are behind the door."

He studied his reflection in the bathroom mirror. The bandage around his throat was soiled and stained, and he was unshaven. He washed and dressed, thinking of Jean and how she had looked lying dead in her apartment.

He recalled the other events of last night. He had told the driver of the samlar to stop on a deserted street not far from Arunee's house, and had walked, limping, the rest of the way.

Arunee had met him at the door. He told her what had happened. She listened, saying very little, and in the lamplight her face looked as if covered with opaque paper. He remembered that with particular clarity. Later, while he rested in a chair, she went into the kitchen to make tea. Before she returned he was asleep. She must have undressed him. He had the dimmest memory of her helping him move to the cot.

She made a breakfast of eggs with green peppers and waited until he finished.

"That bandage looks terrible," she said then. "I'll get you a fresh one."

She returned in a minute with a lighter bandage. Her quick brown hands unwrapped the old one. Carefully and gently she began to massage liniment into the injured area.

"You keep medical supplies?"

"With children around?"

When Arunee finished putting on the new bandage, the massaged area was cool and free of pain. But he was tired again. Arunee began remaking the cot for him to lie down. As she lifted a corner of the sheet, something animated and green jumped out. It was a toad.

"A friend?" he asked.

"You slept with him last night," Arunee said. "I like him. He eats spiders and mosquitoes."

The toad leapt to the windowsill and watched them with baleful eyes. It uttered a loud croak, then wheezily inhaled.

"I think we speak the same language," Brian said. He made a croaking noise, then drew in his breath with a similar wheezing gasp.

"I think you're both very ill. Get back in bed. Take off your clothes."

"Not again. I don't trust that blanket."

"Well, at least take off your shoes."

A soft warm breeze wafted through the open windows, and near the roof two small birds fluttered nervously. He remembered watching them, and it was the last thing he remembered for awhile.

In his dream Diane told him again why she never intended to have children. She asked, "What's so important about breeding? Cows do it without thinking it's a great mystery, and monkeys do it without being struck dumb by the wonder of it all. I have no time for children. They need food and looking after. They need their teeth cleaned and to be amused and played games with. They need help with schoolwork. And they're always underfoot. Always hovering around like restless moths looking for a light source."

When he awoke the sunlight had left the ceiling and was cutting a yellow wedge out of a wall across the room. As he sat up on the cot, Arunee came in from her bedroom.

"I'm glad you're up. I would have had to wake you soon."

She told him she had called Harry Lokma and learned that Colonel Suvit was looking for Brian.

"He thinks you murdered Jean Hudson."

"Mainly he wants to put me back in jail."

"Lokma called again a few minutes ago. He says things are looking better. In a few days we might be able to prove you aren't guilty. Until then it would be better to keep you out of Colonel Suvit's hands."

"How do we arrange that?"

"You are leaving Bangkok. As a guest on a Royal Navy patrol boat."

Arunee explained Lokma's plan. He had worked out all the details, including having a car delivered to Arunee's house. The yellow Toyota was parked outside as she spoke.

"I hope you fit into the trunk. It will be safer."

"I can try."

"There's a small cove two miles from here where a rowboat is anchored. The patrol boat is at midriver. They're expecting you."

Arunee went out to the car first and made sure there was no one around to observe them. Brian hurried out to meet her.

She opened the trunk. It was smaller than Brian thought. He clambered in and wrapped his body in a fetal position.

Arunee nodded approvingly. "I know it's uncomfortable, but you won't have to be there long."

"It's like being back in the womb."

Arunee whispered "Good luck" before she closed the trunk lid. It was very warm inside. The car had been sitting in the sun.

A few minutes after they were under way, Brian felt a spasm start in the calf of his bad leg. He tried shifting his weight a little, but the muscle cramp got worse. Hang in there, he told himself.

The car stopped, and he heard Arunee get out. He heard her voice, speaking in a low tone next to the trunk lid.

"There's a delay. Be patient."

The car started off again. They were traveling faster, and there were more stops and starts. The cramp in his right leg kept tightening.

Damn. *Goddamn.*

The air in the small enclosed space was becoming stale with exhaust fumes. There is a conspiracy against my breathing, he thought. First the suffocating smoke in the hotel room, then the garrote, now this.

The car finally slowed, stopped, and this time he did not have to wait long before the trunk lid opened.

Arunee said, "Hurry. The ferry is pulling out."

"What ferry?" He unwrapped himself and crawled out.

"People were picnicking in the cove. You couldn't have got to the rowboat. I drove to the ferry, using the least traveled streets."

She started off, and he hobbled after her.

She said, "The ferry goes near where the Navy patrol boat is anchored. When you're close enough, drop overboard and swim."

He saw the ferry at the dock. A whistle proclaimed its imminent departure.

"Thanks for everything," he said.

Her kiss was as quick and gentle as a leaf falling on his mouth. "The word in Thai is *khoopkhun maak.*"

"*Khoopkhun maak,*" he said.

TWENTY-ONE

AT THE FOOT OF MAHACHAI ROAD, HE JOINED THE CROWD boarding the ferry. The ferry moved slowly toward midriver. He made a casual survey of the passengers nearby. Most were intent on their conversations, their newspapers, their private worries.

He edged the the rear. A sampan glided past. A motorboat zoomed by in the middle distance, leaving a cutting wake. Further out, a barge was moving sedately upriver like a placid cow.

Just ahead was the yellow and white patrol boat, flying the Thai flag. Uniformed sailors were working on deck.

Brian put both hands behind him, gripping the railing, ready to propel himself backward.

Someone was watching.

The man had a large head, a plump body, and wore a beret. He was staring at Brian with unusual interest.

Brian moved away from the railing. He edged through the crowd of passengers until he reached a narrow passageway bordering the pilot's cabin, where he leaned against the wall, looking back the way he had come.

No one appeared.

"Meestrah Buckley?"

The man in the beret had come around the other way.

"You've made a mistake." Brian said.

"No mistake. I am from police. There is photograph of you at our headquarter."

It was stifling hot. The ferry continued to chug its way toward the opposite river landing.

They had already passed by the patrol boat.

"When ferry land you will please to come with me."

"How do I know you're a police officer?"

The man reached into his pocket to show his identification.

Brian lifted and tossed him. He went flying backward over the railing, facing Brian with a look of pure astonishment. He disappeared into the river with a splash not audible over the ferry's engines. As soon as Brian saw him come to the surface, he swung about quickly.

Two people saw what happened and were registering alarm. One was a young woman carrying a baby in a contraption on her back. The other was a tall, thin young man with high cheekbones.

"Man overboard!" Brian cried. His voice was too weak to carry far, but the cry was instantly taken up by the others. As the crowd surged to the rail, the two witnesses were swept away from Brian.

The young woman instantly lost interest in everything except trying to protect her baby. She grabbed the rail hard and hung on. The tall, thin young man fought to hold his position in the milling crowd. He was shouting something that was lost in the general uproar.

The struggling figure in the water below was rapidly being swept toward the rear of the ferryboat. Someone threw out a life preserver. Everyone on board was watching the rescue. No one would bother about him until they got the policeman out of the water.

Brian ran to the deserted side of the ferry. He dove overboard.

THE WATER FELT COOL AS HE WENT UNDER, BUT AS HE ROSE to the surface, he was no longer aware of the temperature. He swam to the stern. The ferry had come to a near halt, with its engines making a grinding noise. Water bubbled along its sides.

Brian took a deep breath, dove, and counted thirty breast strokes underwater. When forced up for air, he had not made much progress. The ferry was twenty yards away.

He drew in a huge lungful and went under again.

This time when he came to the surface, the ferry was a considerable distance away. A water taxi raced by with its nose out of the water.

He began to swim, slogging on against the water-logged weight of his clothes.

There must be people on the river who saw him, but they were going on about their business. On a hot day, if someone chose to cool himself with a swim, even while wearing his clothes, why not? *Mai pen rai.* It doesn't matter. The national bywords.

Brian's swaddled strokes were slowing. He realized that he was not going to make it to the patrol boat with his clothes pulling him down. He would have to divest himself before trying to swim farther. As he began to do so, he saw a long slender sampan with a cargo of caged mynah birds working its way upriver. A woman in a broad-brimmed straw hat was patiently poling.

Brian reached the sampan and held on to its side with one hand. The woman looked at him curiously. Her sunken eyes made her face resemble a peanut shell.

He pointed to the patrol boat at anchor.

"Take me there, please."

The woman nodded and steered the sampan toward the patrol boat, poling a little harder and moving to the other side to compensate for Brian's added weight.

As they came near, the navigation lights on the patrol boat turned on. Brian, treading water, made a *wai* to the woman in the sampan. *"Khoopkhun maak,"* he said.

Her face broke into a wide grin. *Koonmak! Koonmak!* cried a mynah bird.

Brian swam alongside the patrol boat. A rope ladder dropped down to him, and he caught the lowest rung. He hauled himself to the top of the ladder where a sailor helped him to the deck.

"Buckley?"

An officer's cap perched atop black unruly hair. A uniform and collar insignia gray with a black circle and two stars. A youthful face sporting a moustache.

"I am Roi Tho Takson. We were expecting you, although not the way you arrived."

Brian said huskily, "I missed a connection."

Later, wrapped in a blanket, Brian sipped tea in Takson's compact cabin.

"Shall I call you Roi Tho or Takson?" he asked.

The moustache twitched with amusement. "Roi Tho is a rank. I command the Marine platoon on board. Call me Takson."

Brian heard the noise of the electric windlass and the anchor chain clanking steadily into its locker.

Takson said, "I am surprised they chose an American for an observer."

Brian sipped more tea; it made a nice warm spot in his stomach. "I'll try to stay out of everyone's way."

"Our orders are to show you every courtesy. Is there anything you wish? Your clothes will soon be ready."

"I'm fine."

"The bandage on your throat is wet. Would you like another?"

"It'll dry." He didn't want any questions about the rope mark. "I had an operation recently."

"If I cannot be of service, then I beg you to excuse me. I have duties to perform."

From the porthole of Takson's cabin, Brian watched the city of Bangkok slide backward out of view. The riding lights of boats at their moorings twinkled across the water, rising and falling to the same rhythms that had moved other craft for centuries. At night the magical serenity of an ancient culture prevailed over urban development, defying time and new ideologies. A great civilization once held sway here, flew its arrogant flags, and the evocative air was still redolent with days of glory.

Brian watched until he could no longer see the golden pagodas and the soaring towers and spires of the palace. Then he sat down on the cot and began to massage his leg, kneading vigorously until the stiffness began to loosen and the pain to unbind. He avoided the three-inch seam of scar tissue above his knee.

Another fainter scar on his hipbone he owed to Starbuck, the huge Princeton guard. College football was like a series of skirmishes preceding all-out war in the Pros. In the locker room he saw veteran professional players with bodies so stitched together they looked as if they had just come from Baron Frankenstein's lab.

When he looked out the porthole again the view had changed. The riverbank was sparsely dotted with factory buildings, and houses that were little more than shacks. They passed by a slow-moving teakwood barge pushing on like a great tortoise.

He heard a sharp knock on the door.

"Come in."

A young Thai marine appeared, holding Brian's clothes.

"Put them anywhere. Thanks."

The clothes, including his underwear, were dry and neatly

pressed, but his canvas shoes were a bit damp. As he pulled up his trousers, he noticed that his wallet and the carrying case for his passport and visa had been removed.

Takson entered the room without bothering to knock.

"The Nowa Tri wishes to see you." His tone was firm, bordering on hostile; even the hairs of his moustache seemed to bristle.

"My wallet and passport are mi—"

"Everything will be explained."

Brian followed Takson down the short corridor to a corner cabin, a bit larger than Takson's. A plump, round-faced man wearing a naval uniform was standing behind a table.

"You claim to be a journalist," he said. "Your passport and other papers prove otherwise."

He picked up Brian's wallet and passport from the table and, holding both between thumb and forefinger, held them forward like a prosecuting attorney presenting Exhibit A.

"I'm not a full-time journalist," Brian answered. "I'm on special assignment for the newspaper. If this was not made clear to you, I'm sorry."

"We have received a report on the radio. Colonel Suvit, the police director of Bangkok, has put out an order for your arrest. You are wanted for questioning in a murder."

Brian met the man's probing gaze. "I can explain. Colonel Suvit is angry with me because of a story I helped to publish in the *Bangkok Post*. I'm not guilty of anything, but he has personal reasons for wanting me in jail."

"I find that very hard to believe."

"I suggest that you talk with the editor of the newspaper. His name is Harry Lokma. He'll back up everything I've told you."

"We are observing radio silence. Until our mission is complete, we can receive messages but not transmit."

"Then how can I prove what I'm saying is true?"

"That is not our problem. While you are aboard my ship, you will be kept under guard. When we return to Bangkok you will be turned over to the police."

Brain understood that the Nowa Tri was following a correct procedure, but that did not make his situation easier to bear.

"May I have back my passport and wallet?"

"You may not. Roi Tho, this man is in your custody. You are responsible for him."

Takson, standing straight and stiff, saluted smartly.

Brian was taken to a small, nearly bare room furnished only with a cot, a washbasin, and a chamber pot.

Takson posted a marine guard at the door. Then he closed the door and bolted it from the outside.

AT THREE O'CLOCK IN THE MORNING BRIAN WAS STILL AWAKE, reading a small booklet describing the patrol craft. It was the only reading material he had been able to find. The booklet informed him that the ship was of the Klongyai class, with a one-hundred-and-ten-ton displacement, a three-inch deck gun, antiaircraft gun, and three torpedo tubes. He read the booklet through twice before he put it back where he found it, under the chamber pot.

Thunder had been rumbling for several minutes. Now there was a long breathless silence followed by a great, rushing wind, and rain poured from the sky.

The doughty patrol ship of the Klongyai class fought its way upriver.

It occurred to Brian that he was following the same northward route that Ellen Peterson had taken. She might have transferred at the leper village to a smaller boat and gone on past Lampang to the Golden Triangle. It was probably too late to catch up with her, but if he could question people at the village he might at least find out where she had gone.

He dozed on the cot in the small bare room, and when he awoke the storm had passed.

A few minutes later the patrol boat's engines cut off. Then the lights went out.

Brian's back muscles tightened. They must be approaching the leper village.

He heard a splash. A large heavy object had fallen into the water just below his porthole. He looked out, and as his vision adjusted to the dark, he made out an inflatable raft rising and falling in the small eddy caused by the patrol boat's slow drift. A rope was attached to the raft, holding it close to the boat.

Someone slid down the rope onto the raft. It was the Nowa Tri wearing a dark sweater over his uniform. He cut the rope with a knife, setting the raft free. Then he pushed away from the boat, picked up an oar inside the raft, and paddled.

Brian pounded on the door of his room.

"Takson!" Brian shouted. "Get him at once!"

A sleepy voice answered in Thai.

Brian interrupted: "I must talk to Takson. Roi Tho Takson! *Quickly!*"

The Thai voice turned angry. A rifle butt hammered on the door.

Brian shouted above the noise: "TAKSON! NOW!" Then he hurried back to the porthole. Straining to see, he picked out a glint of lacy foam from an oar dipping in and out of the water.

As he turned back toward the door, the porthole exploded in a hail of fragmenting glass. He hit the floor and stayed there, while the door to the room sprouted a jagged series of horizontal holes. An instant later came the crackling splintering noise of gunfire.

Short staccato bursts evaporated to near silence and burst out again with renewed fury. Brian crawled on his belly to the door. The door was locked from the outside, but so riddled with bullet holes it looked like the target in a shooting gallery. He felt a slight yielding when he pushed against it.

He got up into a crouch and lunged at where the bolt should be. Wood groaned and shuddered. He lunged again, and this time the door gave way, and he followed it into the corridor. A sailor outside was lying with his head propped against the other wall. His rifle was beside him, and his white uniform was crimson from the waist up.

Brian picked up the rifle and ran down the corridor. He started up a companionway, but stopped abruptly because the top step was jumping and smoking.

The deck was being swept by gunfire.

The square frame of the companionway filled with blinding glare. There must be a searchlight on shore. He heard confused shouting and cries of pain.

A Marine appeared in the companionway, clutching his stomach, his foot wavering to find the first step. When he fell, his head struck the floor below with a squashing sound. Brian climbed out cautiously from the companionway.

Smoke and the acrid smell of cordite drifted over bodies sprawled in grotesque positions. A short distance away, a flame rising from a hole in the deck looked like a miniature eruption from a volcano.

A sailor carrying a fire extinguisher rushed toward the hole from which the flame spouted.

Another fusillade raked the deck. Brian ducked. When he looked again, the sailor way lying face down, and the extinguisher was gushing foam from a dozen places.

The patrol boat swung idly on the current and brought in view a wooden pier jutting out from shore. Men were crouching near a toolshed on the pier and firing at the boat. Nearby, other men were reloading a 40mm gun.

Small arms fire answered from the wheelhouse. Brian saw two men up there. One looked like Takson.

The glare of the searchlight dimmed as the patrol craft continued to veer to starboard. The view now included the thatched huts of a village, with chickens and ducks running wildly along a dirt street. Where the street ended, there was a central building with two long barrackslike structures.

On the wooden pier men kept firing. Another explosion rocked the boat, causing bodies to leap into the air and fall limply back. A sailor reeled across in front of Brian with both hands extended before him like a blind man. He reached the railing and toppled over into the water.

The stricken boat yawed further, putting its prow between Brian and the men firing from the pier. During the moment of comparative safety, he raced across the deck to the wheelhouse.

He climbed the ladder. Takson was kneeling and firing through a shattered wheelhouse window, and a bearded man with him was also firing.

Takson stopped to reload. "Where's the Nowa Tri?"

"I saw him drop a raft overboard and row ashore. Before the firing started."

Takson said in a queer tone, "His own ship."

"You can't make a revolution without selling out a few friends. How much damage?"

"The port engine is out. So is the steering. And we've got fires below deck."

"How about the guns?"

"All gone, except for the antiaircraft gun aft."

Kneeling, Brian took aim with his rifle. He fired and a man on the dock seemed to throw his automatic weapon into the water and jump after it.

One for our side, Brian thought.

"How about that antiaircraft gun?" he asked.

"Probably works. But no one can get to it. Several men died trying."

"Where's the ammo?"

"Still in cases near the gun. We're lucky they haven't hit that yet or we'd all be gone."

"Does the boat respond to the helm?"

"He's the helmsman." Takson indicated the bearded man.

"Ask him."

Takson did. The helmsman answered in Thai, then shrugged and held his hands a little apart.

Takson translated. "The rudder connections are severed, but a mechanic crawled into the after compartment and is trying to hold the connections in place. We've got a little control, but not enough to move out of range of the shore guns."

"Move in as close as we can to the dock."

Takson stood motionless. "You're right. When the ammunition goes, they'll die, too."

"That isn't the idea. I'm not counting on dy—"

The wheelhouse was engulfed in a churning explosion as a shell exploded below it. The ladder was blown to kindling, and the tremendous jolt flung Brian down. Glass in the remaining window shattered and flew through the air like tiny knives.

When Brian got up, the wheel was spinning wildly and the bearded helmsman was lying face down. Takson turned him over. His face and throat were shredded with glass.

The wheel was still spinning, and the throttle controls for the engines were smashed.

"Take the wheel," Brian said. "Swing in toward the pier. I'm going for that antiaircraft gun."

He jumped down from the wheelhouse and made a broken-field run across planking slick with blood and water. Bullets moaned about him. A hornet plucked at his sleeve.

The patrol craft swung further to starboard, heading toward the dock, and effectively shielding him from those on shore.

He reached the stern and stripped the shroud from the anti-aircraft gun. He worked the elevator wheel to depress the muzzle to a horizontal trajectory.

Shells were loaded in crates nearby. He kneeled on a crate and ripped the top free, hefted a shell into the antiaircraft gun and set the firing mechanism.

A thin mist had formed on the water as cooling air drew up heat from the river.

He swung the big gun in the direction of the pier. He sighted, lowered the muzzle again, and, bracing himself, pulled the lanyard.

A roar, a flash and smoke, a bucking recoil. The shell landed well beyond the pier, among small boats at anchor, erupting in a gout of flame.

Brian cursed. He would not have another chance. Men on the pier were already aiming their weapons at him.

A violent explosion boiled up on the far side of the pier. Debris flew outward from its center, as if fleeing the eye of a hurricane. Another giant explosion, and another. The small boats were going off like bombs.

Fires sprang up in the village. Thatched roofs blazed like torches.

The river gathered itself in a churning waterspout and fell on the pier. Men were swept off like ships from a gaming table. A few survivors running for safety vanished as though they had run beneath a tidal wave.

THE PATROL CRAFT DID NOT ESCAPE PUNISHMENT. WITH A shrill, metallic shrieking and a crackling of timber, the boat was driven aground. The crates of antiaircraft shells slid rapidly across the sharply canted deck and ended up against the ship's rail, bending it outward.

Brian got up slowly. On shore the only moving things were three men running hard past a blazing thatched hut. One man had his hands raised high as if trying to surrender and run at the same time.

Well, Brian thought in a numbed way, there's no doubt those small boats were carrying a lot of munitions.

He returned to the wheelhouse, trying to shake bells out of his head. A small semicircle of jagged platform remained, with the wheel in its center. Takson was slumped at the wheel, one arm jammed through the spokes.

Brian called to him: "Can you get down?"

Not until Takson moved was Brian sure he was alive. Using his free hand Takson pushed away from the wheel and crawled to the edge of the platform.

"Just push yourself over," Brian said.

He caught Takson as he fell, and lowered him to the deck. What looked like a bone was sticking up through Takson's back. It was a long wooden splinter. Brian eased it out.

"I'm all right," Takson muttered. His face was ghastly.

On the deck littered with bodies, a few were stirring. One lifted a hand asking for help. Several crewmen were coming up from below. One man had a first aid kit and immediately began tending to the wounded.

Other crewmen formed a fire brigade to pour water on the

smoldering inferno below deck. An occasional fierce red tongue leapt up, wavered, dwindled, licked at the edges of a ragged black hole, and expired in a twisting plume of smoke.

On shore villagers were emerging from their hiding places, wandering about dazed and bewildered. A few stopped to watch the burning remnant of a thatched house.

An older man with white hair walked within hailing distance of the boat. He called out to the crew medic who was tying a tourniquet around Takson's arm.

"He wants to know if he can help," Takson said. "He says he's a doctor."

The white-haired man came on board. He had a large leprous patch on one cheek and his nose had collapsed flat on his face. Two fingers were missing from each hand.

Takson exchanged a few words with him before the man went off to tend the wounded.

Takson said, "His name is Pariba, and he's apparently the doctor here in the village."

A PRELIMINARY INSPECTION BELOW DECKS REVEALED HOW lucky they were. They found an unexploded shell imbedded in the port torpedo tube, and a torpedo jarred halfway out of its rack. Another shell had penetrated the main transom but failed to cause calcium flares stored there to ignite.

In the wreckage below deck, an orange glow flickered, darkened, flickered again like a firefly hidden deep in the branches of a tree.

Takson used a blinker, a two-foot-long tube with a light inside, flashing it periodically to signal any members of the crew who might still be alive.

Smoke was coming from the engine room although the fire was out. They found two crewmen dead there from carbon dioxide poisoning. They had pulled the carbon dioxide release to put out a dangerous fire in a fuel tank, and then were unable to escape in time.

A total of thirteen from the patrol boat were dead. One Marine suffering from a head wound was comatose, and several others were badly wounded.

They counted eight dead ambushers, including a partial corpse that washed ashore and a floating body dragged from the water. Many others must have drowned. A large patch of blazing fuel was drifting downriver, and there was no way of knowing how many bodies were trapped in it. There were no wounded. The survivors must have taken their wounded with them when they retreated into the jungle.

In the main building that served as a hospital for the village, two rooms were set aside for medical treatment. A number of villagers had suffered burns and other injuries. Takson ordered the lepers to be treated in a separate area. He told Dr. Pariba that members of his crew were to be given priority in medical care.

Later, watching Dr. Pariba working with the crew medic, Brian told Takson, "He seems to be the nearest to a headman in the village. I have some questions I'd like to ask him."

"Only when I have finished. I have questions to ask also." Takson added soothingly, "Your wallet and passport are safe. They will be returned to you."

"Thanks."

"I am most grateful for your help in the fighting. You are no longer under guard. I know I can trust you."

Takson's interrogation of Doctor Pariba took place in a small room that served as an office in the hospital. It was barely furnished and had a curtained alcove that contained a narrow, straw-filled bed.

Brian waited outside for almost an hour. When Takson and Pariba reappeared, the doctor was clearly agitated, speaking quickly and hardly able to contain himself. Takson did not respond, and finally dismissed him to return to treating the wounded.

"What's he upset about?" Brian asked.

"He is afraid the men who escaped into the jungle will return after we leave and punish anyone who cooperates with us."

"He may be right."

Takson replied impatiently, "My duty is to get the boat repaired and return to Bangkok. I have been in radio contact with the Minister of Defense, and those are his orders."

The call of duty foreclosed Takson's sympathy. It was not so much that he did not understand the villagers' peril as that he did not want to understand it. He was calm and in control because he had his duty to perform. There was nothing further to understand.

The patrol boat had suffered considerable damage. The hull had broken when it ran aground, the steering gear was out of action, there was a broken manifold in the engine room, and damage to the fuel tank compartment.

They discovered a small crane barge used by the smugglers that had not suffered much damage in the explosions that destroyed the other boats. Takson was sure this would enable him to patch his patrol craft so he could get back to a drydock for real repair work. He predicted that, with the help of the villagers, they would return to Bangkok in a few days.

"And what will happen to the villagers after we leave?" Brain asked.

"No one will be harmed. I will ask for government troops to control this area," Takson said with firm assurance. "Meanwhile, if the Nowa Tri tries to recapture the village, I will be ready for him."

At the hospital Brian found Doctor Pariba tending to the wounded, administering morphine, bandaging wounds, giving antibiotics and words of comfort.

Brian waited until Pariba was about to leave, then asked him to change the bandage on his throat. Pariba did so expertly.

"Can you tell me when the last barge arrived in the village?" Brian asked.

"The day before yesterday."

"Was there a woman on board?"

"She did not stay on the barge. She left in one of the smaller boats."

Brian asked cautiously, "A Thai woman?"

"She looked American, or European."

"A tall woman about thirty years old? Dark hair."

"I only saw her most briefly. I can't be sure."

"Did anyone mention her name? Would you know it if you heard it? Ellen Peterson. Is that familiar?"

Pariba answered tentatively, "Yes. That is possible."

Ellen Peterson had passed through here on her way to find sanctuary with Khun Wanchai. And she was not far ahead of him.

"I have to follow this woman. Is there any way I can get a boat?"

"The Roi Tho will permit this?"

"I'm not asking his permission."

"Such a trip would be most dangerous. The tribesmen who live in the jungle between here and Lampang will take your head."

"I'm willing to risk that if I can get a boat."

Pariba's face twisted in a half smile. The lepromatous patch had weakened the facial muscles on one side.

"Would you like someone to go with you? You will need an interpreter and guide."

"Are you volunteering?"

"If I stay here, I will surely be killed."

"Can you help me to find a boat?"

"A small fishing trawler belongs to the men who were stationed in the village. They used it for occasional boating pleasure and also to bring in fresh fish."

"Where is it?"

"Anchored a quarter of a mile upriver. The Roi Tho will discover it soon."

"Then our best chance is to leave tonight. Can you be ready?"

Doctor Pariba's eyes had a strange look. "I do not expect the journey to be a pleasant one. But whatever happens, I will have no regrets. I have very little to live for. If I die, I have very little to lose."

THERE WAS A LUMPY, SWOLLEN, MISSHAPEN MOON, BUT THE river seemed to be steeped in darkness, the waters rolling in place without forward movement. Takson was supervising the work of crew members trying to replace the steering gear of the patrol boat with a hand tiller in the lazarette.

A young marine was patrolling the wreckage-strewn shore. He kept his automatic weapon at the ready as Brian and Pariba approached.

"Ma ha krey?"

Pariba said, "He wishes to know what we want here."

"Tell him we saw someone in the village who may be one of the smugglers. He should go check it out."

Pariba relayed the message. The young marine looked doubtfully toward the thatched huts in the village. He sucked in his breath before he replied.

Pariba said, "He has strict orders not to leave his post. He wants us to inform the Roi Tho."

"Can he be talked into leaving?"

"I do not think so."

The young marine was watching them warily, an earnest, disciplined young man standing between them and the trawler. There could not be, Brian realized, a satisfactory outcome to their confrontation. He hoped for a clean resolution. Nothing messy. It was a simple question of getting close enough to . . .

A concussion like a giant fist pounded the ground. The universe exploded into a giant red blossoming flower. Small pebbles and sand rained down.

Trench mortar!

Brian fell and hugged the ground.

The young marine had been knocked off his feet. He scrambled up, retrieved the weapon he'd dropped, and started off on the run.

He had made only a few strides when he heard sharp chattering noises. He turned while running, fell, and lay spread-eagled.

Machine gun!

Brian tried to dig deeper into the ground. He did not feel compelled to see what was happening. He knew what was happening. The Nowa Tri was launching a counterattack.

There was no telling how many men the Nowa Tri had, but they probably outnumbered Takson's depleted force. This section of beach was on the outside perimeter of the action. The patrol boat was the target. If its guns were rendered useless, the recapture of the village would be easy.

A mortar shell exploded near the patrol boat and lifted it from improvised blocks. The boat settled down awkwardly, its weight collapsing part of the supports beneath it.

Suddenly, men appeared on the boat's tilted deck. Takson was among them. The antiaircraft gun was wheeled into firing position, aimed at the jungle. The gun belched smoke and kept firing.

Part of the jungle leapt skyward. A line of explosions erupted along the edge of thick concealing foliage. Men were catapulted out of hiding on spouts of flame.

"Pariba," Brian called softly.

Pariba was lying prone only a few feet away. He looked up hesitantly.

Brian said, "The Roi Tho has things under control. Time to go."

They got up and ran.

THE TRAWLER WAS AN OPEN STRUCTURE WITH A SMALL SHELtered cabin. Anchored so close to shore and partly camouflaged by jungle growth, the boat gave the illusion of a lurking creature. Misty steam rising from the river's surface was like the creature's vaporous breath.

On board the trawler Brian checked the fuel gauge, which was nearly full. He found the key to the ignition in a small metal box in the cabin locker.

He muttered a short prayer and turned the key.

A whining noise ended in a soft cough. He tried again. More whining, more coughing.

"Let me try," Pariba suggested.

This time the whining was brief, the coughing prolonged, and the engine caught with a muted huffing.

"I don't have much luck with inboard engines," Brian apologized. "I always do well with outboards for some reason."

He took the wheel and guided the trawler to midriver. Then he turned the prow north.

TWENTY-TWO

AFTER BRIAN LEFT ON THE ROYAL NAVY PATROL BOAT, ARU-nee began to investigate the murder of Jean Hudson. She had to clear Brian of suspicion so he could safely return to Bangkok.

With Harry Lokma's permission she enlisted the aid of a reporter and a researcher who'd been working with her on the expose of the H & D Trading Company.

She sent the reporter to question everyone who lived in the condominium building and neighboring houses on the street. Someone might have witnessed what happened on the night of the murder.

She also put a notice in the newspaper's personals section requesting information from anyone who might have been in the vicinity at the time the murder occurred.

An employee at the Bangkok Telephone Company, who per-formed occasional, small favors for pay, provided her with a list of telephone numbers that Jean Hudson had called in the past month.

As she expected, the last call Jean made was to the hospital where Brian was a patient. If the Bangkok telephone exchange listed the time a call was placed and how long it lasted, that would have been all she needed to prove his innocence.

But there was no such record. Colonel Suvit could still claim that after Brian answered the call, he went to Jean's apartment and murdered her.

She assigned the researcher to check out each of the other calls.

Within hours the researcher reported that most telephone calls Jean Hudson made appeared to be routine, but there were several to the American Embassy and several more to the American representative of a gem factory specializing in fine jewelry, precious stones, carved jade, and ivory.

Arunee asked, "What is this person's name?"

"Peter Judd."

From several sources during the next two hours Arunee acquired information about Peter Judd. One of the sources was a business associate of Aelbert, an executive at a gemstone company. He had never heard of Peter Judd, and neither had anyone he asked. Gradually it became clear that Judd's position at the gem factory was a front.

By then Arunee was sure that Peter Judd's real employer was the CIA. The CIA ran hundreds of businesses around the world: airlines, executive recruitment firms, ship chartering companies, aircraft manufacturers, printing companies, newspapers, book publishing firms, and advertising companies. These were called "proprietaries"—apparently legitimate enterprises established specifically as fronts for the CIA. The proprietaries were not expected to make a profit. Money that went through their ledgers was not accounted for in detail.

Through the proprietaries the CIA was able to move supplies and sums of money around the world. These were not labeled as foreign aid and so did not have to be approved by Congress. This provided funding for covert activities into which no other United States government agency was allowed to pry.

Arunee called Peter Judd to ask for an interview. He refused because he was leaving Bangkok that afternoon.

"Another assignment from the Company?" she asked.

There was a silence.

She went on: "I know who you work for. I promise the Company will be kept out of this, if you'll grant me an interview. Otherwise I'll get the facts on my own, and no promises."

"I'll call you back," he said.

He called back in an hour. Probably he used the interval to check her credentials with the CIA computers and his superiors.

"I'm not sure I can help," he said, "and I don't have time for an interview. But on the condition that neither my employer nor I get mentioned, I'll try to answer some of your questions. Provided you're not after the family jewels."

"Family jewels" was the CIA's term for improper or illegal activities they did not wish to reveal to the public.

She asked, "Was Jean Hudson working for you?"

"We used her."

"Did she supply information about the H & D Trading Company?"

"Yes."

"Could that be the reason she was killed? To prevent her from giving you more information?"

"I doubt it. We weren't using her anymore. But she was peddling information elsewhere."

"What makes you think so?"

"We planted a bug in her apartment."

She took a deep long breath. "Then you know who killed her. You must have recorded it."

"All we know is that she went to the door. That was it."

"Buckley was on the phone with her at the time. So you know *he* couldn't have killed her. You can clear him."

"Are you kidding?"

"This is a simple case of eavesdropping. You can help without getting involved. All I need is the tape or recording you were making at the time."

He chuckled harshly. "What tape? What recording?"

The phone went dead. When she called back, there was no answer.

The reporter she had assigned to find eyewitness accounts called in soon afterward.

"A woman who lives in a building across the street says she saw a man run along the street, jump on a motorcycle, and speed off. This was around the time of the murder."

"Did she get the license plate?" Arunee asked.

"No. But she gave me a description of the man."

The description of the man didn't fit Buckley. That helped to corroborate Brian's version but didn't prove the running man was the killer. What she needed was the kind of evidence that would convince Colonel Suvit.

The newspaper's reporter at police headquarters sent in a copy of the official file on the murder. The file had not been cleared for public distribution, but that was merely a matter of putting the right amount of cash into the right grasping hand. By tomorrow every newspaper in the city would have its copy.

The file was slender. A posed studio shot in color of Jean Hudson in life, other photographs in black and white that showed her in death: lying on the rug, on a stretcher, and in the morgue. The morgue photographs featured closeups of both her profiles and her full face. There was also a closeup view of the wound that killed her.

A card with her fingerprints was clipped to a note saying that the prints of Buckley found in Jean's apartment matched those on file at police headquarters. No other prints had been identified, which meant only that the other prints found did not match any in police files.

The lab report on blood samples was stapled to the autopsy finding. The blood sample showed distinct traces of alcohol, although not in amounts considered excessive. The contents of the stomach indicated that the victim had eaten approximately three hours before her death.

The rest of the file consisted of depositions from policemen who found the body and their preliminary questioning of witnesses, all of whom were tenants in the building. Their descriptions of the man leaving the murdered woman's apartment unmistakably identified Brian.

Other questions had not been asked. Was Brian carrying a weapon? Had he made any attempt to avoid being seen? Was there blood on his clothing or on his face or hands? How long after the sound of fighting was heard did Brian emerge from the apartment? Did he utter any threats or warnings or make any offensive or intimidating gestures? Did anyone attempt to follow him?

Arunee went home that evening in a discouraged mood. She made dinner and helped Chakra with his homework while Ajana worked on a kite she was making to fly at the parade ground on Sunday.

In the middle of a problem in arithmetic, a subject in which she was hardly more proficient than her son, she was interrupted by a telephone call. The caller was Elizabeth Spencer, whose daughter Emily was Ajana's classmate at school.

During the flutter of friendly hellos and how-are-yous, Arunee's alarm system began working. She was not close with Elizabeth Spencer. Why was she calling?

"I understand that Emily and your daughter are going to be at the parade ground on Sunday," Elizabeth said.

"Aren't you coming? Some of the kites are marvelous, and they do battle to amuse the spectators. I think you'll like it."

"I'm sure I will. But the point is, well, Emily invited your daughter to our house for dinner that evening."

"If it isn't convenient . . ."

"I'm afraid it's not. There are certain rules we try to live by. We have Thai friends, and we like them very much. But we don't socialize."

"Ajana and your daughter are in the same class at school, and play together every day. I don't know what you mean by socialize."

"Oh, I think you do. There are differences between people. Your daughter goes to a Christian school, but she isn't a Christian. That's one important difference. And there are others we don't have to go into."

"No, we don't."

"I don't mean to upset you. I wish this had never come up, and it shouldn't have. It's our fault, really, because we didn't teach Emily properly."

You will teach her, Arunee thought, and afterward she will know that never the twain shall meet. And the more twains that never meet, the more fragmented the human race will become until we are all again living in small, mutually hostile tribes.

As she hung up, Chakra was staring at her, trying to guess her secret thoughts. She would have liked to tell him what was troubling her, but did not think it wise.

It was very late at night before, deeply tired and quietly depressed, she went to bed.

THE NEXT MORNING IN THE NEWSROOM, SHE WAS AGAIN PURsuing her investigation of Jean Hudson's murder. Somewhere in the maze there might be a single thread that would lead Brian out of suspicion.

The classified notice had drawn the usual quota of crank calls. Only one was worth following up. It was from a businessman who had been driving past the condominium building that night when he saw a man climb out the window of a second-floor apartment and descend to the sidewalk.

Arunee picked up the businessman at his office and drove him to the condominium where he identified the window of Jean Hudson's apartment, and confirmed that he had seen the man around the time of the murder.

She thanked him and gave him a choice of two press passes to Thai boxing or the Bangkok ballet. He chose the ballet. He explained that his lady friend, whom he had been visiting at that hour, thought boxing was brutal. Arunee paid for the taxi to take him back to his office.

She stayed on to question other occupants in the building, trying to find someone else who had seen the other man. She had no luck until she met a woman returning from her marketing. The woman lived on the fourth floor at the other end of the building.

On the night of the murder, the woman said, she was returning from a visit with her sister.

"My sister has been ill with a stomach ailment, but the Lord Buddha be praised, she's not going to need an operation. Anyway, when I came home, I opened the door to the lobby with my key, and this man came in behind me. It made me nervous at that time of night. I was very thankful when he didn't follow me into the elevator."

"Where did he go?"

"He took the stairs."

"Someone was murdered here that night. Why didn't you report this?"

"I didn't know about the murder until late the next day, and by then the police already knew who did it. Anyway, the murderer wasn't the man who came into the building with me."

"How do you know?"

"According to what I've read, the killer is a white man. And very tall. This man was Chinese and not that tall."

"Can you describe him?"

"He was about medium height. He was wearing a white open neck sports shirt and brown cotton twill trousers. But if I had to identify him I wouldn't need to remember all that. He had a mark."

"A mark?"

"A scar below his left eye."

Arunee's next stop was police headquarters, where she presented the evidence to Colonel Suvit. She had proof that there was another man in the apartment at the time Jean Hudson was killed. She knew how he got in, and how he escaped after killing her. More importantly, she had worked out a time sequence from the moment Brian left the hospital to the moment witnesses saw him leave Jean's apartment. There was not enough time for him to have gotten there, committed the murder and searched her apartment.

"The other man did that," she said. "His description fits the man who bombed the printing press at the newspaper and probably killed the sailor Manit."

Colonel Suvit was not impressed. "You have not proved Meesstrah Buckley's innocence. Only that someone else may be guilty."

"If you keep insisting Buckley is the killer, you'll end up

looking foolish. And if the real murderer goes free in the mean-time, you will certainly be blamed. I will personally make sure you are blamed."

Suvit stared at her stony faced. "Meestrah Buckley has committed assault on another police officer."

"When did this happen?"

"On a river ferry. The officer was thrown into the river."

"If Buckley did it, why didn't you arrest him?"

"He was not on ferry when search was made."

"You seem anxious to prove him guilty of something."

Suvit stroked his cheek with long fingers that had surprisingly pale fingernails. "If I may say so, you seem even more anxious to prove him innocent."

"He *is* innocent. The proof will appear in the morning edition of the *Bangkok Post*. After that, no prosecutor will put him on trial for the murder of Jean Hudson. I suggest you withdraw the charges. Otherwise you are going to look like a fool."

Without waiting for a reply, she left his office.

IN THE NEWSROOM, SHE FOUND A MEMO FROM HARRY LOKMA inserted in the roller of her typewriter. *Something important. L.*

She went down the hall and found Lokma interviewing an applicant for Mrs. Phun's job as secretary. The applicant was a neat, shirtwaisted young woman, part of the new wave of Thai women going into business. In the past few years, the status of women had changed more than in the previous five hundred years.

Lokma finished the interview quickly, asking the young woman to leave her resumé with the personnel office.

Arunee knew that something serious had happened when Lokma did not meet her eyes.

"Please close the door."

She did, and sat down in the chair the young woman had vacated.

"I had a call from the Defense Ministry," Lokma said. "The Navy patrol boat ran into an ambush. More than half the crew were killed."

Shock almost anesthetized her. "Buckley?"

"We know he survived the first attack, but there was another and now he's listed as missing. The story is confusing. Apparently the officer in command of the ship was a secret supporter of Khun Wanchai. The battle was fierce and no one is certain the village is securely in government hands. Troops are being hurried there in helicopter gunships.''

A chill began in her bone marrow and kept spreading.

"Please keep me informed," she said.

Somehow she got through the rest of the day. She talked to people who came and went, but she did not remember what they talked about.

Sometime or other it rained. She heard the rain rattling windows in the newsroom. The sky was dull slate and there was a monsoon cloud the color of dark turpentine. She wondered what the weather was like where Brian was. The brief storm passed, and the setting sun poured yellow lava through the windows onto the floor. The roof of a building across the way turned ochre. She wondered if Brian would ever again see such beauty.

She knew how she would react when news of his death came. Her heart would turn to dust.

She stayed late at her desk, waiting for word, checking the news ticker every few minutes. At one point, to keep her feelings under control, she quietly hummed an ancient *sutra*. This helped to absent her from outer reality so she could withdraw to her inner life. For those few minutes, she might have been in a quite corner of a *wat* saying her prayers.

At last, reluctantly, she put the cover on her typewriter and turned off her small, green-shaped lamp.

She looked in at Harry Lokma in his office. He saw her and shrugged. No word.

On her way home she topped at her favorite *wat*, the Marble Temple. She had happy memories of going there as a child with her parents on *Visaka Puja*, the day on which the Lord Buddha was born. They brought flowers and joss sticks and joined in the traditional candlelight procession three times around the *bot* or main temple building, with the monks chanting and the flickering candles casting shadows on the white marble walls.

This evening a short line was waiting to enter the temple. She bought a membrane-thin, inch-square piece of pure gold leaf and affixed it to the gilded image of the Lord Buddha. So much gold had been pressed into place on so many objects and images, that a chaff of golden glitter drifted onto the marble floor.

She went home and made dinner for the children. She ate a little so the children would not notice anything was wrong. She was testing herself, like someone taking her first tentative steps after a long invalidism.

When the children were asleep, she sat for awhile looking out at the dark river. In the deep of Phang Nga Bay lay the bodies of her parents and her brother. A typhoon had roared out of the skies to destroy the ferry on which they were passengers.

We are all on a frail ship, she thought, and the sky is full of typhoons.

All that night she lay awake staring at the ceiling.

TWENTY-THREE

Brian was at the wheel of the trawler when the sun rose on the right, invading the solemn blackness that covered the river. The air took on a rosy blush, the water became slowly luminous.

Pariba was asleep on a pillow on the narrow bench near him. His head drooped to his chest, showing blemishes on his scalp through scanty white hair, and his cheekbones protruded beneath yellow skin.

Brian did not waken him to take his turn at the wheel. He kept the engine throttled down to minimize noise as the trawler chugged along the empty river.

At noon the stillness and oppressive heat became inexplicably ominous. The jungle on both sides was shadowed and guarded by overhanging thick leaves and branches. An eerie feeling came over him, a feeling of imminent danger.

"How long have I been sleeping?"

Pariba was awake.

"A few hours."

"Longer than that. How far have we come?"

"I estimate about sixty miles. I've been keeping an eye on the fuel gauge. We can't go much farther."

Pariba found a map in the ship's locker and studied it. "Kwanpir. We can refuel there. It's a river settlement built by a French tin company. The mine failed, but there's still a small colony of French and Thai workers who chose to remain. They're sure to have fuel."

The trawler rounded the gently curving river bank. Ahead was the first break in the solid phalanx of trees and jungle growth.

A circle of thatched huts and lean-to shelters appeared in a level clearing.

The encampment seemed deserted in the fierce glare of the noonday sun.

"Does anyone live there?"

"A nomad tribe," Pariba said. "They may be out hunting food."

A short distance farther along the river they encountered a long, hollowed-out canoe making its way downstream. The canoe was piled with vegetation and what looked like a fresh killed pig. The brown-skinned paddlers glanced at the trawler and quickly looked away.

Pariba said, "It is taboo to look on one like me. If the evil eye of a leper holds theirs too long, they believe they will catch the disease."

Pariba's eyes seemed to float in pale, dead sockets. The origin of the superstition was not hard to imagine.

"It would be wise to put as much distance between us and them as possible. This boat would be a great prize."

At dusk, as the last rays of a bloodred sun were striking white sparks from the water, they dropped anchor at midriver. On the opposite banks close-packed walls of huge trees were bound together by climbing creepers and thick growths of feathery bamboo.

"The fuel gauge is pointing to empty," Brian said.

"We are almost there. This place is called the Forest of the Cold. It once stretched almost to Ayuthia, but is much smaller now. Kwanpir is just beyond."

Pariba volunteered to stand watch. Brian had put off sleep for so long that he was toxic with need for it. As soon as he put his head down on the bunk in the cabin, he was unconscious.

He dreamed a nightmarish jumble in which Diane had the dead-white, rotting face of a leper. She got into bed with him. "I'm frightened," she said, "because I can't help being needful." Her skeletal hand clutched at him . . .

He opened his eyes to find Pariba tugging at his shoulder. In closeup Pariba's face was like a skull with moving jaws jerking on wire.

Pariba whispered, "They are coming."

Pariba pointed. Brian looked hard, expecting a clear sign, but he saw only a red gleam wavering in the jungle.

Then in a flicker of torchlight a brown body slipped with stealthy movement into the river.

"Let's get the hell out of here!"

He hauled up the chain with all his strength, bringing the heavy, claw-footed anchor over the side.

Pariba cried a warning.

Behind Brian, a native, knife clenched between his teeth, was coming over the stern. Brian whirled and put his weight behind the swinging anchor. It struck the native in the side of the head, and his face split into lines like cracked pottery. He fell back into the water.

Pariba started the trawler's engine. As the headlights came on, a pirogue was revealed directly ahead. Three natives in the hollow interior, startled by the light, paused with their paddles streaming water.

The prow of the trawler struck the pirogue squarely in the middle. Two men seemed to leap upward and back into the river. The hull passed directly over the third man as the pirogue capsized, and the trawler continued on through the wreckage. A high-pitched scream came from the rear as someone was sucked into the boat's propeller.

The trawler began moving haphazardly, colliding with more men swimming in the water. The headlights wavered.

"Pariba!" Brian called.

No one was at the helm.

Brian took the wheel and straightened the trawler's course.

"Pariba!"

The silent river gave no reply.

Perhaps the leper had been flung overboard by the collision with the pirogue. Perhaps he had been seized by the attackers. In all the noise one more cry of distress would not have been heard.

Going back to search for him was senseless. There was no chance of finding him.

Brian accepted the futility even as he brought the wheel hard over. The trawler swung around and started back into the indistinct vapor of its own exhaust clinging to the river. The headlight revealed splintered pieces of wood floating on the surface and the capsized rear end of the pirogue jutting out of the water, holding up a man's severed hand and forearm like a trophy.

Brian moved the trawler closer to the shore, describing a wide semicircular path to expand the area of search.

There was no sign of Pariba.

Brian turned the trawler north again. He anchored several

miles beyond the place of ambush. The river, with its unknown, tortuous turnings, would be much safer to navigate in daylight.

HE STAYED AWAKE ALL NIGHT TO GUARD AGAINST SKULKING enemies.

With daylight the black forest on either side turned miraculously green.

Except for a grainy irritation of the eyelids and a tendency toward inattention, he suffered no ill effects from his sleepless vigil. But he was very hungry. He had eaten nothing in thirty-six hours, and it seemed as though each empty cell in his body was registering its need.

He started the engine and resumed the journey to Kwanpir. The fuel gauge had been pointing to empty for some time, but gauges often gave premature warning. Kwanpir could not be far away.

The rising sun glinting on the river blinded him, and he shielded his eyes. He had the impression of a dark blur ahead on the horizon.

As he drew closer he saw what the dark blur was.

Doctor Pariba was dangling from the branch of a tree overhanging the river. He was naked and his head drooped in a posture of submission. The sharpened end of the tree branch protruded from the center of his chest.

Brian's stomach gave a dry heave. He had to take a firmer grip on the wheel as he guided the trawler past the grisly figure.

Half a mile farther on the trawler's engine gave an apologetic cough. That was the last sound it made.

Brian turned the helm, using the trawler's residual momentum to move toward the riverbank. The current turned the boat slowly sidewise. He picked out a spot to go aground, a nearly obliterated channel that led into a tangle of dendritic growth.

The boat managed to plow through the undergrowth and come to rest against a tree that had bamboo roots wrapped around its bottom.

Brain leapt down into a scraggly growth of liana vines, giant ferns, and gnarled banyan trees. He pushed small branches and foliage out of his path, and waded into the channel. Mosquitos swarmed, feeding on him like maggots on a carcass. A monkeylike creature swung and gibbered through the vines overhead.

Brian followed the channel until it dwindled to a slender silver snake writhing forward beneath grubby ferns and creepers. Then he used a trailing liana vine to pull himself out. In the shelter of a tree, the ground was warm and damp and soft, a fertile breeding ground. He lay with his face pressed into the ground, digging with his fingers for tubers or roots or edible insects.

A sudden, crackling noise made him look up.

She was a sturdy peasant, with a broad face. She wore a dirty blouse and trousers that were blended with many shades of earth, and she carried a rifle in her knuckly grimed hands.

As Brian sat up, the woman quickly brought her rifle to bear on him. She spoke to him harshly in Thai.

"I am American." Brian pointed at himself for emphasis. "American." Without hope that she would understand, he said, "My boat ran out of fuel."

She replied, "Boat."

"That's right. Boat. You speak English?"

As he stood up, she grasped her rifle tighter.

"I need fuel and fresh water and food," he said. "My boat is nearby."

Brian heard a rustling in the bush, and two men stepped out. They carried rifles crosswise on their chests, and bandoliers strung over their shoulders.

The woman turned to them and apparently gave a brief interpretation. They looked at Brian in a most unfriendly manner.

The woman turned back to prod Brian with her rifle. "You come."

He was led back to the trawler.

The woman prodded Brian again with the rifle. "You help."

They began camouflaging the boat. The two men and the woman worked with machetes, cutting down scrub and tree branches that Brian piled on the trawler until the boat looked like part of the jungle. The dense overhead growth was an impenetrable shelter.

The work was heavy, and Brian was tired and hungry and weak. Mosquitos bit viciously. He slapped at them without energy.

Once, when carrying a load to the boat, he stumbled over a buried root and fell. The woman and her two companions laughed heartily.

Then they fell silent, listening.

After a moment, Brian heard it, too. A deep thrumming, like distant thunder.

The steel muzzle of the woman's rifle thrust under his jaw.

She held the rifle there, her hand on the trigger and her eyes glowing like live coals in a charcoal stove.

The deep thrumming came nearer. Brian saw the helicopter a quarter-of-a-mile downriver, flying slowly, as though searching.

It was a Boeing Vertol, armed with enough power to obliterate half a mile of jungle. The trombone sound of the helicopter's engine rose to a crescendo, faded, played a few wavering notes, ceased.

Only then did the woman remove her weapon from the underside of Brian's jaw.

With a quick gesture she ordered him back to work. The afternoon sun no longer penetrated the dimness, and the trawler had disappeared into the shadows.

The woman disappeared also. Brian faintly heard communications going on, her voice and a disembodied voice. She had a shortwave radio hidden nearby. When she returned, she said nothing.

An hour later a thin, disheveled-looking man appeared, bare to the waist, struggling with two large tin containers of gasoline. He put the containers down and climbed up on the foliage-shrouded deck of the trawler.

One of the men passed a tin container of gasoline up to him.

Brian decided to venture a bit. "I will pay you for the gasoline," he told the woman.

She looked at him blankly.

"Boat b'long Hmong," she answered.

For the first time Brian knew the identity of his captors. They were not members of the nomad tribe he had encountered before.

The Hmong people lived mostly in the inhospitable area around Chiang Rai and Nan. They had been fighting the Thai government for years, ever since their profitable slash-and-burn farming techniques were outlawed because they were denuding the forests.

"You keep the boat," Brian agreed. "It belong Hmong. But I need some way to get to Lampang."

The woman moved her rifle so that it pointed at Brian's chest.

"No go Lampang," she said. "Go Nan."

This was good news. The city of Nan was in the far north near Laos, much nearer to the Golden Triangle.

"Will you take me there?"

A fleeting smile wrinkled the woman's broad face. She turned to interpret to her companions, mimicking Brian's tone. What she said struck them as hilarious. They laughed and slapped their thighs.

Smiling, the woman leaned toward Brian. "You go Nan to die," she said.

TWENTY-FOUR

BRIAN SHARED AN EVENING MEAL WITH HIS CAPTORS, AN UNsavory looking concoction of meat and rice, before he helped to remove the camouflage from the trawler and push the boat a short distance down channel to the river. Within an hour, they were on their way.

The heat and quiet lulled Brian into somnolence. The river was brown and heavy with mud. The thought that he was going to meet his death seemed ludicrous. His fate would not be determined by this small guerrilla group. He was being taken to Nan on instructions the woman received on the shortwave radio.

Beyond Lampang, the Chao Prya joined the Nan River, and they passed through a cool, mountainous area heavily covered with forests of immense trees. here the river slid past as smoothly as green silk, breaking into coruscating drops wherever the trawler's screw broke the surface.

At one place a powerful elephant, guided by a *mahout* seated between its ears, was nudging huge logs to the edge of the river where workers branded them and tied them into rafts to float down with the current.

The mountains were succeeded by a sparsely inhabited landscape of sandy soil, obviously where little rain ever fell. The varied countryside dispelled Brian's lingering impression that Bangkok was downtown Thailand. The City of Bangkok was a glittering outstation, a prodigy, an anachronism dwelling in a world all its own.

On the morning of the third day, the trawler stopped at a wooden pier. The pier was old and in disrepair, with crumbling planks, and behind it was a two-story warehouse with a broken window on the second floor.

The only human being in sight was a wispy man fishing with his toes in the mud of the riverbank.

The trawler tied up at the pier. They disembarked and waited beside the warehouse. Brian's hands and face felt parboiled from exposure to the sun. He had not shaved in four days. The bandage on his throat was dirty and dry. He removed it. The woman barely glanced at his bruised throat.

Half an hour passed before a bus came, honking to announce its arrival as it rounded the corner of the warehouse. The driver leaned out the window to talk with the woman leader, while her companions kept Brian under tight scrutiny.

The woman signaled that they were to board the bus. Obviously this meant they were not going on to the harbor at Nan. They had stopped at this disused pier to avoid disembarking at the large port.

They all boarded the bus. The exterior was dust-stained, but the seats within were of solid teak and looked shiny new.

Unfortunately, the seats were designed for smaller passengers. Brian overflowed the divider to the adjoining seat, and after an hour he was sure the hard ridge had permanently indented his left buttock.

The bus was then traveling across what appeared to be a saucer-shaped plateau, following a route that could only have been laid out by a drunken camel. Yellow patches of flat earth were broken by gray sand and black rock. A fine layer of dust drifted in through the open bus windows, coating the shiny teak seats. While negotiating axle-breaking turns, the driver peered through the layer of obscuring dust on the windshield.

They passed through a hamlet where straggly chickens hunted and pecked between tree stumps. Young, barefoot women wearing flimsy shifts worked sullenly in the white glare of the sun, while naked brown children scampered on the dirt road. The driver leaned on his horn continually until they were safely beyond the hamlet.

After another barren stretch they came to a wooden countryside with several farmhouses. The hills in the distance were covered by a thick mist.

The bus turned on to a short paved road and jolted to a stop near a large farmhouse. Several men and women were clearing away shrub and piling waste into smoldering bonfires. The men wore work shirts and cut-off trousers. The women wore horizontally striped skirts, and their long hair was fashioned in knots on the sides of their heads.

Two soldiers emerged from the front door of the farmhouse. Each wore a khaki blouse and trousers and carried an automatic rifle. They came to the side of the bus, and the driver opened the door.

"Go," the woman ordered Brian.

Brian descended from the bus, but when the woman started to follow, a soldier presented his weapon as a barrier. Scowling, she retreated into the bus. Apparently she was not to have the honor of accompanying Brian.

The two soldiers escorted Brian to the farmhouse. They were greeted by a young monk who wore a robe girdled about his waist and draped over his bare shoulders. He indicated that they should follow him.

They passed through an open kitchen where a pot was warming on a charcoal fire, and then through an open doorway where he saw a bed with a mosquito netting that was drawn aside. The living room they entered was equally bare. A low, round teak table, a few rattan chairs, and a small statue of Buddha with a lone worshiper—a pink lizard that gave out with a throaty burble.

Nothing gave any indication that the owner of the farmhouse was wealthy, and the only connection with the military was the presence of two armed soldiers.

Brian wondered about the person the Hmong woman and her companions had brought him to see. They had undertaken an arduous river journey to bring him here.

Why?

The young monk led the way down a corridor with plastered walls that led to a high door set into a wall. It was painted as white as the plaster wall, but made of metal, perhaps steel, and confronted them like a blank stare of suspicion.

The monk placed the palm of his hand flat against the left side of the door.

The door opened, and the monk preceded them into the room. Brian looked about him. One wall was covered with a sumptuous drapery depicting a battle scene in which a warrior in resplendent costume was leading his troops. The facing wall was lined with an opulent silk hanging of a fire-tongued dragon.

Directly ahead, across the wide, carpeted area, a man was seated at a long table eating with chopsticks from a silver bowl.

He wore an embroidered red kimono; a black tiara of hair circled his head, and a large ornamental comb was set in it.

The windows behind him were slitted steel embrasures through which shafts of sunlight cut like white knives.

He continued to eat, using his chopsticks with delicate precision.

After a moment the young monk said shyly, "Lord Wanchai."

Wanchai put down his chopsticks and turned to look at them. He waved a languid hand at the young monk, who bowed deeply and backed away. Another gesture brought Brian forward. The two soldiers stationed themselves slightly behind Brian, their automatic rifles at the ready.

Wanchai had a strong, angular face with a nose as cruelly hooked as a falcon's. His voice was deep and had an upper-class British accent: "I know who you are and why you are here. If you lie, you will be punished."

"I have no intention of lying," Brian answered.

Wanchai held him in a steady gaze. Brian felt a strong urge to blink, but did not. He had a childish notion that this was a contest in which he could not afford to show even the most trivial weakness.

"Then you may begin your confession."

"I have nothing to confess."

Wanchai's thick, dark eyebrows rose. "I advise you not to persist in a deception that is already exposed. You are an American intelligence officer who came here to spy on my military preparations."

There seemed to be a total lack of any military preparations worth spying on. No encampment with barracks and fortifications, no airfield or planes. Brian did not think it wise or politic to remark on this.

"Your mission has failed," Wanchai said. "It is no shame now to try to save your life."

"I have no quarrel with you, and I wasn't coming here as a spy. I had a personal reason."

"What reason?"

"There is a woman here. I have some important questions to ask her. She is the only one who knows the answers."

"What is this woman's name?"

"Ellen Peterson."

Wanchai's face was as impassive as though fashioned by an ivory carver.

Brian said, "If you allow me to speak to her, you have my word that I will not tell anyone about my visit here."

Wanchai answered with heavy irony, "Perhaps you do not clearly understand your position. You have no reason to expect to leave here alive."

The thought that death might be imminent was not quite as ludicrous to Brian as it had seemed a short time ago.

The young monk entered, approached Wanchai, and, at a respectful distance, bowed deeply. Without raising his shaved head, he delivered a singsong message.

Wanchai pushed back his chair and rose. He was a tall man, about six feet, and the kimono he wore did not conceal the breadth of his chest or his powerful shoulders.

Wanchai said, "Government planes are approaching. Since you came here to spy, it should interest you to see how we defend ourselves."

Wanchai strode to another door in the room, opened it, and descended a wide stone staircase. Brian followed, with the two soldiers directly behind him.

The stairs led down to a large basement with stone walls. An air-raid shelter, Brain guessed, although it would be flimsy protection. A single, powerful, aerial bomb would reduce Wanchai's headquarters to rubble.

At the far end of the basement was an open doorway, and with no appearance of urgency Wanchai entered it. Brian followed him onto a wide viewing platform forty feet above an immense area where men and women were working at scores of desks, each with its own computer.

Wanchai said, "This is our administrative area. Beyond it are conference rooms, storage rooms, and sleeping quarters for personnel."

Brian was impressed. "How many work here?"

"Over a thousand."

More than in Hitler's vast underground bunker in Berlin. There must be corridors traversing north to south and west to east into other areas. This was a fortress, crouching underground like an armadillo with a protective covering of bony plates.

An open passage from the viewing platform led into a short hallway. They entered a room that was like a private study in an elegant home, with indirect lighting, upholstered chairs, a television set on a swivel table, and walls lined with books. Most of the books dealt with military strategy and tactics.

When the door closed, the quiet was so profound that the walls must have been cork-lined.

Wanchai said, "If you are wondering if I am armed, I am. And guards are just outside the door. It would be most foolhardy of you to attempt anything."

"I wasn't planning to."

Wanchai sat in a lounge chair and pressed a remote control device. The television screen lit up to show the main road outside the farmhouse. A farmer was driving a pair of oxen yoked to a cart.

The screen image tilted upward to a sky smudged with black dots. A distant crackling of explosions could be heard. Antiaircraft batteries were hidden in the forest.

Two tiny planes kept coming.

"Your gunners don't seem very effective," Brian remarked, watching the steadily approaching planes.

"We have no wish to shoot them down. We want them to return and file their reports. It would appear suspicious if we did not offer some resistance."

If they drop their bombs here, Brian thought, I hope I live long enough to dance a jig on your grave.

"What will happen?" he asked.

"They will pay no attention to our farmhouse. In a short while, they will fly to an airfield not far from here, where they will strafe planes on the ground and bomb the hangars. On their return to their home base, the pilots will receive the Honorable Order of Rama for bravery in combat."

"Letting planes and hangars be destroyed is a pretty expensive proposition."

The merest trace of amusement showed on the carved ivory features. "Perhaps you have read how the British in the Second World War deceived the Germans."

Brian knew what Wanchai referred to. To confuse the Germans about where the Allied forces planned to open a second front, the British had established an entire army base with barracks and construction vehicles and airfields. The barracks had no floors, no foundations, nothing inside. The vehicles were rusting and useless, the flimsy plywood planes were roped to the ground and camouflaged. From the air, however, the army base appeared convincing, and the Germans deduced that the Allied forces intended to strike at Calais across the channel. The real attack at Normandy caught them unprepared.

To Brian, Wanchai seemed to be leaving out an important

point. If the Allies had not been planning an invasion elsewhere, the deception would have accomplished nothing.

On the television screen, the planes were no longer coming. They had turned aside to bomb the forest where the antiaircraft batteries were concealed, but they were flying too high for the bombing to be effective.

Suddenly one plane veered off from the other and began a steep dive. For a few moments it seemed as though an invisible force was pulling it downward from a sky where everything else remained motionless.

The plane was diving toward the deeply rutted main road.

The farmer riding the oxcart heard the plane approaching. He pushed back his wide-brimmed straw hat to search for it. Then he began to lash his oxen. The slow-paced beasts, unaware of danger, did not hurry over the washboard ridges. They plodded on.

The farmer looked back nervously at the rapidly descending plane. At the last moment he leapt from the cart and flung himself into a shallow ditch bordering the road.

The ground erupted in narrow geysers of dirt, and the cart exploded into flying pieces of debris. The stolid oxen began spurting blood and sank slowly to their knees before keeling over inside the traces.

The plane zoomed sharply skyward.

The farmer did not emerge from his shallow shelter.

Brian felt sickened. "What was the point of that?"

Wanchai shrugged. "Target practice."

RELUCTANTLY WANCHAI TURNED THE AMERICAN OVER TO HIS persuaders. He gave orders that there was to be a brief waiting period in which the American would have an opportunity to change his mind. This was in accord with Buddhist justice, which allows a person to meditate on evil deeds before a sentence is carried out.

Vajir answered his summons, and Wanchai told the young monk what he wanted.

As Vajir began the preparations, Wanchai composed a suitable poem for the ceremony.

> Over the spirit lamp
> How softly, palely the drops swell and bubble
> Carry it to the bowl

Tip the bowl to the flame
Ah, Opium!

The stem of the pipe at his lips, he drew the white smoke into his lungs. The effects rushed in upon him until he drifted in somnolent joy and became one with his ancestors. He immersed his soul in their wisdom.

A vigorous knocking at the door roused him from his dreaming. He felt momentarily disoriented. Who dared to interrupt him so rudely?

Subduing anger he rose with leisured movements and went to the door.

A bare-chested, muscular Malay in tight-fitting cut-off jeans bowed and *wai*'ed.

"Forgive me, Lord Wanchai. You left orders to be told when Boonsong's time is near."

"I will come."

Boonsong no longer resembled the proud, lovely woman she once had been. She drooped from shackles attached to pulleys in the ceiling that bound her wrists. Her dress was a soaked, twisted garment that clung to her ravaged body.

"I have kept her alive as long as possible, Great Lord."

"Is she conscious?"

"Not fully, Great Lord. Death is near."

"I wish to be alone with her."

The Malay *wai*'ed and bowed out of the room.

"Boonsong."

Her head had fallen forward on her neck like the head of a turtle. She did not respond at first, then her head lifted slightly.

"My agent is already on his way to Kuala Lumpur. You might have spared yourself. I hope your suffering will make you wiser in your next life."

Her mouth opened, drooling blood.

"There is no joy for the soul without despair," he intoned. "No liberty for the soul without imprisonment. No rebirth for the soul without death."

She made no reply. The Malay torturer had robbed him of the pleasure of hearing her voice. Her tongue had been torn out.

Her body underwent a convulsion that was fascinating and terrible to see. As he watched, he felt a strong, erotic compulsion.

He stripped off his kimono and underclothing and stood naked before her. She was writhing in her death agony when he ripped down the front of her dress. A full breast appeared. He held its plump softness and squeezed tenderly.

Her vacant eyes turned in their sockets. She had the merest remnant of life. This was the last possible moment to send her into her next existence with a gift of love.

She did not seem to be aware as he entered her. His body arched as he drove hard. As her death rattle began, he experienced with her the spasm of final release.

"Sawat dee khrop," he whispered.

Were those tears of gratitude in her blank eyes? He hoped so.

TWENTY-FIVE

BRIAN WAS ALONE IN A SMALL, WINDOWLESS ROOM. HE HAD been brought there by armed soldiers.

There was nothing in the room except a small, narrow cot placed against a far wall. A wan overhead light gave him a queer sensation of being displaced into an alternate reality where the things about to happen were commonplace.

Waiting itself was torture. There was nothing to think about except what they were going to do to him. He might stall for time, invent answers to questions, make up replies that seemed suitable, but in the end he would undoubtedly pay extra dividends in pain.

There was no way out, no way to stay alive or make a deal. Knowing nothing sealed his fate.

The most I can hope for, he thought, is to abandon hope. No blindfold, no last cigarette.

Too restless to stand still, he paced the room.

The door opened to admit a bare-chested, potbellied man in tight-fitting jeans. His shoulders and arms were so heavily muscled that they rippled with each movement, and each ripple in turn caused a further rippling in the dragons and snakes coiled in a rich demonology of color from his navel to his clavicle.

"My master, the Great Lord, wishes to know if you are now ready to confess."

Brian took a deep breath. "I don't have anything to tell anybody, except that I am not an intelligence agent."

The Malay moistened his lips and spat on the floor. He turned his back, revealing a new kaleidoscope of tattooed images as he left the room.

A short time passed before the door opened again. Wanchai entered with the Malay, while two armed soldiers waited outside.

Wanchai said, "I hope the message I was given is in error."

"I can't tell you what I don't know."

"I warn you, the Malay is an artist at his trade." Wanchai exuded a strong sense of power withheld, of innate reserves that his nature had not drawn upon. "You may find it instructive to meet someone as stubborn as you, and to see what the stubbornness accomplished."

The soldiers entered the room, and used their rifles to urge Brian ahead of them. They walked a short distance through the underground fortress.

The Malay opened a door and turned on the lights inside. Brian was assailed by nauseating odors of blood and body waste.

Boonsong was hanging by her shackled arms from pulleys in the ceiling. Her arms were unnaturally elongated because the shoulders and elbows had been pulled out of their sockets. Brian knew she was dead. There is a posture of death that the human body cannot easily duplicate.

"Do you recognize her?" Wanchai asked.

Brian was full of suppressed rage. "What did she do to deserve this?"

"She did not answer questions."

This is no time to lose control, Brian warned himself. Then the barrier of his self-control broke, and fury swept through like a tidal wave.

Without warning, he lunged and sent a soldier reeling. The other soldier was trying to level his gun when Brian hurtled into him, slamming the weapon back against his chest. His big arms clamped about the soldiers, hoisted him into the air, hurled him headfirst into the wall.

He whirled quickly, looking for Wanchai.

The Malay appeared in his path, his feet planted like a bull in an arena.

Brian charged at him.

The Malay stepped nimbly aside and chopped hard at the nape of Brian's neck. Brian felt as though he had been struck by an axe blade. He grunted, and drove his head into the Malay's chest. Dragons and snakes wheezed. Air rushed out of the Malay's lungs like a bellows collapsing.

Then another decapitating blow fell on the back of Brian's neck. Blackness momentarily closed off his vision. He was on his knees, blindly holding to the Malay's stout muscled leg, trying to pull himself up, when what felt like a grenade seemed to explode inside his skull.

He fell on his back, barely conscious, unable to move. He felt himself slipping away like a rolling coin wobbling off into darkness.

Wanchai said, "Such a foolish man. I expected better of him."

Brian slid into the abyss with that remark as his epitaph.

HE WAS IN A VAST DARK PLACE FULL OF ECHOES. I AM NOT DEAD, he told himself, because my head wouldn't hurt as much. He sat up with an effort and leaned his head back.

He was in his windowless cell. Why had they brought him back here? Why had they let him live? The Malay could have killed him with a good foot stamp on his throat while he lay helpless.

The only explanation was that Wanchai still hoped to get information from him. He was being saved for a session of torture with the Malay.

Brian had two separate reactions. The first, like a sharp lance in his vitals, was the certainty that since he had nothing to tell, he would end up as Boonsong did. The second was a surge of animalistic hatred so intense that he would willingly have accepted his fate just for the chance to kill Wanchai.

He heard a click, click, click, and a flat heavy slapping. Footsteps were approaching. A woman wearing high heels and a man wearing moccasins or slippers.

The ponderous door opened, and he caught a glimpse of the Malay outside. A glimpse was all he needed to trigger the hate reflex. He forced himself to his feet, swaying as he tried to focus his eyes.

A woman stepped out from behind the Malay.

"One hour," the Malay said. He stepped back to let her enter and then closed the door.

The woman wore a sampot and a loose-fitting blouse. Her skin was sun-burnished, and her small-breasted supple body was familiar.

So was the startling white lock of hair.

Brian blinked slowly, allowing time for the retinal image to fade.

The image did not fade.

"You make a very attractive ghost," he said.

She came closer. "I'm no ghost."

He ran his fingers through the dirty tangle of his hair. His fingers came away dark-stained with a blood clot. If the blood was real, so was she.

"Diane?"

She looked at his stained fingers. "My poor darling, what have they been doing to you?"

Ridiculous. Even in closeup he felt as if he were seeing her through a blurred lens. He could not accept what his eyes told him. This woman may be real, but she is not who she's pretending to be.

He said, "If you're Diane, prove it."

"How?"

"Where did we live?"

She smiled. "We lived in New York, in my apartment at 221 East Eighty-third Street. We both worked for the firm of Cochrane, Stevens, Elliot and Alkorn. I was born Diane Hochberg. Does that satisfy you?"

He had not believed the official story of how she died, but he had truly believed she was dead.

"I don't understand what's going on."

"I'll explain everything, my darling, but there's no time now. We have to get you out of this mess."

"Wanchai thinks I'm an American intelligence agent."

"Once he gets an idea into his head, nothing can change it. He's determined to find out what you know. That's why he let me come. I'm supposed to persuade you to talk."

"I don't have anything to tell."

"I suspect your being here has something to do with me. You couldn't have come at a better time. Now we're in it together."

"In what?"

"We're both going to get out of here."

He had barely convinced himself that Diane was alive. That was all he could manage for the moment in the way of accepting miracles.

"How?"

"I've bribed Wanchai's chief security officer."

"I won't let you put yourself in danger to save me."

"I'm not doing this just for you, my darling. It's for me, too. There are urgent reasons why I must get away. Trust me, and for now just accept what I tell you."

Speaking rapidly, keeping her voice low, she told him she had come to Khun Wanchai looking for his help.

"But everything is different. He's planning to start an invasion any day, and he needs money badly to pay for weapons and to pay his troops. He'll stop at nothing to get it. I saw what he did to Boonsong. No one is safe with him."

"I agree with that."

"I've got a plan to escape. Captain Wisarn will help us." She kissed him. "I'll be back soon, darling. Very soon."

She left, and the ponderous door closed.

As her footsteps dwindled in the corridor, Brian wondered if he would see her again. Everything that had happened was so incredible. He would not have been surprised to discover he was having an hallucination.

Meanwhile he had to deal with the situation as if it were real. Her plan would not work. It was beyond the scope of reasonable risk.

Suppose they actually managed to get out of the underground fortress. Even if it were possible to avoid pursuers, there was no place to hide in the desolate rugged terrain. Wanchai would hunt them down.

After awhile Brian heard the flat slapping sound of moccasined feet approaching the door. The Malay was returning too early. There was no way to explain why Diane had left.

He decided not to try to explain.

As soon as the Malay entered Brian drove into him. His hands went to the man's throat, squeezing thick flesh.

Abruptly, bewilderingly, Brian was rolling on the floor. As he started to get up, the Malay landed on him like an avalanche.

Brian worked a knee hard into the Malay's side, and brought a growl of angry surprise. He put his fist deep into the man's solar plexus and took his breath away.

Brian quickly got to his feet. The Malay was up, too, making do without breath for awhile. His brows were curved downward over eyes glittering with strange, wild exhilaration.

He performed a strange whirling dance, and his foot shot out to strike Brian heavily in the side. That part of his body instantly went numb. Brian charged into him, and the Malay caved backward under the heavy impact. At close quarters, they grappled, reeling together across the room, their bodies straining against each other.

Brian found another grip, his fingers almost met in the flesh of the man's throat. The Malay's mouth opened wide, slanting at an angle to reveal part of his lower jaw. His teeth were touch-ing at oddly matched sharp points like canine teeth.

A sudden cleaver of pain ripped through Brian's right shoul-der. It was as if his arm had been struck by a lightning bolt. The arm hung limp and useless.

The Malay was about to strike again when Brian swung hard with his good arm. The blow landed flush, and the Malay went spinning heavily into the wall.

He came off the wall quickly, shouting with fury. Then he paused, and his expression changed to indignant astonishment. A split second later all expression vanished in a red haze. He raised one hand tentatively to where his face had been before he slumped to his knees and toppled onto his side.

Diane and a slender, moustached man in uniform were in the doorway. The man was holding a gun from which a wisp of smoke curled.

Brian had not hard a shot, only a *humphing* noise. A silencer.

There was a small hole in the back of the Malay's head where the bullet had gone in. The uniformed man turned the Malay over. The center of his face was a crimson hollow.

"Is he dead?" Diane asked.

The uniformed man nodded.

"Good. You acted quickly." Diane turned to Brian. "I'm sorry I took longer than expected. But we're all set now. Come on."

He could tell from the clipped, dry phrasing how tense she was.

As they moved into the corridor, Diane said to Brian, "Don't forget. Act as though you're in Captain Wisarn's custody."

They made several turns along the curving corridor before they reached a grilled door with a sentry on guard behind it. Captain Wisarn spoke to him, and the sentry released the grille to let them through.

They reached the end of a tunnel before they were challenged again. This time the guard behind a locked gate did not seem satisfied with Captain Wisarn's explanation. He glanced at the identification papers Wisarn showed him, handed them back, turned on his heel, and went to a wall telephone.

Brian heard the *humphing* sound again.

The guard went down as if his legs were pulled out from under him. He lay beside the wall where he fell.

Wisarn put his gun muzzle against the gate lock and fired. The lock shattered, he opened the gate, and they went through.

Stairs led up to an underground courtyard, and the courtyard had an exit passageway. At the end of the passageway was another staircase leading up to a trapdoor. Wisarn pushed the trapdoor open.

They were in a barn. Bundles of hay completely circled and hid the trapdoor. They pushed the bundles aside.

Several oxen stood in their stalls, feeding, and one swung its head from the trough to look at them.

They slipped out the barn door into the night. The air was warm and an almost-full moon shone out from behind luminous clouds. The farmhouse was a hearing distance away.

A military jeep was parked on a side of the barn not visible from the house. Captain Wisarn was apparently careful about details like that.

Wisarn got behind the wheel of the jeep, and Diane, without hesitation, got in the front seat beside him.

Brian got in the back of the jeep. A tarpaulin covered the luggage carrier behind him.

Wisarn turned. "Weapons are under there. I hope we do not have to use them, but if . . . ?"

"I know how to use them," Brian said.

They took off across a field that led to the main road. In the moonlight someone was running at an angle to them, moving with surprising swiftness, his arms pumping like cylinders. Captain Wisarn swung the wheel hard over. The jeep veered toward the man, who stopped running. He tried to draw a weapon.

When the jeep crashed into him, he gave a high-pitched, terrible cry, like a horse in agony.

The jeep came to an abrupt halt and the motor cut off. Wisarn got the motor started again, but the wheels wouldn't turn. The man's body was blocking the jeep, his arms clasping a front wheel, his legs twitching. Brian saw that he wore a soldier's uniform.

He helped Wisarn to pull the body out of the way. It was like dragging a heavy bag full of loose bones.

Wisarn leapt back into the driver's seat, and the jeep started forward so violently that Brian barely got aboard.

At the end of the open field they turned onto the oxen-pounded dirt road. In places the ruts were two- or three-feet deep, and small stagnant ponds of water had collected inside them. They were riding without lights. Wisarn twisted and turned the jeep around rock outcroppings and fallen logs.

"It's only a few miles to the boat," Diane said.

"I didn't know there was water around here."

"An inlet from the river."

Despite his misgivings Brian was experiencing a feeling that Diane often created, a sense of being involved in something exciting with someone special. It was frightening and exhilarating, like a giddy ride on a rollercoaster that at any moment might leap the tracks.

They were passing a forested area when they saw lights above the trees, and heard the loud sonance of a helicopter engine. The helicopter came into view, its searchlight probing the woods.

Wisarn kept the jeep's gas pedal pushed to the floor and rode along the extreme left side of the road. The jeep bounced and leapt over ridges.

The searchlight swept ahead of them and, as though sensing something overlooked, quickly switched back.

The jeep was starkly outlined in blinding white light.

Brian ripped off the tarpaulin to disclose a few semiautomatic rifles and boxes of cartridges. He chose a rifle, checked it, and found it was loaded.

Balancing the semiautomatic on his left knee, he took careful aim at the glaring white eye. He pulled the trigger and held the weapon on rapid repeat.

The helicopter abruptly zoomed upward.

Wisarn turned the jeep sharply and raced for the woods.

He almost made it.

The jeep was traveling at high speed when the rough terrain curved up suddenly like the rump of an elephant. The front wheels veered in soft, deep-packed vegetation, and with a wrenching groan the jeep toppled, gave a last shudder, and lay still.

Brian and Diane scrambled out. Gasoline was spilling from the ruptured tank of the overturned jeep.

Wisarn was trying to pull himself free of the jeep. His leg was caught. Brian started toward him.

The rapid chattering of a machine gun winged the air with bullets. Brian grabbed Diane and pulled her down. They lay belly down while bullets ricocheted and caromed off nearby trees with a curious singing sound.

A furrow cut toward the overturned jeep. With a hushed rustle like a thousand candles being blown out at once, the lagoon of spilled gas went up.

Brian held Diane's head down as a searing hot flash passed

over them. The nearby trees exploded, their branches dripping fire. Small trickles of orange flame crept across the leaf-strewn ground.

In the midst of the conflagration Brian saw the jeep and a blackened, skeletal figure.

The helicopter hovered over the road. Its whirling blades were creating a fierce draft that sucked flames away from the woods and revealed a narrow tract of untouched trees like a dark roadway.

Brian got Diane to her feet, and they ran. Soon they were concealed in dark glossy foliage. Branches knotted overhead to shut out the moonlight.

"Captain Wisarn?" Diane asked.

He was grateful she had not seen.

"Never had a chance," he answered shortly.

They moved on through the woods. It was like being in a tunnel. The clangor of the helicopter circling the burning area gradually faded. There was a good chance the crew believed no one had escaped the flames.

They walked for almost an hour. Brian was starting to feel splinters of pain in his weakened leg.

"Is it much farther?"

She pointed. "It's right over there."

Through the trees he glimpsed water tipped with tiny white crests in the partial moonlight. A speedboat bobbed at anchor not far from the shore.

"Is there a pilot?" he asked.

"We'll have to do that part ourselves."

Her face was streaked with sweat and dirt, and she had never looked more beautiful.

THE SPEEDBOAT WAS A SPEEDING PROJECTILE, ROARING WITH unleashed power. Its headlight punctured the darkness.

At the wheel Brian concentrated on following the inlet's winding course, while Diane studied a map showing the route from the inlet to the Chao Prya. She measured a distance on the map with thumb and forefinger and checked the mileage per inch.

"About a hundred miles to Sakhut Sakhaen," she announced. "We should be there before daylight."

"After Sakhut Sakhaen, where next?"

"Kuala Lumpur."

"Where you've got a safe deposit box in a bank."

She glanced sharply at him. "How did you know?"

"It seems to be a popular place for having safe deposit boxes. Is it in the Bank of Bhumipitra?"

"You're full of surprises." Her voice had an edge of suspicion.

"I know that's where George Denison had his."

"Who told you that?"

"His wife, Boonsong. Did you know they were married?"

"I guessed it."

"We confirmed it."

"Would you like to tell me more?"

He told her everything that had happened since he arrived in Bangkok. She listened without interruption until he finished.

"Now you," he said. "I want to hear your side. From the beginning, and don't make a long story short."

They were speeding out of the inlet onto the river. Level fields stretched away monotonously toward shadowy hills.

"I don't know where to begin." She was silent for a few moments. "That safe deposit box in Kuala Lumpur. That's what it's all about. That's why I took the chances I did. It isn't a very pretty story, I'm afraid, but I'm not apologizing for it."

"How much is there in the safe deposit box?"

"More than you think." With a touch of pride she added, "Quite a lot more. I'm a rich, rich, lady, beyond my wildest dreams." She used the term mockingly, deriding the cliché even as she found it useful. "It's there under a pseudonym you'll appreciate. Mrs. Brian Thomas Boru."

"I don't suppose I should ask how it was acquired."

"From a lot of sources, none of which will bear scrutiny."

"Smuggling?"

"Everyone in Thailand is involved in that. It's part of the culture. Wanchai was my particular lucky charm. I sent him a letter by courier, enclosing some publicity about the H & D Company and asking if we could be helpful. He was rumored to have an eye for a pretty woman, so I sent along a photograph of myself, too. Sure enough, I got an invitation to visit and make a sales pitch. From then on Wanchai was a mighty valuable customer."

"With a payoff in drugs?"

"I knew nothing about that. That was strictly George and Ellen. They had a private deal. Modern weapons in exchange for the poison oozing out of all those pink and white poppies.

Ellen cooked the books to hide what was going on. It was irresponsible of me to trust them. I was careless."

"Mistakes usually have fingerprints on them. This doesn't look like one of yours."

"I've never cared for the nitty-gritty of bookkeeping. When I found out what they were up to, I threatened to expose them. I didn't realize I was putting my life in danger. They were in too deep."

"Did George Denison rig your car with dynamite?"

She nodded. "He would have succeeded in getting rid of me if it wasn't for one of those ironic turns. Ellen's car was in the garage because it failed to pass an emissions test. When I drove her to work that morning, she was in a very excitable state, quite sure we were all going to jail. And she was depressed and very angry at George."

"Why?"

"She had just learned about George and Boonsong. She had a spinster crush on George."

"So I heard."

"You do get around. That very afternoon she apparently decided to save her skin, and get even with George, by becoming a government witness. She was going to the Royal Palace to put herself under their protection. She took my car from the parking lot. She didn't know George had rigged it. He hadn't told her what he was going to do."

"After she was killed in the explosion, why didn't you go to the police?"

"I couldn't prove anything. And I had just found out my partner was trying to kill me." A slight shiver passed through her. "I also was in deep trouble with the Thai government. They weren't pleased by our arms deals with Wanchai. My best chance was just to get away."

"Disguised as Ellen?"

"A wig, no makeup, and dressed as plainly as she usually was. People tend to accept you're who you say you are."

"You came to Wanchai."

"There was no one else. I knew it wouldn't be long before he was the man in charge. Look what he's accomplished. Within a few years he's welded the seven major hill tribes and the guerrilla forces of the northeast region into an army. General Prapha, commanding the army of the south, is on his side. He's even got an agreement with the Republic of China. They persuaded the government of Laos to allow him to station his troops and build an airfield just inside their border.''

"Going to Wanchai didn't turn out to be such a good idea.''

"No, it didn't. But we're safe now." She rested her head on his shoulder. "I'm tired, and I'd rather not talk anymore. You know what I'd really like? To find some nice quite cove and put up anchor for awhile and make love." She lifted her face, full of wistful yearning, put her hand on his cheek and whispered, "I know I've hurt you, but that's all in the past. If you take me back you'll never be sorry. You don't know how much I regret—''

Brian drew in a sharp breath.

The searchlight prying into the darkness ahead picked up a hummocky line stretching from one river bank to the other. It resembled a row of submerged humpbacked whales.

He reacted quickly, wrenching the wheel and jamming on the brakes. There was an unpleasant shriek of metal. The speedboat yawed and careened, then sheered off and struck the obstacle broadside with a sound like thundering surf shattering against a barrier reef.

TWENTY-SIX

BRIAN WAS THROWN PARTWAY ACROSS THE WHEEL. DIANE WAS in the cockpit behind him, lying in water with one bare knee protruding.

She asked dazedly, "What was it?"

"Logs," Brian answered. The speepboat's side had cracked open and water was pouring in. "We're about to go under."

He lifted her to the gunwale now only a few inches above water, pushed her over, then slipped over the side after her.

The boat made a gargling plunge; its searchlight glowed eerily underwater for a moment before going dark.

They swam a few strokes, and Brian grabbed hold of a huge log lashed to others behind it. He climbed onto the log, and pulled Diane up to join him.

He filled his chest with a deep, painful inhalation. "What the hell is a log raft doing in the middle of the river?"

"It's how they ship teak. Cheap transport. They tie big logs together and float them downriver."

"This one is anchored."

A woman's voice called from shore, "You come this way."

After a moment Brian said, "I know who that is. I'm afraid we've underestimated Khun Wanchal."

They eased into the water and swam slowly toward shore.

DAYLIGHT ARRIVED WITHIN THE HOUR, TINTING THE SKY OCHER and streaking the river with warm red glints. Brian and Diane sat with their backs against a tree trunk.

Tribesmen squatted in an irregular semicircle near them. With curved fingers they were scooping up squashy food from their bowls.

Brian and Diane kept their hands clasped behind their necks as they had been ordered to do. A blue swarm of mosquitos tormented them.

She said, "As a young girl I always wanted to visit distant, romantic places like this. One of my favorite games was to spin a globe of the world and stop it with a finger. 'Here. This is where I'll go next.' Then I'd go to the library and read all I could find out about the place. *Damn*. Another one just bit me."

"Are they talking about us?" Brian asked.

The semicircle of tribesmen was conversing animatedly with gestures.

"I'm sure they are, but it's a patois I don't understand."

Brian said loudly, "Hey! We're thirsty!"

No one in the semicircle turned to look at him. They were too intent on their talking.

"Well, they're not paying much attention to us. We can speak freely."

Diane said, "I'd like to take my hands down before gangrene sets in."

"I'll try first."

He unclasped his hands from behind his neck and slowly lowered them. No one noticed.

Diane lowered her hands also.

"What makes you think Wanchai is behind this?" she asked in a low tone.

"I had a run-in with this same bunch. They brought me to Wanchai. They keep in touch with his headquarters by short-wave radio."

"Then we didn't just have an unlucky accident."

"No. They were expecting us."

She looked thoughtful. "Any chance we can get away?"

"I'm open to suggestions."

"Fresh out. I can't stand these mosquitos. If there's nothing else to do, I might as well try to nap."

She was dozing when he first heard the deep binaural sound of powerful diesel engines. Diane sat up at once, almost as though she had been waiting for a signal.

A stir of excitment set the tribesmen in motion. One ran down to the shore and stood there, gesticulating wildly.

A long, sleek yacht came into view on the river. Sailors were on the foredeck, and an unfamiliar flag was flying from its mast.

"That flag isn't from any country I know," Brian said.

"Siamese. That's his dream. Back to the days of glory."

"Wanchai?"

She nodded. "He intends to be the first absolute monarch of a new and greater Siam."

"I admire a man with ambition."

"That's his yacht. He calls it the *Prince Bowaradet*, after his grandfather."

The yacht had a large steel hull and a medium-sized super-structure. Sailors dropped anchor at midriver. A crewman with a hailer called out a message to the shore.

"Did you get what he said?" Brian asked.

Diane had fallen into a reverie. He had to repeat the question before, with a start, she came to.

"Wanchai is on board," she said. "They're lowering a boat for us."

"Wanchai in person? What an honor." Brian forced a smile. "If it wasn't for the honor of the thing I'd just as soon pass it up."

She squeezed his hand. "Look, I think I can handle him. Let me do the talking. Trust me."

He nodded, admiring her spirit. "I have no choice. I'd like to make being alive become a habit."

She must be aware that Wanchai would not be charitable, having lost several men and an expensive speedboat during their attempt to escape.

A small dinghy neared the shore, manned by two sailors. One sailor was carrying a machine pistol at chest level.

The dinghy stopped in shallow water. The woman guerrilla leader waded out with Brian and Diane.

Brian helped Diane in, then clambered in himself. When the woman tried to follow, the sailor with the machine pistol blocked her way.

There was an angry exchange between the woman and the sailor. Finally she threw one leg over the gunwale. The sailor made a half-hearted attempt to stop her. She got in, and perched on a seat triumphantly.

The tribesmen pushed the dinghy into deeper water, and the small boat chugged to the yacht. They maneuvered alongside and Diane preceded Brain up the courtesy ladder.

On deck everything looked bright and tranquil in the sunlight. Khun Wanchai, wearing a white kimono, was seated in a canvas chair beneath a bright red and green parasol.

Diane walked directly toward him, her shoulders back, her lithe figure plainly outlined beneath her shapeless dress.

Her gaze remained fixed on him as she began to speak. She spoke in Thai although Wanchai had a perfect command of English. Brian thought she made the right decision. To speak in English would establish a distance, however small, between her and the warlord. Speaking Thai was a form of deference, and this was a very good time for deference.

He surveyed the situation. The sailor with the machine pistol had moved unobtrusively to a position from which he had a clear line of fire. The other sailor was keeping a watchful hostile eye on the woman guerrilla leader.

Two more sailors were on the deck above. They carried automatic weapons.

Wanchai, his face lanquered with boredom, was listening to Diane. The ornamental red comb sticking in his hair looked like the ruff of a horny rooster. When he answered, whatever he said caused Diane to clench her hands at her sides.

Wanchai turned to Brain. "She says you forced her to accompany you, against her wishes. Is that true?"

"Yes."

"I will hear your version."

Diane had not prepared him to invent a scenario.

"At first she tried to convince me to cooperate with you. I told her that I was not an American intelligence agent, so I couldn't do what you wanted."

"And then?"

"Your Malay came to get me."

"And you killed him. Where did you get the gun?"

"She had it. She'd brought it for protection."

"How did you get possession of the gun?"

Even a glance in Diane's direction might inform him how he was doing, but he couldn't risk it.

"When I heard the Malay coming, I overpowered her."

"And used her gun to kill him."

"Yes." He had the feeling of someone slowly sinking into quicksand.

"It was careless of him to let that happen. He was not usually so careless." Wanchai's gaze was drilling. "Why did you take her with you?"

"As a hostage."

"Did you take Captain Wisarn as a hostage also?"

"Yes."

"How did you arrange for the jeep?"

"I didn't. I happened to find it there." Brian realized this was unconvincing, and tried to change the emphasis. "I don't feel I did anything wrong. This is like wartime. A prisoner has a duty to try to escape."

Wanchai's ivory-carved face was remote and chill. "Captain Wisarn was bribed, and so was the man who was supposed to guard my speedboat. Both have now departed this earth, and so cannot testify to the truth." He turned toward Diane who had said nothing throughout the brief interrogation of Brian. "This is my decision. I know you have a considerable treasure stored away. If you tell me where to find it, and I am satisfied with the amount, I will spare your life."

Diane's only answer was an almost imperceptible shake of her head. "There is no treasure."

"You acquired most of it from profitable dealings with me. It will be better for you to speak now. We are well-trained in the art of extracting information. You are not equally disciplined to resist."

"You know I would not lie to you."

Wanchai arched an eyebrow. "Perhaps you do not think I am serious. I will demonstrate how serious I am."

Wanchai gave a command. Brian was watching Diane, whose stunned expression was all the clue he needed about what was going to happen.

The sailor with the machine pistol bowed to Wanchai, and moved close to Brian. He positioned his weapon directly against Brian's head.

Wanchai raised his hand. "When I lower my hand, it will be the signal to fire," he said to Diane. "At this close range that weapon will literally cause his head to explode. Will you watch?"

Diane was looking at Brian with an expression of pure anguish. Brian's sphincter muscles tightened, and his mind became a blank, beyond fear.

"Do not delay," Wanchai warned. "Or you will discover your mistake too late."

"Great Lord, I cannot believe—"

The sailor's attention was fixed on Wanchai's hand, awaiting the signal. Brian made his move. He lunged forward and seized the machine pistol.

The sailor pulled the trigger, but the deadly hail of lead swerved past Brian. Across the way a sailor fell, bright red spouting from his body like water from a riddled garden hose.

Brian grabbed the sailor with the machine pistol and pulled him down. As they hit the deck and rolled, Brian seized the sailor's arm and wrenched it until the bone snapped. The machine pistol clattered to the deck.

Brian retrieved it and whirled, firing the machine pistol toward the two sailors on the upper deck. One gave the kind of wail a swimmer might make who was attacked by a shark. The curving stream of bullets had severed his leg. As he toppled over, the other sailor began firing.

The sailor with Brian had gotten up, reeling blindly in pain. The bullets thunked into his body, and his pain ceased.

Brian's machine pistol poured a leaden stream that passed like a scimitar blade across the sailor above. The man reared up, then crumpled like a sawdust figure over the railing.

Brian swung the machine pistol around to cover Wanchai, who was sitting immobile, his hand frozen in an upright position. The massacre had taken only seconds.

"Try something foolish," Brian said.

Wanchai lowered his hand. "Nothing was further from my mind."

Diane screamed, *"Look out!"*

Without thinking, Brian flung himself down. Something hissed close by him. A ship's officer was standing in the companionway holding the pistol he had just fired.

Brian fired back. The officer's pistol wavered and he turned partly round as if he intended to go back for something he had forgotten. Then he folded up at the joints like a beach chair and disappeared down the companionway.

Wanchai kept both his hands in full view on the arms of his canvas chair.

Brian got up, his weapon fixed on Wanchai.

"If someone else shows up, you go first."

"You are in command. Tell me what you want."

"We're taking over your ship."

"I assumed that. You understand that we're under-staffed at the moment. We ordinarily have a crew of six and the captain."

"Where's the captain?"

"At the bottom of the companionway. You killed him a moment ago."

"Where are the others?"

"A lovely young woman named Deva is probably hiding in her cabin, quite terrified. The cook is undoubtedly under a table in the kitchen. There are two crew members unaccounted for. I'm afraid that is all."

Diane said, "That's enough to run the ship."

"I disagree. Handling a yacht with two sixteen-cylinder engines generating 5000 horsepower, and with a fuel capacity of 1500 gallons, is not a job for amateurs. I know nothing about it. Neither does the cook, and certainly not Deva, who is only fifteen years old and not in the least nautical."

Something flew swiftly out of the blinding sunshine. A flying stick. A pencil line drawn between the ship and sky.

It found a target. Diane looked amazed at the slender wooden shaft protruding from her arm just above the elbow.

The woman guerrilla leader on the upper deck broke into a run. She reached the railing and leapt over.

"*Goddamn!*" Diane said.

She picked up an automatic weapon and ran to the lower deck railing. She pointed the weapon down at the water and fired a long burst.

Brian went to Diane's side. The woman's body floated away from the side of the yacht, face down within a circle of crimson water.

Brian tore away Diane's sleeve to examine her arm. The wooden silver seemed joined indissolubly to her flesh.

"It hurts," Diane said, wincing as he tugged at it.

"I have to pull it out. Keep Wanchai covered."

She bit hard on her lower lip. "Please hurry."

He took a firm hold and with a strong twist pulled the dart free. Diane gave a small gasp. A little blood oozed from a hole in her arm, and a brownish pink circle had formed around it.

Wanchai sat, unmoving, as self-contained as an egg. He watched with a slight frown as Brian led Diane back to him.

Breaker said, "You have medical supplies on board. Where are they?"

"The infirmary is down one deck and to the right. The door may be locked."

Brian told Diane. "If he moves, shoot him."

The door to the infirmary was locked. Brian rammed his shoulder into the door, and it opened. In the cramped, closetlike space, he found antiseptic and bandages and a small medical scissors.

When he returned Diane still had her gun pointed at Wanchai in his chair. She was looking very pale.

Brian was shocked at how the reddish circle on her arm had spread. He used the medical scissors to widen the wound so it would bleed freely. He put his mouth to the wound and sucked until he filled his mouth with blood, then spat it out. He felt her trembling.

Her voice was faint. "Is it . . . poison?"

Brian turned to Wanchai. A new alertness had entered the warlord's posture.

Wanchai shrugged. "Probably. The natives use a poisonous substance similiar to curare on their arrows."

Curare attacked the central nervous system. If a similar poison was in Diane's bloodstream, it would be fatal. The only cure was to suck out enough of the poison.

He pressed his lips to her skin again and sucked in more blood. Suck in. Spit out.

Too little blood was coming.

She said, "I'm dizzy. You'd better take this." She offered him the gun she was holding.

He ignored her. Suck in. Spit out. Her skin had a cool, wet, soft feeling.

"Let . . . me . . . lie down."

He lowered her gently to the deck. Her breath was tremulous, and her face was moist. Her hand moved spasmodically, and the gun slid out of her loosening fingers.

"Dear God . . . don't . . . let me die."

He took her wrists and rubbed them vigorously. She was making mumbling sounds, and not until he learned closer did the the faint sounds become words.

"I'm going . . . to miss . . . my . . . lovely animal. . . ."

After that her lips moved, but no sounds came.

A shadow fell across him. He looked up blankly at Wanchai, who was holding the semiautomatic and pointing it at him.

"You can do nothing for her now," Wanchai said.

An icicle penetrated Brian's heart. Diane seemed to have

shrunken; she really was quite a small woman. She had seemed so much larger in life.

He held her close.

He said to Wanchai, "Go ahead. This is as good a time for me to die as any."

TWENTY-SEVEN

THE DECK HAD BEEN SWABBED OF THE EVIDENCE OF RECENT slaughter. No blood, no suffering, no death.

The yacht's gentle rocking motion caused a slight lapping of water at its sides.

"Why didn't you kill me?" Brian asked.

He was standing before Wanchai on the deck. Wanchai was seated in his canvas chair beneath the red and green parasol.

In the heat of the sun Brian felt drained of both hope and memory. His hands were chained behind his back, and his leg was hurting badly from the strains he had put on it. It was difficult to keep standing. He was gripped in shock, not even aware of how much time had passed since Diane was taken away.

"You have put me to a great deal of trouble." Wanchai spoke as calmly as if he were discussing the weather. "You deserve death, but I am willing to let you live if you help me to find the money your wife has hidden away."

Brian shook his head.

"You must know where it is. You were her confidant. Please consider carefully. I am presenting you with a clear choice. If you are dead the money will be of no possible use to you."

To his own surprise, Brian heard himself ask, "If I tell you, will you let me go free?"

"Of course. I will have no further interest in you."

"How do I know you'll keep your bargain?" He had no illusion that Wanchai would.

"You have no alternative except to trust me."

Brian said, "The fact is, I don't trust you."

241

Wanchai looked reflective. "Do you have a better suggestion?"

"Let me go as soon as I tell you where the money is."

"That is not a serious proposal. Before I knew whether you had told the truth, you would be out of my hands."

"Maybe you can improve on the idea."

"I will send someone for the money. As soon as I am informed they have it, you will be at liberty."

"What protection would I have? I'd still be around after I'm no further use to you."

"We appear to be deadlocked."

Brian had been in a drowning mood, but now he saw a shaft of sunlight turning the water pale green above him.

He struggled upward toward it. "I'm willing to go with your men to get the money. But I won't tell them what they need to know until we get there."

"That is not practical. We will need to make arrangements before you leave."

"What kind of arrangements?"

"If the money is in a bank, we will need a facsimile of your wife's signature and a letter confirming that she appeared before a magistrate with her lawyer to authorize you to withdraw funds. These will have to be forged. We will also need an accompanying letter from the lawyer. These details can be arranged, but they will take time."

"I'm in no hurry. Let's do this thing right."

"You must at least tell me where the bank is located, if it is in a bank."

Brian thought about that for a few moments before he replied: "Kuala Lumpur. And that's all you'll get. I won't tell you the bank or the name the account is under."

"I will make the necessary arrangements. To save time someone will meet you at Klang—about an hour from Kuala Lumpur. This person will supply the documents you need."

"That sounds all right."

"You will travel by boat across the Gulf of Siam. Two of my men will go with you. They are both very capable. If you default on our agreement, your life is the forfeit."

Brian nodded.

"You will leave early in the morning. Until then you are a guest on my yacht. Under guard."

* * *

IT TOOK SEVERAL HOURS FOR WANCHAI TO COMPLETE THE NECessary preparations. He met with the replacements for the lost members of his crew and with two men who received special instructions. One man was short and muscular, the other big, quiet, and purposeful.

Wanchai had chosen them to accompany the American on the trip to Kuala Lumpur. No instruction was needed for a return trip. The American was not going to return.

Wanchai had been arriving at a new equation in his mind, subtracting one thing, adding another, and he was no longer sure that the American was an intelligence officer. Measuring him, he did not fit the role; there were no secrets hidden behind his eyes.

Nevertheless recent events showed he could be dangerous. Far wiser to negate the danger, and to gain control of the fortune to which the American now had the only access. That money would expedite a shipment of M-60 tanks now being withheld by arms merchants in Singapore. They would be needed for the offensive at the end of the monsoon season.

A native Hmong woman came on board to remind him of the ceremony about to take place. The bodies of those killed in the battle on the yacht were to be consumed together. She requested that the place of honor on the pyre be given to their leader. From shore they had seen what happened. Their leader had caused the death of the *fahrang* woman and so deserved the honor.

Wanchai agreed. "Your people will be well regarded for the courage your leader showed."

"Will you attend the ceremony?" she asked in her barbarous patois.

"I shall watch from here."

She backed out of his presence, making small bows of appreciation.

A tumultuous day was coming to an end, one that would remain marked forever on the calendar of his mind. In the eyes of Buddha, time is an unbroken flow, and we only deceive ourselves by cutting it up into segments. All is part of an inexorable plan. Days, nights, weeks, months, years are meaningless designations; time has no beginning and no end. In our perception, an hour can be longer than a day, a day longer than a year, and a year longer than a lifetime. One must be patient, and let time devour itself like a snake eating its tail. Everything must proceed as written; nothing can be singled out or divided.

Very soon I will achieve victory and sit on the throne of Siam, as I was meant to do from the beginning. It will be a time for rejoicing throughout Greater Siam, for I am the *Naga*, come to reclaim my heritage.

Later, from the large picture window of his stateroom, he observed the funeral pyre like a vivid red fabric hanging against a backdrop of green jungle growth. The color turned gradually to pulsating orange and then to intense white.

In the heart of the blazing pyre dark oblong shapes were arrayed on a platform. In the center, raised on a smaller platform above the others, was another oblong shape.

The pyre began collapsing in separate pools of flame, vanishing in smoke that faded into a stain against the twilight sky. Death was flying upward through the air.

He thought of Diane and felt a slight tingling in his skin. Life is a little sad, a little strange, and the wise man must learn to be ready for any fate.

Deva served his dinner. He had little appetite; the sanguinary events of the day had sated him. He sampled a small portion of shrimp soup with mushrooms and scallions laced with red pepper, scarcely touched a salad of minced chicken with mint leaves and lime juice, toyed with sates of pork broiled in yellow curry. Finally he ordered Deva to remove the dinner tray.

Watching her slender figure and graceful hands as she stacked dishes on the tray, his interest stirred. He ordered her to return, and drank tea while she began her ministrations. She was young and unskilled, her mouth as untalented as her hands. He soon became impatient and sent her away. She would cry through the night, and perhaps in the morning she would seek the counsel of older, more experienced women.

He brought out the hookah and the opium-making equipment. The small sand-colored grains of powder wrapped in tinfoil soon caused a chemical change in a deep hidden core of his body, inducing pleasant repose, a sweet bondage to his visions.

He was one with Buddha sitting beneath the Bo tree.

He was *Naga*.

There was hardly enough light in the room to perceive his shadow on the wall. Idly he watched the very last reflections of the crimson sun cast upward into a dark blue sky. A band of thick clouds extended to a great height.

Before midnight, the hour of the tiger, winds converged at low levels, and a heavy mass of twisting humid air began rotating slowly on its way to the Gulf of Siam. Its development could be watched with accuracy, but nothing could alter its course.

All is written.

THEY HAD BEEN UNDERWAY FOR TWO HOURS WHEN THE SKY turned dark. The launch was buffeted by wind-driven waves, each larger than the one before.

The powerful launch fought the stormy gulf, its prow lifting surprisingly high, the tarpaulin aft bellying and flattening with loud flapping noises.

Brian was inside the cabin with two men. The short, stocky man was checking map references, and the large, quiet, purposeful man was at the wheel. Both wore gunbelts. Brian had no doubt they knew how to use their guns.

There was little likelihood they would need to. His wrists were securely tied behind him and his ankles were bound. He sat in the port side of the cabin on a narrow bench beneath which gear was stored.

From time to time, at very brief intervals, one of the men turned to look at him. He was helpless, but they were not the kind who took anything for granted.

Trying to forget the terrible recent events, Brian made a deliberate attempt to fill his mind with pleasant thought: walking with Diane through Central Park in autumn with the brown leaves deep and glorious on the path, watching her show off at parties, visiting museums with her, attending Broadway plays, dining at one of the restaurants that she favored. His mind rattled on, making random connections with happier times.

A sudden, odd query was actually a prompting from his subconscious: did he trust her? No. He had always distrusted her; that was his only defense against her ability to manipulate and control. If people are a mixture of good and bad, how can we avoid ambivalence?

A new thought struck him with stunning simplicity and force. Denison said he saw Diane crossing to the parking lot to get her car to drive to the Royal Palace. That was a lie. It was Ellen Peterson. Therefore he must have known Diane was still alive.

She had to leave Bangkok because the threat of arrest was too great, and so was the danger that Denison would try again to kill her.

The cabin windows on the launch lit up with startling brightness, then the whole sky flared with lightning.

There was a clear solution to her problems, and that was why she did not leave Bangkok for two days after the bombing. Denison was not murdered by Wanchai's agents. That was not how it happened.

A brutal, boisterous squall hit them head-on.

The launch veered sharply under the impact of pounding wind and rain. The window behind Brian cracked. He kept his head low, almost between his knees, and hunched his shoulders as fragments of glass blew in.

Whatever her original plan, it changed to a crime of opportunity when she returned to the office and found Denison unconscious. It would have been easy to take his gun and stand close enough to put a bullet through his head. A fitting revenge on the man who had tried to kill her.

Could she have done it?

Suddenly Brian remembered what Denison had told him. The partnership agreement called for the surviving partner to get everything. With Ellen and George out of the way, all the money would have been hers.

Yes, she could have done it.

The short man came over to nail a square of oilcloth in place over the broken window, then hammered in several wooden slats behind it as support. A makeshift solution that would work for a time.

Brian sat up, soaking wet. He kept perfectly still, his hands behind his back. Even these two careful men could not foresee everything, he thought.

Rain came in a downpour, rattling the roof and the tarpaulin like volleys of buckshot. The cabin door sprang open and water gushed in. The short man forced the door closed and fell to bailing, gathering full buckets from the sloshing interior.

Neither the tall man wrestling with the helm nor the short man bailing had time to watch Brian.

Brian searched behind him with his fingers until he located a large piece of broken glass. Patiently, determinedly, he began to work on the leather binding on his wrists. He cut through the binding on one wrist, and began with his free hand to loosen the binding on the other.

The launch rode up to the crest of a mountainous wave, hung at the top, made a stomach-dropping plunge. As they wallowed in the trough, another giant wave raked the launch from stem to stern. Part of the cabin roof tore away.

Inside the cabin the three men were driven down beneath a

rowdy tumult of water. The tall man was clinging to the helm, and the short, stocky man was grappling for his lost bucket. Brian was on his knees beside the narrow bench he had been sitting on.

Shuddering, shaking herself like a half-drowned bitch, the launch staggered upward.

When Brian looked up, both men were watching him.

The short man abandoned his search for the bucket and started toward Brian.

The prow of the launch was wavering skyward at that moment, and the backward surge of water pulled the short man's legs from under him. He sat down on the bucket he'd been looking for and rolled off to the side, floundering. The effect was quite comical.

It also gave Brian the few seconds he needed to free his other hand and loosen the binding on this ankles.

The short man reached him, and slammed his fist hard against the side of Brian's jaw. Brian held on. The short man hit him again. Brian reached up, found the man's testicles, squeezed hard.

The short man doubled over. Brian hit him. The short man blubbered down into the water. Brian pulled off the binding on his ankles and stood up.

The gun he confronted was held in a remarkably steady hand, considering that the tall man's other hand was still gripping the wheel.

Brian was sure the tall man had no intention of killing him. If he was killed the whole purpose of the mission would be lost.

Fortified with this knowledge, Brian felt he could safely ignore the gun.

The bailing bucket rolled against his leg, and he swung it up to use as a weapon.

The tall man fired.

Brian felt a crashing blow on his temple. He dropped the bucket, lurched, almost lost his balance.

The tall man did not fire again. Perhaps he had not meant to kill, Brian thought. He might be a better marksman than I gave him credit for.

He dragged his feet toward the tall man, moving through a dark mist. His concentration was fixed but purposeless. He knew where he was going but no longer knew why.

The tall man turned the gun butt forward to strike. Just like Denison.

Brian used his forearm to block the powerful downthrust of the gun butt, then drove forward with bull-like strength to . . .

Not Denison.

Starbuck, the huge guard from Princeton who had stopped their running game all day. Goal line. Fourth down and a yard. He drove into Starbuck so hard, he lifted him off his feet. There was a sound of glass breaking. Starbuck dropped away, and he went over the goal line. Safe.

Far from safe. He was hanging halfway out of a broken cabin window.

His arm floated in the water a dozen feet away. It waved at him.

A face surfaced with a mouth frantically open and yelling. The wind roared the sound away.

A foaming, swirling wildness of green and white swept forward. The face disappeared, and so did the arm.

The wave drenched Brian, partly reviving him, but he had trouble focusing his eyes. His head blazed. He staggered to the helm and fought the wheel.

The launch slowly came around until the wind was behind it. No more water was pouring in. Brian throttled back and put the launch on automatic pilot.

He began to bail, using the bucket with a will. He fell into a rhythm, swinging down, filling up, hurling out. Long after his arms ached unbearably, he kept on.

Something slid into his leg. It was the short man, lying face down in the few remaining inches of water.

The tall man drowned in the sea, the short man in the boat.

Brian lifted the body to the rail, spoke a few words about consigning a soul to the deep, and pushed it over.

He found a map wrapped in oilskin in a compartment beside the helm. Steering with one hand, he set new coordinates. Toward Bangkok.

He had a terrible headache.

TWENTY-EIGHT

WHEN THE LAUNCH, NEARLY OUT OF FUEL AFTER ITS RETURN voyage, limped into the port at Sio-cha-kin, Brian was so weak he was barely able to walk. A worker at the rice mill helped him to a telephone. He did not call the police or a government official or the American Embassy. He called Arunee.

She brought him to the American hospital, listened to his incoherent rambling, and put it all together into an urgent message to the Prime Minister. Wanchai had considerably more men and armor than had been reported, including a number of advanced aircraft. He also had a secret agreement with China, and the support of General Prapha, commanding the Thai-Malay forces in the South.

The next morning, the doctor returned to examine Brian. The doctor and Arunee left the hospital room, and Brian heard them conversing in low tones in the corridor.

When Arunee returned, she was smiling. "The doctor says you are recovering nicely. He wants you to rest. The concussion will clear up in a week or so, and so will the double vision."

"I don't mind the double vision. I see two of you."

"You must be feeling better." She came to the bedside. "Horace Calisher and John Nixon arrived a while ago. They're waiting. Shall I tell them to go away, or will you see them?"

"Nixon first," he said.

Nixon came in as eagerly as a ferret. "Do you have anything to tell me?"

"About what?"

"You know. The money. Denison's. Your late wife's." Nixon sounded impatient. "What they owe the government."

"Forget Denison. Wanchai got that. But you might have a consolation prize. My wife kept her money in Kuala Lumpur. The Bank of Bhumipitra. I can tell you the name of the account, but I have no idea how much is involved."

Nixon said happily, "Write down all the particulars. The tax liability will have to be settled first, but if there's anything left over, the money might go to you as nearest of kin."

Nixon left, nodding and smiling, looking pleased.

Calisher came in next. His face had a gray hue, and his forehead was furrowed. "I have to talk to you alone."

"Arunee can hear anything you want to say."

Calisher said to her, "This is highly confidential. I can't speak freely with anyone else here."

"I'll wait outside," Arunee volunteered.

As soon as the door closed, Calisher said, "I owe you an apology. I thought you had something to do with Jean's death. I realize now I was wrong."

"I hope Colonel Suvit agrees."

"I'm sure he does. It seems clear that Wanchai's agents were responsible. I still find that hard to accept. After all, Wanchai is a grandson of Prince Bowaradet, and went to Eton and the Royal Academy."

"I suppose good breeding and background aren't everything."

Calisher studied him. "I suspect I'll never know the whole story of the part you've played in recent developments."

"I don't know what you mean."

"Several companies of soldiers from the Bangkok garrison have been confined to barracks and their weapons taken. Apparently an uprising in the city was supposed to accompany an invasion from the northeast by Wanchai's troops. A number of top rank naval officers are also under arrest. And General Prapha who commands the southern army is being relieved of his command."

"What makes you think I had anything to do with that?"

"I understand that the Prime Minister is acting on information supplied by you."

"I doubt that. He must have developed his own sources of information."

Calisher shrugged. "We've picked our side. The present regime has had bad press back home, but we don't have much choice.''

"It's not always easy to pick the white hats from the black hats.''

Calisher's eyes made a small sideways movement, as if looking for a way to evade putting his next question. "Did you ever find out why your wife was trying to bomb the Royal Palace?''

The truth was not only hard to believe, it didn't matter anymore.

"No, I never did.''

"Well.'' Calisher stood up, and reached into his breast pocket. "This arrived yesterday. It was addressed to you in care of the Embassy.''

Brian took the envelope. "Thanks.''

"Good luck. If there's ever anything I can do.''

Brian waited until Calisher was gone before he opened the envelope. The letter inside was from Tim and Nancy.

> *Dear Brian: Nancy and I don't have an address for you, so we're sending this to the Embassy in Bangkok with a copy to General Delivery.*
>
> *Yesterday we received a call from the hospital telling us that Martin had lapsed into a coma. He never recovered consciousness and died this morning. The doctor assures us that he suffered no pain. That is merciful, and we hope you'll see it in that light.*
>
> *Since you won't be here, we'll take care of what has to be done. Burial will be in your family plot. We've ordered a simple headstone. When you return we'll take you to visit his grave.*
>
> *Sometimes things happen for the best.*
>
> *Tim and Nancy*

Brian sat still, his heart beating hard. He felt a sharp tingling in his sinuses, a quick film in his tear ducts. Martin had been the last link to his childhood, to his father.

There was a startling interruption, a terrifying whooping noise like an air raid siren swelling, fading, swelling again. He got up, put a robe over his pajamas. In the hospital corridor, a number of frightened, bewildered people were milling around, patients, visitors, and staff. Someone was crying. A radio was blaring the national anthem.

Arunee fought her way to him through the crowd.

"What's going on?" Brian asked.

"It's begun. Khun Wanchai's invasion."

WANCHAI HAD WANTED TO WAIT UNTIL THE END OF THE MON-soon season, but his hand was forced by the actions of the Thai government, especially the order to General Prapha to turn over command of the southern army. General Prapha ignored the order, and they began the long-planned invasion at once, with Prapha coordinating his attack with Wanchai's.

The long period of waiting was over. It was as if a plane had been gliding along an interminable runway unable to get off the ground, and now with a single upward lunge, it was in the air. Wanchai had no doubt he would prevail.

Power, unquestioned power, was the ultimate freedom. He had lived within limits too long. Although his soul would have future incarnations, he was not content to let his present life end until his ambition was achieved.

If only my grandfather were still alive! Wanchai thought. A word of approval from Prince Bowaradet would mean more to him than paeans of praise from others. On his deathbed Bowaradet had prophesied, "You will carry out what is foreordained. It shall come to pass."

At last, the time had come.

Chiang Dao fell in the first hours of the assault. The badly mauled Thai forces in the northeast retreated to join the main body of the army.

In the south Prapha's army swept up from the peninsula. There was almost no opposition. Prapha's fervent Moslem fighters in-spired terror in the ranks of the irregular militia confronting them.

The two-pronged offensive became a giant pinchers move-ment. Town after town fell. Phrae fell. Utatadit fell. Nakhon Pathom fell. The Thai army's retreat became a rout. Soldiers fled, casting aside their weapons, stripping off their uniforms.

The Thai generals sent an elite regiment to stem the tide, moving the troops up the Chao Prya in naval vessels com-manded by officers loyal to the government.

The elite regiment held Wanchai's forces for two days of un-equal combat. Then they gave way, and the survivors joined the general retreat.

The next day the weather turned. Torrential monsoon rains

changed roads into quagmires and *klongs* overflowed, inundating the rice fields.

The invaders lost their advantage in mobility because artillery caissons sank to their hubcaps in mud; airplanes were grounded by runways two feet deep in water. M-48 tanks stalled in muddy terrain where M-60's would have rolled through.

The Thai army used the lull on the battlefront to reorganize and regroup. They attacked at Nakhon Pathom, now a drowning city where water had risen to the courtyard of the tall Buddhist pagoda. Monks gathered robes to their knees to wade out from the temple, and workers paddled boats and rubber rafts to their places of work.

Prapha's forces patrolled streets that were little more than deep reeking pools, with crabs and other aquatic life swimming underfoot.

When the government troops attacked, the invaders abandoned the city. They fled through brown waters choking with effluent from overflowing *klongs*.

The Thai army then counterattacked in full force, striking between the parallel prongs of the invading armies.

This was a critical moment. Wanchai and Prapha had been fighting simultaneously on separate fronts. Now their armies were in danger of being split off from each other.

Prapha ordered his army to pull back. His supply lines were overextended and his troops were exhausted. Morale was low after the rout at Nakhon Pathom; they had lost momentum, were fighting on unfamiliar terrain, and as Moslems they were among a hostile people who regarded them as infidels.

Wanchai countermanded Prapha's order for withdrawal and demanded a broad frontal assault in order to reach Bangkok as soon as possible.

Prapha obeyed. His army began an all-out attack without benefit of the artillery, tank and air support lost to the weather.

The Thai forces were driven back, fighting for every town, village and hamlet. At last the contending armies swayed and reeled in battle less than thirty miles from the capital.

The Thai forces held.

General Prapha isolated himself in his tent, wrote a letter of apology to Wanchai for having failed to carry out his orders, wrote messages to his family and close friends, then put his revolver into his mouth and pulled the trigger.

Wanchai assumed full command of Prapha's forces as well as his own. His combined armies drove forward to the outskirts of

Don Muang Airport, reaching the very spot at which his illustrious grandfather, Prince Bowaradet, and the Royal Army met final defeat.

There, the embattled government troops held again. The airport remained in their control.

Wanchai settled down to begin a siege.

Within Bangkok the supreme Buddhist religious leader, confronted by Moslem forces at the gates of the sacred temples, urged all loyal Buddhists to resist to the death.

The city garrisons responded, even those soldiers who had been confined to their barracks. To show their devotion, they spent a day cleaning the pagodas, using their shirts, towels, and underwear as dust rags. They shared rations with the monks and made offerings to the temple. Then they marched out to join the troops defending the city.

The United States Government announced that an airlift of military supplies would begin to aid the beleaguered city. A quiet warning was also given to the leaders of the People's Republic of China. When Wanchai pleaded for their help, silence was the only reply.

Thai government troops, bolstered by the supplies flown in from the U.S. base in Singapore, mounted a fierce counterattack. Wanchai's troops wavered, then began a slow retreat. The government troops pressed hard, and the retreat became disorderly.

On the twenty-sixth day of the invasion, Khun Wanchai's cause was clearly lost.

Wanchai's officers placed him under arrest. Unwilling to shed the blood of Prince Bowaradet's grandson, they carried out a sentence applied two centuries earlier to another royal victim. They tied Khun Wanchai into a bag of velvet and beat him to death with clubs.

Then they sued for peace.

TWENTY-NINE

SHORTLY AFTER THE INVASION BEGAN, THE HOSPITALS IN Bangkok and in many other cities were evacuated of all but the most critically ill patients. Hospital rooms and medical services were urgently needed for wounded soldiers sent back from the fighting front.

Brian was moved to a small hotel at Chonburi, south of Bangkok, an old frame building with connecting passageways and roofs of different heights. It was surrounded by acres of overgrown gardens with rusting fountains and a few bungalows in need of repair.

He spent his time reading and strolling through streets where oxcarts moved cheek-to-cheek with bicycle rickshaws. Automobiles and three-wheeled samlars were not to be seen, because their fuel had gone to war.

Arunee telephoned every day to tell him the latest news. The Bangkok telephone exchange had never been reliable, and now, with wartime pressures, it was whimsical. Her call might take two hours to be put through, but he didn't mind waiting, for the sound of her voice was a chime of joy.

A cycle of his life had ended with Diane. She had exerted such a magnetic hold that only now was he able to view her from a distance. The many memories they shared that now had no mind but his to inhabit, the tangled bonds of their conflicted and ambivalent relationship, were gradually unraveling. Looking back, he remembered most of all their slow drift into the big chill, the arctic time.

* * *

ON THE DAY AFTER KHUN WANCHAI'S ARMIES SURRENDERED, Arunee came to visit. In the slim sheath she wore, she resembled a lovely flower stalk.

They strolled together through the main street. Everyone was in a festive mood. The stores were filled with silks and lacquered parasols, pottery, and hammered silver. Portraits of King Rama and his lovely Queen Sirikit were displayed in every store window. They spent two hours in a small shop looking at umbrellas and glazed antique celadon ware, and the owner seemed more than willing to have them spend all day there.

"Thais have a different concept of time," Arunee explained. "We do not think of it as passing by. It is like a large, mysterious ocean in which interesting things are happening."

"That's a difficult idea for Americans to grasp."

Arunee smiled. "I used to think your people had a religious rite in which they worshiped clocks and calendars."

"HOW IS HARRY LOKMA?" BRIAN ASKED.

Arunee said, "He's starting a new campaign. He wants the King to dismiss the military government and call for democratic elections."

They wandered beyond the town and stopped near a big bamboo wheel turning steadily on the edge of a klong. The silence between them grew awkward.

She said, "You will be going home soon, to your own country."

"This is a country one can't leave except as a stranger. And I'm no longer a stranger."

She looked puzzled. "But you must go back."

"I can't."

"I do not understand."

Leaving was intolerable because it meant he would not see her again.

"I know what my life there would be like without you, and I don't want it. I think you care for me. I know I love you. Why can't we be together?"

She shook her head sadly. "You are not sufficiently aware of difficulties."

"If we love each other, there are none."

"My children."

"What about them?"

"They could not relate to . . . one who does not speak their language."

He smiled at the absurdity. "They speak English. They can teach me to speak Thai."

She hesitated, seeming to taste unsavory words before uttering them: "You are from a different land, a different culture. I am not suited to love you."

Brian said gently, "That wasn't a problem when you were married to Aelbert."

"Aelbert understood I could not be part of his world, and I never was. I am Thai. I shall live and die and, with the blessing of Buddha, be reborn a Thai."

Caught at a moment of uncertainty, he did not press the point. He was afraid that she might be trying to spare him from a greater hurt.

They returned to the street where cyclists were pedalling like wiry insects. Before they reached his hotel, she slipped her hand into his.

"I am not leaving Chonburi until tomorrow." A roselike stain appeared on her cheeks. "I am hoping that I may stay with you tonight."

SHE WAS BEAUTIFUL AND UNREAL IN THE MOONLIGHT GLOW that came through the vine-covered window. In his arms she was as light as a willow branch and as softly yielding. Her black hair tumbled about her oval face with its small straight nose and cupid's bow mouth partly hidden in shadow.

A ray of light caressed her slender bare shoulders, her tiny waist, her flat belly, and smooth-as-silk thighs. He reached for her in a zone of light and dark. She came to him willingly; he felt her warmth enclose him.

Her scent was like cherry blossoms.

IN THE MORNING HE READ THE NOTE SHE LEFT. HE WAS STANDING in his shorts near a rickety wooden bureau. He had seen the note a moment after discovering she was not there, and had put off reading it, shrinking from reading it.

My dearest, I am ashamed that I cannot tell you this in person but if you were to look at me I would not have control of my feelings. It is better to part this way. We must not meet again.

She added a postscript: *Last night I always will remember, and cherish.*

The writing blurred before his eyes. The words did not explain anything.

A surge of love for her rose in him. His first impulse was to call her. Then he was swept by a fierce refusal to pursue where pursuit was not welcome. He had a feeling of rejection, a signing off. It was impossible to understand her inner life; it was hard enough to understand his own.

The vision he had of a future with her and her children, of becoming a family who cared about each other, might be an illusion. Buddhists were always talking about happiness as an illusion. Until a soul went through different incarnations in its search for perfection, there was no chance of finding *Nirvana* and eternal happiness.

He did not ask for that kind of happiness, it was enough to be happy in one place and one time. Deal with the here and now; everything else is nowhere and never.

He had been certain there was no unbridgeable gap. Now he had to consider the possibility that she was right, and there was no way they could be together. He was a foreigner in this country, a man without roots.

And then he thought: there is a country where I am always welcome, a country that I need. Whatever else I have been running away from, it is not the United States of America. At a low point, angry and unsure, he made up his mind to stop building sand castles against the tide. Everything must have a beginning, a middle, and an end.

He called an airline to reserve a flight from Bangkok to New York.

WHEN HE ARRIVED IN BANGKOK AT HUALAMPHONG RAILWAY Station, an eager host of baggage carriers jostled and pushed for the right to carry his small bag. He shouldered past them to a line of taxis waiting for passengers.

A taxi driver opened the rear door of a vintage vehicle. It was Phibul, wearing a slightly soiled white bandana about his head, and smiling with slightly crooked teeth.

"You go hotel?"

"To the airport."

Phibul held the door open to the rear seat. "You are leaving Bangkok?"

"My plane takes off in ninety minutes."

Phibul got into the driver's seat. He looked at Brian in his rear-vision mirror. "You will return."

"I don't think I will."

"Oh, yes sir. You are not tourist. A tourist goes and often does not return. You are not that kind. You will not rest until you see the golden temples again."

I am a different kind of visitor, Brian thought, who cannot return because I have pushed my luck too far.

The day was hot and still. The taxi stopped at a traffic light and a noodle vendor rode by on a bicycle with a blue awning, balancing a large food cabinet behind him.

His impressions of the city had been changing almost from the time he first arrived at Don Muang Airport. Bangkok had seemed like any modern urban metropolis, streets gridlocked with traffic, a gaseous smog enclosing buildings, hurrying crowds surging in all directions.

Now he had come to love this colorful, exotic city where the *klongs* sparkled in the sun and were dotted with lotus flowers and water hyacinths, where even government buildings with their whitewashed walls and colorful swooping or tiered roofs were pleasant to look upon, and the shabbiest lane might lead to the soaring gilded spire of a temple set among tropical trees.

"How is Colonel Suvit these days?"

"He is living in jail, sir. He has much poor luck. The new government discovered many of his family working for police. Including this unfortunate person."

"Are you still with the police?"

"Oh, no sir. Now full time drive taxi. Must support large family." Phibul looked depressed, then his jauntiness returned. "Those white walls, sir, are at entrance to Temple of Emerald Buddha. The wall surrounds whole palace, but is shut off on holy days and royal fest—"

"Phibul, I'm leaving Bangkok."

"Oh, yes sir, so sorry. No time for tour."

Along the Chao Prya the floating market was filling up with farm produce. Brian heard the soft splash of boats moving through the water. The river smelled sweetly of flowers and burning joss that mingled with other complex and humid scents into a tantalizing aroma.

In Arunee's small riverfront home, the day would be beginning. She would be getting Chakra and Ajana off to school.

The taxi passed a sidewalk vendor offering passersby his delicacies—lizards on sticks ready for basting and dried frogs pressed together in bunches like packed figs. All around them cars were weaving and angling their way through traffic lanes. Gasoline was on sale again, and the Thai romance with the automobile was flourishing. Car horns honked as if the drivers had their palms surgically attached to them. Bicyclists ignored the warnings and, smiling and waving, cut across in front of cars and daringly traced out personal routes through bedlam.

A smiling city, Brian thought, full of smiling people. He felt a real kinship, as some years before he had felt a kinship with Asian people supposed to be his enemy. Others must have felt the same, for many of his fellow soldiers had taken Vietnamese brides. After the war they had struggled against endless red tape to bring the women they loved back to America. . . .

You are from a different land, a different culture. I am Thai. I shall live and die and, with the blessing of Buddha, be reborn a Thai.

He sat up straight. Had he been *that* simple-minded?

"I have to make a stop on the way, Phibul."

"Must charge wait time after five minutes."

"I may not be long."

ARUNEE WAS PREPARING BREAKFAST WHILE THE CHILDREN dressed. She was glad it was daylight, and she had the routine of the morning to comfort her. Last night she had made the pillow damp with her crying.

She had chosen to set herself apart from her desires, and she still believed she was right. During the night, though, the reasons seemed to fade into the background, while the anguish of what she had lost stood out from it. She had substituted a desolate logic, a barren foresight, for something that mattered very much. Without love a life might be judged not worthy to live. Without love . . .

She told herself: be still. You are not wise enough to know what is worthy.

Over the subdued clatter she was making in the kitchen, she heard a motor and through the open window saw a taxi stop in front of her house.

He was coming to the front door.

There was no time to compose herself. She hurried into the bathroom and threw cold water on her face to deny the hot blood rising into her cheeks. In the small cabinet mirror her dark eyes stared back at her with confusion.

Forgive me, dear Lord, please, oh please, for I am helpless and bewildered. Teach me to live with a cool heart.

He knocked softly.

"Who's there?" she called out in Thai, keeping up a pretense of not knowing.

"It's Brian. May I come in? Just for a few minutes."

She could keep her composure that long. She went back to the stove, and called out in English: "Come in."

He loomed in the doorway, his large body stooped beneath its unwieldy strength. His neck and back muscles were thick and deep, and his massive shoulders rounded with power.

He came toward her. "I was on my way to the airport."

She was a little frightened. Even a touch, a brush against him, might stir buried desires. She remembered too well how she had lain in the dark after they made love, her body mellow and satisfied, all tension and urgency having left her.

She drew back a little. "I'm getting breakfast for the children. They have to be ready for the school bus."

His hand was resting on the counter near her. She had to resist an impulse to reach out to it.

Only a few more minutes.

She put scrambled eggs and green peppers onto a slow fire and went into the bedroom. Ajana was half-dressed and half-awake. Waking was difficult for a child. The transition back from a dream world is not easy for anyone.

"A friend is here," she said.

"Who?"

"You'll find out when you come to breakfast."

She went into Chakra's bedroom to tell him to hurry.

Reluctantly she returned to the living room. He was standing where she had left him.

"I must speak to you," he said.

She moved the children's breakfast onto their plates. Ajana came out of her bedroom, fully dressed and rubbing sleep from her eyes. When she saw Brain, she ran to him.

"Lift me."

Arunee said, "Not this morning. There's no time."

When Chakra came out, he looked at Brian with fondness and triumph. "Can he have breakfast with us?"

"Would you like to?" she asked Brian.

He sat at the table but didn't touch the food. Arunee was scarcely breathing. She heard the minutes ticking away while she searched for phrases that would circle about meaning. This last farewell must be short, not too freighted with sadness.

"Arunee." He was standing up, towering over her.

"Yes?"

"Over here."

He led her away from the table. Her hand was in his, and she felt her fingers warming as her blood went to him.

They sat down next to each other on the sofa.

"What time is your plane leaving?" she asked.

"I can't go without you."

She felt a salt sting behind her eyes. This is unfair, she thought. I have made a difficult choice, and now you are forcing me to make it again. You have my love; let me live my life.

"We cannot be together. I will keep saying this until you believe it."

"You said you could never be a part of my world. You never asked if I would be willing to be a part of yours."

"I know you could not."

"I will be unhappy wherever I go," he said, "if you are not there. No one will ever fill the space for me where you have been."

Everything inside her seemed to be breaking up. Lord Buddha, help me. She hoped Buddha understood that she was leaving everything in his hands.

"We must do what is best," she said.

"Yes. We must." His hand touched her shoulder and turned her toward him.

A deep, hot, painful fever was in her chest. What is the matter with me? she wondered. I know the dark side of the moon, but I am not looking at it.

"If I have one life to live," he said, "I want to live it with you."

Then he kissed her, and her lips took the feel of his mouth, and she was seized by a powerful, astonishing thought: *This* is kharma, and nothing can change it. How wonderfully his chemistry works on me.

She sensed a yielding in him; a change that would not stop until his true face was revealed. There can be a merging without surrender, she thought. We need each other. His world will change because of me, and my world will change because of him.

Thank you, dear Lord, for showing me the way.

Ajana and Chakra had left the table and were standing nearby, Ajana looking anxious, Chakra pretending not to be.

"Mama, is he staying?" Ajana asked tremulously. "Will he be here when we come back?"

Brian put a finger to Arunee's lips, silencing her.

He answered, "I'll be here. You kids are going to have to put up with me for a long, long time."

Outside, the taxi horn honked loudly.

Arunee smiled.

"You'd better tell him not to wait."

ABOUT THE AUTHOR

WILLIAM WOOLFOLK IS THE AUTHOR OF EIGHTEEN BOOKS OF fiction and nonfiction, many of which were chosen by major book clubs. His books have sold a total of over six million copies in all editions. Some years ago he was chief writer and story editor for the television series *The Defenders*, which is still on everyone's list of the best dramatic series ever to appear on TV. Mr. Woolfolk has also been a successful magazine publisher and is the founder of *Space World*, the first popular magazine of astronautics.

Mr. Woolfolk's novels include MY NAME IS MORGAN, OPINION OF THE COURT, THE OVERLORDS, THE PRESIDENT'S DOCTOR, THE SENDAI, and others. Among his nonfiction bestsellers are THE GREAT AMERICAN BIRTH RITE and DADDY'S LITTLE GIRL, which he coauthored with his daughter Donna Woolfolk Cross.

Mr. Woolfolk currently resides in New Canaan, Connecticut, with his wife, Joanna, who is also an author.